Triangles

Triangles

A Novel by Ruth Geller

THE CROSSING PRESS / Trumansburg, New York 14886
The Crossing Press Feminist Series

Also by Ruth Geller:
Pictures from the Past
Seed of a Woman

Copyright © 1984 by Ruth Geller
The Crossing Press Feminist Series

Cover design by Beverly Rosen
Book design by Allison Platt
Typesetting by Martha J. Waters
Back cover photograph by D. Geller

Library of Congress Cataloging in Publication Data

Geller, Ruth.
  Triangles.

  (The Crossing Press feminist series)
  I. Title. II. Series.
PS3557.E39T7 1984   813'.54   84-15632
ISBN 0-89594-152-X
ISBN 0-89594-151-1 (pbk.)

Acknowledgments

Many people helped me in the writing of *Triangles,* either by sharing their experience and knowledge, or by offering criticism of the manuscript in its varying stages. My thanks go to Sue Dinsmore and Audrey Mang, Patricia McDermott, Karen Lands, Verdia Jenkins, Lisa Albrecht and Bev Sorensen, Colleen Evans, and Kathleen Fallon, and to all the people I annoyed with my weeks of frantic last minute phone calls. I would also like to thank Barbara Smith, who reminded me that if everything is connected then everything should be connected; Bonnie Zimmerman, who has been criticizing me since the old S.C. days; and Evi Beck, who taught me viewpoint and gave me encouragement. I am grateful to my editor at Crossing Press, Nancy K. Bereano, who was patient and understanding with me, and who gave me the most important thing—a chance.

In addition, my family shared their anecdotes and stories with me and answered many questions, and their help was invaluable. I especially want to thank my grandmother, Sophie Dorenz Geller, for her wonderful and varied memory; my sister, Janet Geller-Lesko, for her continuity; my uncle, Harold Pokras, for his *Pesach* memory; and my uncle and aunt, Joseph and Flora Sadetsky Geller, for all their memories and complaints. My gratitude goes to my Auntie Coo, Claire Geller-Kolchetski, for being herself in spite of everything, and to my mother, Hilda Pokras Geller, not only for her typing of the early drafts of *Triangles,* but for all the years when she told me in her slightly defensive but nevertheless supportive way, "Well, *I* think you're a good writer. . . ." And I want to offer my belated but warm thanks to my dear grandpa, Sam Geller, for listening to me.

Finally, I want to thank Shane.

It is not *easy* (or so she has told me often enough) to live with a writer, especially a writer who is almost compulsively driven. Any partner might understandably resent the enormous amount of time and the outrageous mental preoccupation that writing involves. It is true that during the years it took me to write *Triangles,* and during the years before, Shane complained mightily. But in spite of her complaints, I knew she was on my side.

In the more than twelve years that we've been together, Shane has become a partner not only of my life, but of my writing: talking over ideas, criticizing innumerable drafts, giving me advice about what to say and what not to say to this or that person, and most important, seeing me through the disappointments that were for many years the emotional atmosphere in which I lived.

In addition, in the fourteen years since I began writing, I have applied for a multitude of awards and grants. I have not received one. To have to continually put my writing on hold while carrying out the duties of a full-time job could have destroyed that writing. But during the past twelve years, Shane has supported both of us. In the face of my half-hearted offers, she has consistently argued that I should *not* take another teaching or typing job, but instead concentrate on my writing. While working at a job both physically and emotionally wearing, she never once suggested that I give up my writing to make money.

I can truly say that without her friendship, love, loyalty, and understanding, her honest criticism, and her support and generosity, *Triangles* might well not have been written.

Dedication

In July 1983, my family gathered for a party to celebrate my sister's marriage. Coincidentally, my grandmother—Sophie Geller—had just celebrated her 90th birthday. I'd brought along an excerpt from *Triangles* that I planned to read to her, thinking she would be pleased and flattered.

I'd been telling her about the book for years and about the character, Rose, I'd based on her. But it seemed to make little impression one way or another. She'd smile and say, "Dot's nice," as though I'd told her I'd slept well the night before or was thinking of painting my house. I hoped that reading from the actual book would make the difference.

A little while before she was due to leave, I took her into the bedroom, closed the door, and sat her down. I was very uncomfortable. My Yiddish accent is not so hot, and I'd never before read to a person who was my conscious inspiration for a character. She was the real thing.

Well, I began to read. At first I thought she understood it and loved it. She was leaning forward, frowning with anticipation, smiling, nodding. I felt great. Especially when she laughed in what seemed to be all the right places. Once I paused and asked, "Do you understand it, Grandma?" and she answered, "*Oy*, it's vondehful!"

As I continued reading, however, I sensed that her reactions were not based on what I was reading, but took their cue from my facial expressions and tone of voice. Finally, I paused. I gave her a questioning look and asked, "What do you think, Grandma?"

She grinned more widely, shaking her head in amazement at how terrific I was, and exclaimed, "*Oy*! I t'ink it's vondehful dot you could read vidout glesses!"

I groaned inwardly and, trying not to laugh, hurried through the rest of the excerpt. I couldn't believe it. All my work, all my years of writing, and she's impressed by my eyesight.

But what can I say? Except that this book is dedicated to Sophie Geller, a real character.

Chapter 1

The Quarry I

It was the last Sunday in September. On a side street toward the lower end of Elmwood Avenue, the front door of a gray-shingled house opened, and an old man and woman emerged. They did not speak, but it was clear that they were in the midst of some ongoing dispute. The man, after carefully placing a rag on the stoop, sat down with a critical side glance at his wife. She seemed to squat carelessly, though in reality she'd placed herself so that she landed insultingly half on and half off the rag. He shook his head in disgusted resignation, and reaching into his shirt pocket for his tobacco and rolling papers, glanced around at the street where he had lived with his wife and family for almost sixty years.

As a young man, he'd come to this country from an Eastern European border town whose rulers had changed so many times that he wasn't sure what to claim as his native land. He'd been born Shlomo Rosinsky. Sam Rosenthal was an Ellis Island name, one he did not like, but accepted. He was a passive, unassuming man who'd never felt secure in his adopted land, and his calloused hands and sad eyes spoke of a life that had not been easy. His family in America was important to him for he'd lost everyone in Europe; and more and more as the years went by, he contemplated the past and his irretrievable mistakes. He sat on the front step, his forearms resting on his knees, smoking and thinking.

His wife, Rose, sat in a similar position. On her, however, the posture appeared sprawling and aggressive, for she was a person who demanded attention even with her silences. Her thin gray hair was cut into a modified Dutch Boy style that was neither fitting nor flattering, but Rose was not one to care for appearances. Her favorite outfit of late was a pink jogging suit that she'd "borrowed" from the locker room of the Jewish Center on Delaware Avenue and never returned, and she wore it in defiance of considerable family pressure.

Today, yielding to her son Morris who had repeated several times, "Ma, do me a favor and don't wear that goddamned jogging suit," Rose had worn a dress. In an additional show of cooperation, she'd donned nylon stockings. But since she was not one to lose an argument, the stockings were of different lengths, one reaching to the knee, the other to mid-calf. Technically, however, they were stockings, and when her son gave her an exasperated stare, as he undoubtedly would, she would be entitled to look properly aggrieved, as in: What does he *want* from my life, my son. . . .

Rose was a clever woman whose shrewd eyes were always on the lookout for whatever she could use to her advantage, and given other circumstances, she might have been a prosperous businesswoman, a successful lawyer, a popular politician. But her life had been largely determined by two factors: that she was a Jewish woman born in the last decade of the nineteenth century, and that in the new century's first decade, she had fled from pogroms in Europe and come to America. As her domineering father expected, she got married and raised children. And being Rose, she became involved in the various intrigues of her family, friends, and neighbors. She was known far beyond the confines of the neighborhood for her energy, intelligence, and audacity. Everyone who knew Rose had a story to tell.

The Rosenthals had two living sons, Harry and Morris. When the boys were young and Sam was out of work, Rose became pregnant and gave herself an abortion with a crochet hook as women in the neighborhood had taught her. After that, she miscarried at early term several times. During the Depression, she again became pregnant and again considered abortion. But her father, who lived with them, said no. The child would be a girl, he said, and she listened to him because she wanted a daughter. The child was a girl, but a rebellious girl, a girl in such continual conflict with her grandfather that he came to regret ever having spoken. Her life was a troubled one, and she died before she reached the age of thirty.

Harry, the oldest son, had once aspired to a career on the stage, but now he made his living mainly by appearing in television commercials for carpet stores and muffler shops in New York City. Morris, after some years of moving his family from one upstate New York town to another in various unsuccessful bids for advancement within the Civil Service system, had returned to Buffalo where, to his humiliation, he'd been forced to take a low-paying job working for a cousin he'd always resented.

Sam and Rose were waiting for Morris this morning. He was going to bring them to his house for a Sunday brunch of bagels and lox, *matjes* herring, boiled potatoes, cottage cheese, and sour cream.

It was a lovely day. In years past, the autumn air had smelled wonderful, like the canopy of yellowing leaves from the elm trees that towered overhead. But in the fifties, the trees had succumbed to blight. The air was less pleasant now, and the street had the stark appearance of a neighborhood in decline. Here and there a house had been abandoned, the windows boarded, the door posted with an official notice prohibiting entry.

In the middle of the block, across the street from where the Rosenthals lived, there was a vacant lot littered with debris. But underneath the debris there was soil in which tenacious weeds had germinated and flourished. Dandelions and ragweed grew there, goldenrod and blue-flowered chicory; and in the back, young ailanthus trees with graceful branches of slender dark green leaves. Beyond this was a back yard with a small garden and an old maple tree, and between the tree and the house hung a clothesline weighted with freshly washed sheets.

Sam had been gazing at the yard and the sheets. Placing a newly rolled cigarette between his lips, he struck a match, glancing at the meeting of flame and tobacco before returning his gaze to the billowing white sheets that waved and slapped in the breeze. The silence did not last. Soon he and Rose began to bicker in Yiddish, picking up their dispute where they'd left off.

For the most part, Rose won their quarrels. She could offer several different opinions on any one topic, presenting diametrically opposed arguments with equal force of conviction. Her memory and hearing were selective: she was a blank slate when urged to recall a day old error, but was miraculously blessed with virtually superhuman memory when she could win a battle by recalling a slight detail of thirty years past. Usually Sam refrained from criticizing her since he knew it would do no good.

But this time was different. On Friday, she'd promised to read him a two-page letter they'd received from their grandson, Jack. Now, after two days of her avoidances and Sam's pestering, she finally admitted that Jack's letter was misplaced, though she was careful not to say that she had misplaced it. She'd shifted her position so many times that the rag on which she'd been half sitting was no longer under her. And she decided that the best method of minimizing her guilt was to fling a few accusations of her own. For example, if Sam knew how to read English, he would have read the letter upon its arrival, and its subsequent disappearance would be irrelevant. She was about to do this when she saw their son's car turn down the narrow one-way street.

Morris, or "Mo," as most people called him, drove with both hands on the wheel, frowning at the road ahead. He was a heavy-set man whose once handsome face had been marred by bitterness. Like his father, he had a passive and fatalistic attitude toward life, but he was not easygoing like Sam. For though he lacked Rose's strong will, he had her intensity. He was a man filled with frustration by the world's injustices: he felt he could not change things, but neither could he forget them.

The doctor had told him to lose sixty pounds, and he was currently on yet another in a series of unsuccessful diets. He'd wanted badly to stop for doughnuts on the drive downtown and had used every psychological trick at his disposal to avoid doing so. He knew of three or four doughnut shops along the route he'd taken, and each block between his home and his parents' was a struggle and a victory. But he was not one to acknowledge his own victories.

By the time Mo pulled up in front of the gray-shingled house, Sam was standing at the curb, his hands in his pockets. He stuck out his thumb and bent down, looking into the car's open window. "Goin' my vay, kid?"

"Hiya, Papa," he answered. "You ready?"

Though Mo's voice was gruff and his utterances sounded like complaints, or even threats, Sam took no notice. He did notice, however, a bag of groceries on the front seat, and seeing it, gave his son an injured look.

"It was on my way, Pa," Mo said, answering the look. "Come on, let's go. Sylvia's waiting." Rose was getting into the back seat, and he inquired, "You okay, Ma?"

"On deh go, kid," she answered, and gripping the door handle, used the weight of her body to pull the door shut.

"I can't believe she didn't wear that *shmatte* from the gym," Mo commented to his father; and, unwilling to believe she'd actually dressed properly, he turned and looked her up and down. . . and saw the stockings. "Christ, where'd you get those socks, the Salvation Army?"

This was Rose's chance, and she took it: she looked properly aggrieved and shook her head in bewilderment. "Dot's a lovely outfit," she said, fingering the dress material and purposefully misunderstanding his criticism. "Mrs. Villiams give it to me. Vhen she vashed it. . ."

"All right, all right, I'll take your word for it," Mo muttered. He said to his father, "Your wife is unbelievable."

Sam shook his head as if to say that his wife's behavior was beyond his control, and he could not be held responsible. As far as he was concerned, the main issue was yet to be resolved, and as they rode away, he reached into his back pocket for his wallet.

Mo put out his hand to stop him. "Put away your money, Pa. This week it's my treat. Next week you pay."

"Next veek, next veek, ev'vy veek it's *next* veek," Sam complained, sat back and sighed. He needed an ally, and since he would not ally himself with Rose, spoke to the invisible but omnipotent entity beyond the windshield who was sure to understand. "My son, he t'inks I'm an old man, I can't afford to buy food."

As Mo rounded the corner, he glanced into the rear view mirror and saw Rose frowning studiously, avoiding both her son's glance and the vacant corner storefront that had, up until last week, been a neighborhood grocery.

Its closing was for Mo one more argument as to why his parents should move.

Knowing that it was useless, but trying nevertheless, he said, "The corner store is closed now, Ma. Where're you gonna buy milk?"

"Milk?" she said, as though it were a foreign and rather disdainful word. "*Hak mir nisht kain chainik* about milk."

"Milk-shmilk," Sam said. "I'll buy a cow."

Rose leaned forward and began inquiring about her three granddaughters. Mo's responses regarding Norma and Meryl were rote: his oldest and youngest daughters were fine. But when Rose asked about Sonia, he hesitated uncomfortably. Whether or not she was fine, he could not say with the same bland conviction with which he reported the well-being of the other two, regardless of his actual knowledge concerning their condition: his middle daughter was not only divorced and disinterested in remarrying, but disinterested in meeting men. To him, her life seemed undecided, unprotected, undefined. Her absence this morning was difficult to understand and something he could not explain to his mother. Unlike Norma, who lived in Boston, his middle daughter lived right here in town; and unlike Meryl, who was married, she could therefore have, to his mind, no legitimate overriding commitment that could keep her away from the brunch.

Finally he said, "Sunny's fine, Ma, but she's not coming."

"Not coming?" Rose demanded. "*Vuss* is duss, she's not coming. . . ."

"Ma, don't *hak* me a *chainik*. She's not coming."

"*Vuss* is *duss* she's not coming!"

Sunny's refusal to come to brunch had irked Mo, and his mouth tightened in annoyance at the memory of that morning's phone conversation in which she'd informed him that she was going to, of all places, the quarry. He knew well enough not to tell Rose this, but knew also he'd have to be careful what he said since Rose always could tell when he was lying.

He was approaching an intersection as the signal changed. As a diversionary tactic, he stepped on the gas, scooting under the light just as it changed to red. A man in the oncoming lane had wanted to turn left and beeped as they passed.

"Moishe," Sam murmured, "excuse me, but I'm too young to die."

"Sorry, Pa." He glanced in the rear view mirror, wondering if his mother were going to pursue the topic of his daughter's whereabouts, and to forestall this possiblity, he said, "Listen, Ma. Pa. Jack's home."

"*Oy!*" Rose cried, "Jackeleh?" She leaned forward so that her face was almost flush with the two men's. "Uh-*huh!*" she commented to Sam, meaning that his concern over the lost letter had been foolish, for now that Jack was home, the letter was of no consequence. And to prevent any retaliating comment from Sam, she turned to her son. "*Nu?*" she prompted, anxious for the details of Jack's arrival.

There were few details. Jack had moved to Boston with his girlfriend, but they'd parted company, and since he'd gotten laid off from his job some weeks earlier, he'd decided to move West. He had come to Buffalo for a visit before he left.

Rose already knew about the layoff and was most interested in the girl. "Deh blonde *shiksa?*" she inquired.

"No, Ma, not the blonde *shiksa.*"

"Vhat hoppen to deh blonde *shiksa?*"

"Ma, he stopped going with the blonde *shiksa* two years ago."

"*Nu?* So long?"

He nodded, keeping a judicious silence and seeing no need to tell what other *shiksas* there had been.

Sam had not been listening to the conversation. He was thinking about Jack. He could hardly believe that Jack was now a man, for it seemed like only a few moments earlier that he'd held him at his *bris.* "Yacov," he murmured aloud, and Jack's Hebrew name, coming from his lips, sounded like a sorrowful endearment.

Rose didn't notice that he'd spoken. Monday was large trash pickup in her son's neighborhood, and as he parked the car in front of the mint green house, she'd seen a perfectly good wooden chair in his neighbor's garbage and was trying to figure out how she could retrieve it without her son and daughter-in-law finding out.

Mo noticed that Sam had spoken, but was concerned with other matters: he was reminding himself to tell his wife not to mention in front of Rose that Sunny had gone to the quarry.

From the bordering ridge, the quarry appeared to be a magnificent but barren expanse of sand and rock; it was necessary to walk down to its midst to sense the intensity of its life. An intricacy of plants and animals coexisted in the fine variations of earth, air, and water—a universe of living things, each its own center in the world of the quarry. The sky dominated the landscape of sand, clay, rocks, and pebbles, and in the pools of water, its blue depths shimmered. By one secluded pool, a woman stood naked at the edge of the water.

On her face there was a self-absorbed expression, and she seemed hardly aware that she was naked. She had not yet accepted who she was or how she looked, and occasionally tried to starve herself into a contemporary American standard of slimness. But her thick strong body came from another mold, and in spite of her wishes, would follow its own destiny. She loved the quarry fiercely, perhaps because here her appearance ceased to matter. In the marks and scars of her flesh could be read the stories of her life, and that was their importance, not how they measured up against some unattainably smooth ideal. The pale diagonal stretch marks across her hips, fleeting as strokes from a silvery brush, were like the muted colors that marbleized the most common and beautiful quarry stones. She was another living creature, part of the same cloth of which the quarry itself was created, and like the quarry, she simply belonged.

Her features were large and striking. Her thick black hair was curly and flecked with gray, and around her deep blue eyes, faint age lines had begun to tell the passage of years. Sunny was twenty-nine, an introspective and self-critical woman whose proud, almost arrogant demeanor was a defensive expression of her determination to make her way in a sometimes hostile world. She had been an independent and rebellious child, and as a woman had remained essentially the same. But the events of the past few years—the accidental drowning of her daughter and the subsequent breakup of her marriage—had thrown her life, her self-confidence, and self-image into turmoil. These days she was a woman filled with doubts and plagued by guilt, determined to survive yet not knowing exactly what that meant. She could not see where she was going, perhaps because she hadn't yet seen from where she'd come.

She felt a deep pervasive despair about what had been done to the natural world. Every day the news got worse. Every time she turned around there was a new crisis whose portrayal was so distorted that sometimes she felt she must be mad. Her despair was like a paralysis, and feeling so powerless, she had decided (though it was not a conscious decision) that she must tend to her own life and leave the world to itself. But the terrible injustices and cruelty on one side, the misery and suffering on the other, did not go away. It took all her energy to keep her vision narrowed and confined. She had become a woman without faith: without faith in the future, without faith in the survival of life itself. It was only here at the quarry that her anxieties were soothed, for the quarry seemed like an island, untouched by the torturous twistings of human history.

The quarry, however, was private property, and trespassing was forbidden to nonauthorized personnel. For five days of the week, the area was busy with human and mechanical activity—digging, sorting, crushing, and carting away the earth which was then sold. The topography changed continually as the Company exhausted one area and gouged into another; and the landscape was characterized by a myriad of levels, from the unmined surfaces to the scooped out sandy flats through which filtered the underground springs.

But on weekends the machinery was still. The air was quiet except for the buzzing of insects and the call of birds. Everything was clean colors here, the sky a deep shining blue, the water an elusive dark moss green. Above the water, two iridescent blue black dragonflies darted and stopped in fine erratic flight. The air was like a massive invisible network, shared by all it touched. She breathed deeply and gazed at the far sloping ridge, thick with quaking aspen. Their flat, silvery-undersided leaves fluttered in a sudden breeze. She saw the leaves tremble and heard them rustle, and in a long smooth moment felt the breeze touch her body, tickling at her pubic hair and hardening the nipples of her soft, gently sagging breasts.

Innumerable histories had created the world in which she lived and the person that she was; and they were like another mesh woven into that of the natural world. She was only vaguely conscious of those histories, for what she'd been taught had been a calculation of lies that were sifted, bleached, and empty. She felt it all had nothing to do with her, and if she had an inner vision of herself, it would be as she was now: a woman standing naked and alone before a pool of water. Yet the histories remained like fine invisible webs. Unknown perhaps, obscured, denied, forgotten. But daily she breathed them, and they coursed through her veins as surely as did her blood.

Scanning the horizon from the quaking aspen to the edges of the boulders, off to the line where the earth met the sky, she sensed that the quarry was changing, and changing fast. Coming here in years past, she'd encountered people who came for the silence. In recent years, she'd seen adolescent boys roaring on dirt bikes over the land, using the peaks of small hills as springboards into their fantasies. That drilling sound of bikes would suddenly invade what she preferred to believe was the immutable quarry silence. It struck her now, as she stepped into the shallow water, that the silence she cherished was only the silence of the weekend, the winter, and the night, for daily the machines pierced the air as they dug into the earth.

This was the first summer after her daughter's death that she'd been back to the quarry. Last year she stayed away: it had been too soon. But this summer she'd longed for the hot sandy vista, the hot blue sky, the empty horizon. She'd forgotten about the water. Seeing it was a recognition of an old pain, and it had taken several visits before she'd dared to submerge herself. She hadn't cried that first time, but now her throat ached. She looked down at her naked body, then stepped forward, took a breath, and dove into the water.

After the shock of cold came a glorious weightlessness, for the water cradled her, making her forget the distinction between her body and the element in which it moved. Here in the dark watery depths, she felt comforted; and open-eyed, she swam underwater, imagining herself a fish. She would be protected by an encircling school of fish, not merely her "family" or her "friends," but her species. She would move in instinctual unity with her kind.

But she was not a fish. She surfaced, gasping for air, and dove again and again until the continual necessity of stopping for air, the reality of her body, disheartened her, destroying her fantasy of freedom and of being an animal in the wild, a creature in its natural environment. She dove for the last time and surfaced with a burst of water into the sunshine.

On the land, Kay had watched in silence. She was thinking her own thoughts about her own life and had hardly noticed how long Sunny stood by the water, how suddenly she'd dived, how many times she'd surfaced and gone under again. She, too, was naked, and her slim body had about it an air of competence and sent out waves of energy and impatience. She was an impulsive and enthusiastic woman who at twenty-four tended to be thoughtless in regard to the consequences of her actions.

She was unimpressed with the quarry. For Sunny it might have been a refuge, but for Kay it had no such special meaning. To her it was nothing more than an old sand and gravel quarry where on Sundays they could go skinny-dipping. She was bored now and anxious to leave. She walked to the edge of the water and stood there, her demeanor expressing martyred patience and misery. When Sunny surfaced and looked toward shore, Kay let out such a woebegone sigh that Sunny laughed. Kay, seeing she'd gotten the message, shot her a silent testy *thank you* and turned away to dress.

Sunny swam to shore. As she emerged from the water, the leaves of the quaking aspen rustled in a sudden gust of wind, and it sounded like rainfall. Dripping, she stood once more facing the pond and the expanse of quarry beyond it, and her gaze was so intent that she seemed to be trying to imprint the water, sand, and sky on her mind as if she thought her memory could survive the long winter until she returned in the spring.

Kay was standing at the blanket. Clad in faded jeans, she was looking at her shirt as though contemplating a decision. Her wiry brown hair glistened reddish in the sun, and in contrast to the rest of her deeply tanned torso, her small breasts looked pale and vulnerable. She turned a face to Sunny that was determinedly earnest, and finding her still gazing at the water, she frowned. "Really," she said, "I don't see why I have to wear a shirt. Guys walk around with their hairy chests hanging out *all* the time. I don't see what's so awful about my two little boobies." She regarded her breasts, then gave Sunny a playful look, holding out her hands in a stance that demanded justice for her cause.

Sunny had turned to her and smiled. They'd had this conversation before. Or rather, they'd played these parts before: Kay the young idealist, passionate about how things should be; and Sunny the mature realist, seeing the world as it was.

"I mean really," Kay went on. "Right? *They're* the ones who get all bent out of shape about women's naked bodies. Why should *we* have to suffer because of it." She gave Sunny an impish smile. "Maybe I won't put my shirt on. What do you think they'll do if we drive into the city like this?"

Sunny walked to the blanket. "Well. . . first of all," she began, "*we* won't drive anywhere like that, because I intend to be fully clothed when I face that world out there. And second of all, what'll happen is that some cop will probably come up and tap you on the shoulder and arrest you for indecent exposure."

"Indecency is in the mind of the beholder!" Kay declared pompously.

"That may very well be true, my dear," Sunny said, reaching for the towel, "but since the beholder makes the laws, you're outta luck."

Kay let out a giggle. Then remembering the part she usually played, she pouted, murmuring, "That's discrimination."

"You got it, kid. That's the name of the game." She began dressing as she listened to Kay consider the consequences of her possible arrest for indecent exposure. By the time she was dressed, Kay, too, had buttoned her shirt, having reached the unwilling but pragmatic conclusion that society was unjust but that she would have to pattern her outward behavior according to this unjust society since an arrest record might, as she said, screw up her chances of getting accepted in law school.

They picked up their things and walked back to the edge of the quarry, their fingers linked in casual affection, an affection made bittersweet by the knowledge that it must end when they left the quarry and returned to the main road.

When they reached the edge of the quarry, Kay, who'd with some difficulty walked back barefoot, soothed her feet in a patch of mud at the base of the hill. These patches, some of them quite large, were scattered throughout the quarry, usually at the perimeters of ponds. When Sunny had first brought her here at the beginning of the summer, they'd gone to such a spot near one of the more secluded ponds and taken a mud bath, laughing as they slathered their own and each other's bodies with the cool wet mud. Sunny had insisted that the mud bath was therapeutic, though whether it was therapeutic for the skin or the spirit was not clear.

It had been a moment of purely delightful abandon, but after they were covered chin to foot and waiting for the mud to dry (which it must before they washed it off, Sunny insisted, otherwise they would not get the full benefit of the treatment), Kay had become fidgety. "It itches," she'd complained.

"It's *supposed* to itch. That means it's working."

"Working on *what?*"

"On... on your pores. It's cleansing your pores."

"I think it's *clogging* my pores."

"Well then go wash it off. No one's stopping you."

"No," she'd said, the picture of enduring misery.

Sunny had observed her and laughed. "It's not a contest, you know," she'd said, and Kay had smiled.

She would have liked them to take mud baths today, not so much for the thing itself but to recapture those moments of joy. But she saw that as they'd neared the edge of the quarry, Sunny's mood had changed and the playfulness between them had vanished. "Why don't you take off your shoes and cool your feet in the mud," she suggested, but Sunny shook her head and started up the hill to the flat sandy rock.

On the rock she sat down, succumbing at last to the apprehension that had nagged at her all day. She was filled with the sense that she'd done something wrong, made a mistake that was irreversible and unforgiveable. She knew the feeling well, and for some time now had slipped resentfully but passively into its shackles whenever it beckoned.

She looked out over the landscape. From her vantage point the quarry might once again seem, to someone who did not love it, a drab and lifeless place whose only asset was that it showed to good advantage the bottomless blue sky. But to her it was a solid backdrop for the mirage of memories that came and went, transient images against an enduring earth. Sometimes she remembered the times she'd taken Meryl here, and Jack; and they'd pretend all sorts of great adventures. Sometimes she remembered the times she and Jack would sit on this very rock, and look out over the quarry and talk.

But today she remembered Debbie, and the memory was so powerful it was almost like a vision. She saw her the day she'd sat at the pond's edge, slapping the water with her small hand and yelling fiercely. "You tell 'em, kid!" she'd called to her daughter. "You tell the world...."

Now the memory made her angry. Tell the world *what!* she thought bitterly and stood up, her face betraying only a cranky peevishness. "Let's go!" she called to Kay.

Kay looked up and opened her mouth to speak, but Sunny was already heading toward the narrow path between the trees that led out of the quarry and up to the main road.

On the way home Sunny was preoccupied, thinking about that morning's phone conversation with her father.

In spite of her attempts over the past few months to ease him into an awareness of Kay's existence by subtle though frequent references, he refused to acknowledge it. When he'd said, "Why don't you come over this morning?" she knew that the *you* referred to her alone.

"Because *we*," she'd replied tartly, emphasizing the joint decision, "have been planning all week to go to the quarry."

"Who's *we*?"

"*We* is me and my friend Kay."

"Oh for Christ's sakes, and *that's* more important than spending time with your *grandparents*?"

After they'd hung up, she'd stood in the kitchen and let loose a stream of complaints and threats as she watched Kay prepare the egg salad sandwiches that were to be their picnic. In the car heading out to the quarry, she'd muttered darkly, though it was obvious that her annoyance was passing, and she was trying to hurry the process by teasing herself. At the quarry, she'd forgotten the phone call. But gradually, becoming aware of her deepening apprehension and unable to trace it to any other source, she came to the conclusion that it must be the phone call; and as they drove toward the Expressway that would take them into the city, she fell into a brooding silence.

Once again she had disappointed her family. Like so many other times in the past. She could not avoid feeling that she had not lived her life as they'd wanted, that she was not what she should be, and that when measured up against their expectations, she was, quite simply, a failure. The fact that she was independent enough to live her life as she saw fit in spite of their disapproval did not enter her mind, and the silence became a misery of self-doubt and self-castigation.

"Well, I'm glad going to the quarry cheered you up," Kay murmured dryly.

It was the perfect thing to say, and Sunny smiled. "Hey, how do you think I got my name? It's my cheerful disposition."

"Yeah, I'm sure of it," Kay murmured. "Who's going to be at your folks' house?" she asked, sensing what was on Sunny's mind.

"Oh, my mother and father, my grandmother and grandfather, probably Meryl and Joe. And I have the feeling Jack's going to be there."

"What do you mean, you have the feeling. Don't you know?"

She shook her head. "When I was on the phone with my father, I thought I heard my mother say something about him being there. Or *start* to say something, but my father shushed her and then wouldn't tell me what she said. He's such a pain in the ass."

Kay smiled. They were on the Expressway, and she watched as they passed one exit after another. As they neared the exit that could take them to the Rosenthal home, she suggested, "Do you want to stop in and say hello?"

"No, it'll be a madhouse."

"I can drop you off if you want."

"No. My father knew I was spending the day with you. He could've invited both of us, but he didn't; and if you're not invited, I'm not going either."

Kay shrugged. They had already passed the exit. "Don't forget we have to stop and pick up milk."

"Yeah, we need a couple things. There's nothing for supper."

"We won't be in the mood to cook when we get home. Let's just get a pizza."

"No, I don't want a *pizza.*"

"How about some wings, then."

Sunny laughed. "You out-of-towners and your wings. . . let's just buy something and cook."

Kay agreed reluctantly. But by the time they pulled up in front of the two-family house where Sunny lived in the upstairs apartment, Sunny had changed her mind. She did not want to cook either, she said. Perhaps they *should* call and order a pizza.

Smiling, but keeping a judicious silence, Kay picked up the damp and sandy things and headed toward the pathway to the back yard and the clothesline.

Sunny got the bag of groceries and the empty thermos and walked up the front steps to the porch. Opening the outside door, she heard the phone ringing from inside her apartment. "Damn," she muttered, and took the steps two at a time. At the door she fumbled with, then dropped, her keys. The phone rang for the fourth time and she said, "All right, all right, take it easy, I'm coming."

As she inserted the key into the lock with her right hand and reached for the handle with her left, the water thermos slipped out of the crook of her arm and bounced down the steps. Hands poised to open the door, she was caught for an instant by an image: the inside of the thermos as a mass of shattered silvery splinters. She flung open the door and ran to the phone. "Hello?"

"Sunny?" It was her mother. Her voice sounded tired, seemingly empty of emotion.

She knew now that something was wrong, knew that the source of her apprehension was here, confirmed by her mother's voice. She steeled herself. "Yeah, Ma. What happened?"

There was a moment of silence, and her mother said: "Sunny. . . you've got to come home. Your grandfather's dead."

Chapter 2

The Funeral

Jewish laws and customs regarding death, like those regarding life, are specific and detailed. Though Sam Rosenthal was not a religious man, and in fact except for the High Holy Days had not been to *shul* for almost twenty years, when he died the laws and customs were respected.

According to Jewish law, embalming is in most cases forbidden, and the funeral and burial arrangements had to be immediate. The responsibility for everything fell on Sylvia, Sam's daughter-in-law. In his life, Sam had belonged to the Workman's Circle, an organization of Socialist laborers, and some years ago he and Rose had bought adjoining plots in the Workman's Circle section of the old Jewish cemetery. Nevertheless, there were other arrangements to be made. Sylvia had to contact the *Chevra Kadisha,* the Jewish burial society. She had to call the Memorial Chapel. She had to arrange for food and beverages, to remember that the mirrors had to be covered, and that a pitcher of water must be placed outside the front door. Her daughters did what they could, but it was being at the center, overseeing it all, that she found so exhausting.

On Sunday night, the *Chevra Kadisha* came to care for Sam's body. They bathed and clothed him in a pocketless white shroud, and a *shomer,* or "one who watches," stayed with him all night, reciting psalms, because it is a sign of disrespect to leave the dead unattended. The shroud was made of cotton and the coffin of pine and without nails so that all could decompose in a simple and natural way, as did the body. A packet of soil from Israel was placed under Sam's head. The coffin was closed to show respect for the privacy of the dead.

On Monday morning, the mourners gathered at the Memorial Chapel. The service was simple. There were no flowers. After Harry stood to say *Kaddish,* the mourner's prayer intoned by the oldest son, the Cantor approached Harry and Mo and with a small pair of scissors, snipped a piece of black material that had been pinned to their lapels. This symbolized the times of old when people tore their clothes in the passion of mourning. Then the Cantor returned to the podium and gave the eulogy.

From the time Sam settled in Buffalo, he'd belonged to the old *shul* on Pearl Street, a few blocks away from his home. But as the older people died and the younger ones moved away, membership fell off, and eventually the *shul* closed down. For awhile he'd tried attending services at the synagogue where Mo and Sylvia belonged, but he hadn't felt comfortable there and stopped going. The Cantor was from their synagogue and hadn't known Sam personally. His attitude was one of faint apology or regret. His comments were brief: Sam had been a good man and a good Jew; he had worked hard all his life and loved his family.

Afterward, the family drove to the old Jewish cemetery on the outskirts of the city. Sam had had eleven brothers and sisters, all of them with families, all of them—along with his mother and father, his aunts and uncles and cousins—murdered in Europe. All that was left was his family in America. Harry was there with his first wife and his children by that marriage (his second wife having stayed at home in New York with their two-year-old son). Mo and Sylvia were there, and their children.

Norma, the oldest, was still ill from her morning flight and trying to breathe deeply of the dewy air. Meryl, the youngest, was weeping bitterly: she was three months pregnant with her first child, a child that would never know Sam, a child Sam had not lived to see. Sunny was crying sporadically. She did not want to cry and brushed the tears away as they fell. Jack was off to one side observing the service, the mourners, the cemetery. Occasionally he glanced off toward the main gates, past which cars could be seen speeding by.

Rose was in a daze. She hardly seemed to know what was happening. But when the service was done and the mourners turned away leaving Sam behind, Rose suddenly let out a piercing Yiddish wail. It was a cry that came from deep inside her, and her sons stepped to her side because she seemed about to fall. She struggled for a moment to break free from their grasp, grew quiet, and fell back into her daze.

They had driven from the Chapel to the cemetery in a cavalcade of cars, but after the service they drove without procession to Mo and Sylvia's two-family house in north Buffalo.

On the front porch was the card table Mo had set up that morning and the pitcher of water Sylvia had placed atop it. Before the mourners entered the house, they paused to pour a trickle of water onto their hands. This was meant as a symbolic act of purification, for the ancient Jews believed that demons followed the dead and hovered around their graves.

But Jack, when he walked up the steps, did not pause to wash away his demons. Instead, he headed directly to the door.

His Uncle Harry, who was behind him, murmured. "Jack. . ." and gestured to the pitcher of water. "It's tradition."

Jack grimaced slightly to indicate he thought the tradition was a stupid one, and when he washed his hands, he did so in a vaguely insulting manner.

Harry, who was thinking about his father and his own life, hardly noticed Jack's performance.

Inside, the dining room table was set with the Meal of Condolence. Besides the pastrami and corned beef, besides the salami and cheese and potato salad and cole slaw, there were the foods such as rolls, bagels, and hard boiled eggs, which symbolized the cyclical and eternal nature of life.

As Jack stood off to one side eating, Mo got a hold of him and began to shepherd him around, reintroducing him to family friends.

Jack was adopted, and Mo made a special effort to integrate him, as it were, into the family. It was an effort Jack had always misunderstood and resented. Now, chewing potato salad and cole slaw, he glanced occasionally at Mo's hand resting unwanted on his shoulder and greeted the family friends with an exaggerated politeness that hovered on the edge of contempt.

After awhile, he made his way through the people, heading into the kitchen and toward the back door.

"Where are you going?" Sylvia asked. She was standing at the kitchen counter slicing tomatoes. She looked exhausted. She'd been crying, and her eyes were red and puffy. She usually wore some make-up, but today wore none. Her face was pale and vulnerable.

Between them, people stood around the kitchen table, pouring soda water, reaching for liquor. Sylvia needed Mo to go down to the cellar and get more ginger ale. She'd thought he was with Jack, and now here Jack was, giving her one of those looks that always made her feel she had to examine herself too closely. "Where's your father?"

"*I* sure as hell don't know. Do you?" he asked, and the statement reverberated with meaning.

She sighed because being with him was so exhausting at times. "Where are you going?"

"Up to my room to get some peace and quiet," he said, and opened the door and climbed the stairwell to the attic.

The roughly finished room at the far end of the attic had been his since he was twelve and the family had returned to Buffalo and moved into this house. Over the years, he'd furnished it with castoffs he'd found and claimed, and in his grimly resourceful way, he'd made it look homey. The bed was a mattress and box springs placed on the floor and covered with a faded red chenille spread; the lamp was made out of old pipes and painted black. Against the side wall stood an old bureau, its veneer chipped and warped. Its mirror was covered with a sheet.

When Jack unlocked the door with his skeleton key and saw the sheet, he knew that Sylvia had been in his room, and he regretted not having put up a deadbolt lock as he'd considered. More than that, the covered mirror angered him; he took it personally. He walked to the dresser and hesitated, his hand outstretched. Then he pulled away the sheet and let it drop to the floor. The mirror was an old one. The mercury had chipped away in places and gave a blotched silvery reflection.

Jack, with curly brown hair and a dimple in his chin, was strikingly handsome. When he wanted, moreover, he could project a disarmingly boyish quality. He hardly looked boyish now.

He closed the door and sat on the bed. The subdued murmurings of conversation could not possibly have reached up two flights of stairs to his ears, yet he felt so connected to the gathering below that no amount of space or closure could make him forget them. It was this connection he had for years tried to strengthen, though he believed it was in vain, and now was trying to sever, though he knew this effort was equally futile.

He had in the past few years moved from one city to another, always further away. But always, he was drawn inevitably back. Of late he'd called Boston his home. He'd been considering a move farther west, a permanent move, and he'd returned to Buffalo yesterday to get the money his grandparents had been putting aside weekly almost since he was born. He'd calculated that at a dollar a week for the first ten years, and a few dollars thereafter until his twenty-first birthday, the money, with interest, should now have reached about $2500. If he intended to break all ties, he wanted the money in hand. Yesterday afternoon, he had gone into the back yard and broached the subject with Sam and Rose. Sam took the request at face value, but Rose had demanded to know why he had to have the money now since Morris had placed it in a high-yield account, and it was her intention to leave it there until she could give it to Jack as a wedding present. Sam had insisted that a gift was a gift, and the money was Jack's to do with as he pleased with no strings attached. If he wanted to stand up on a mountain top and throw every penny into the wind, however foolish that might be, they had no right to stop him.

As the discussion grew more heated, more Yiddish filtered in, and though Jack felt repulsed by its rich gutteral sound, it seemed to him that the subject of debate had changed: they were no longer arguing about the money but about something else. Then Rose pointed at him and said something about his mother—and Jack understood enough of the language to know what she meant. Or perhaps it had less to do with the language than the fact that he just knew. He had sensed it for years, and now he knew.

Several times the day of the funeral Sunny had tried to catch his eye, but he'd avoided looking at her. He knew he had to come to some decision, but he was unable to think clearly. He was trapped between his abhorrence of confrontation and his need to accuse.

Sunny. His friend. His *sister*. What a liar she was. All those years saying she was his friend, that she loved him. All that time she'd been lying.

His chest tightened and he swallowed hard, cursing because he felt tears come to his eyes. He wanted only to know if she would stop lying now. Then he would decide what to feel, what to think, what to do.

The Rosenthals lived on the first floor of a two-family house typical of many in that neighborhood. Long and narrow, the living room, dining room, bathroom, and kitchen followed one another, with bedrooms across the narrow hallway. The mourners gathered here and there in small subdued groups, standing around the beverages and the food, sitting on aluminum folding chairs in the back yard. Some of them had not seen one another since Meryl's wedding three years ago, and they commented about the passage of time, remarking that it was too bad that the reason for *this* gathering was not a happier one. Some of them had come to the funeral for Sunny's daughter, and if they said anything about this, they glanced to make sure Sunny was not within earshot.

Sunny was standing in the corner of the living room. Beside her, Rose sat in a wooden chair, her hands curved listlessly around an old jelly glass filled with *shnaps*. Sunny's attitude and stance were protective, but she realized that her posture was for her own protection and not her grandmother's.

Sunny had reacted to the news of Sam's death calmly. Though it was unexpected, it did not shock her or, for that matter, even seem real. It was not that she disbelieved her mother. Rather, the information was like a piece of abstract data that had little meaning to her life.

When she stepped out of the car outside the Memorial Chapel, however, she understood that her grandfather was dead, and tears came suddenly to her eyes. Her father was standing at the door. After a brief perfunctory embrace, he'd held her by the shoulders, his eyes at once accusing and forgiving, reminding her that she had chosen not to be with her grandfather on the last day of his life. Her mouth had tightened. She'd wanted to say that if she had made that choice, it was he who put her in a position forcing her to do it. But she couldn't say this, and ashamed that any hint of her relationship with Kay should arise on the day of her grandfather's funeral, she walked quickly into the Memorial Chapel where she'd sat down, covered her face and burst into tears.

Her face was pale, and though she'd washed away the tear stains on her cheeks, the grief was still visible. She seemed at one and the same time vulnerable and defensive, as though she were suffering but would not admit it and would reject any offers of sympathy that came her way.

She was standing in between the curtained window and the sheeted mirror. Past the sheer curtain she could see the porch, the card table, the pitcher of water. She kept picturing Sam on the day of Debbie's funeral: he was standing on the porch, pouring a trickle of water into his open palm, and he was crying.

Sighing, she looked away from the window. Her eyes swept the room. Most of the people were involved in conversations, and one or two met her glance. Several times that day when she had caught someone's eye, she'd gotten the feeling that they were talking about her. But she'd ignored the feeling as paranoia or conceit, as though it were preposterous that she could exist in anyone else's mind but her own.

At the end of her glance was the rectangular wall mirror, now covered with a sheet. She'd forgotten about the sheet. She'd expected the reassurance of her own image, and it shocked her to see nothing. It was as though she too had died or ceased to exist. After the funeral service for Debbie, she'd stood in this same corner, and turning to see the sheeted mirror, she'd felt the same shock—as though now that Debbie was gone, so was Debbie's mother.

Her gaze returned to the living room. She was uncomfortable in the ill-fitting dress she hadn't worn in years, in nylons through which were clearly visible the legs she had several months ago stopped shaving. Her mother had told her to wear a dress to the funeral. Any dress, as long as it was a dress, was better than slacks, no matter how nice they were. But she'd worried about her legs, and although she'd felt embarrassed to be thinking about such a thing, she'd asked Kay for advice.

She sighed. Coming to her family's house was sometimes like coming to another world. How many relatives in inquiring about her life had asked about a man, and finding out there was no man, looked puzzled, or sympathetic, or encouraging. Don't worry, their attitude said, you'll find someone.

19

She felt invisible. The woman who'd stood in naked pride at the edge of the water had vanished. This creation—a large awkward girl in a too-tight dress with legs (one could not help but see) that needed shaving—she had been created for the family and would, in a few hours, be removed with a sigh of relief.

She felt a movement beside her and saw Rose bending forward, her hand on the arm of the chair for support as she prepared to rise. Sunny touched her shoulder. "What is it, Grandma?"

"I vahn a *bissel shnaps.*"

"You got some in your glass, Grandma, see? Right there, in your glass."

Rose looked, then raised her hand and drained the liquor. She handed the glass to Sunny and repeated, "I vahn a *bissel shnaps.*"

"Okay, Grandma," Sunny said, and walked into the kitchen. She poured some *shnaps* into the glass, added a fresh ice cube, and turned to her mother who was standing at the sink making coffee. "I think Grandma's getting pretty drunk."

"Seven, eight, *nine,*" Sylvia said in annoyance, because she was counting scoops. When she was done, she turned to Sunny, trying to focus on what it was she'd said.

"Ma, is there anything I can do?"

"No, no, everything's done. I just had to make coffee, that's all."

"Oh. Well, I think Grandma's getting kind of drunk."

"That's all right. It'll do her good," she said, then saw the jelly glass imprinted with a cartoon character. She let out a sigh of exasperation that was almost a laugh. "Your grandmother," she said, and it was a statement in itself. "She can't use the nice glasses. She has to use Yogi Bear."

Sunny shrugged. "Have you seen Jack?"

"He's upstairs."

"Upstairs. . . what is he doing *upstairs?*"

Sylvia gave her a look that said, Do you expect *me* to know the answer to that?

"Well, I'm going to bring this in to Grandma, and then I'll be upstairs if you need me."

"It would be nice if he came downstairs awhile," Sylvia suggested.

Sunny shrugged, as if to say that she would try, but she didn't have much faith in the results.

"Well, *mention* it," Sylvia pressed, and Sunny nodded, carrying the drink in to her grandmother.

Upstairs, she walked across the attic floor and knocked gently on the door to Jack's room. "Jack?" she called in soft inquiry, but he didn't answer. She knocked again and opened the door. He was standing by the window, his back to her. "Jack. . ." she said, and walked toward him, holding out her arms to offer an embrace.

Her bearing expressed sorrow and the sense that whatever their past differences, they should now stand together in the face of death. When he turned to her, however, his eyes said more than she wanted to see, and she kissed him rather awkwardly on the cheek, feeling a rising and confused mixture of anger, frustration, love, pity, guilt. She couldn't decide whether she wanted to hug him or shake him, and not knowing what to do, sat down on the bed, on the spot he had lately vacated. Out of all the churning of unexpressed emotion, she managed to salvage an attitude of wry conspiratorial humor, as though by one glance there sparked between their eyes a common understanding and a common bond. They had once been close; that feeling had sprung up naturally between them so that despite the six-year age difference, they were allies against the family. *The Family.* That was how they had said it, with their dry, ironic condescending humor. They had put great meaning into that word, and what they meant was the same thing. But as they remained there in that silent room—she on the bed, removing her shoes and rubbing her sore feet, he motionless by the window—she saw that time had changed them both in different ways, and *family* had changed its meaning. Their alliance was an empty pretense forced by her silent insistence. She remembered that when they'd been together the last several times, he had been cool and distant.

Now she wasn't sure what to do. Small talk was out of the question. Barefoot, sitting on the low bed, it struck her that she was in the traditional pose of sitting *shiva,* when barefoot mourners sit on low stools in darkened rooms and give themselves up to grief. She felt suddenly and totally drained and wished she were alone to cry out her unhappiness. Wishing this, Sunny knew that for the first time she felt vulnerable in front of Jack. But she chided herself on her distrust: she was tired and imagining things.

After awhile he sat down beside her. "I think I'm moving out West," he said casually, as though the other moments had never happened. "Either that or I'm moving back here. What do you think I should do?"

It was the way they usually began conversations, jumping into the middle of a topic even after a long separation, almost as if they were so close they could disdain small talk and social amenities. It struck a familiar chord, too, because he was coming to her for advice. She inclined her head thoughtfully to the side, and as she usually did, answered him with a question: "Well. . . what do you *want* to do?"

He sighed, and shook his head wearily. The question seemed to mean more than a simple decision about geographic location.

When Sunny was sure he would not speak again, she asked tentatively, "How have you been?"

He shrugged in response to indicate that he had been all right but not wonderful, and asked, "How have *you* been?"

She grimaced slightly to indicate that she had been all right but not wonderful, and they smiled.

Encouraged, she said, "You know, Jack, I think we ought to talk."

He seemed to stiffen but didn't otherwise respond.

"Mom said that you were the last person to see Grandpa alive."

"Who?"

"*Grandpa,*" she said, annoyed at what she took to be a foolish game.

"He wasn't my grandfather."

There was a silence. She opened her mouth to speak. Jack stared straight ahead. "Did anything happen in the yard yesterday?" she asked.

He gave her a quick glance, the meaning of which she didn't understand, and stood up and walked to the window.

"Did you two have. . ." She stopped, for as he'd crossed the room, she'd seen that the mirror was uncovered. "Why isn't your mirror covered?"

He shrugged. "I guess Mom forgot to do it," he said, his voice innocent of deception.

Not seeing the sheet that lay on the floor in a heap, she nodded and looked at him. His back was to her now, his thumbs crooked in the pockets of his jeans in studied casualness.

"Jack?" she prompted, but he didn't answer. "Jackie?" she appealed teasingly, speaking in a heavy Yiddish accent and sounding like Rose.

"Dont *call* me that!" He turned to face her. "That's not my *name.* That's a *kid's* name. I'm *not* a kid, I'm a *man!*"

She regarded him coolly. "Obviously."

He flushed. "I don't mean *that.* I mean. . . I wish you'd just. . . ."

He sighed and shook his head, but whether this expressed his inability or unwillingness to go on, his impatience with his speaking or her listening, Sunny did not know. The conversation was as ill-fitting as the clothes she wore, and she felt as encumbered by other people's silences as by their expectations. She longed to toss it all aside and reach out to him, and from this longing she asked, "Do you remember when we used to go to the quarry?"

"The quarry!" he said, and there was something hateful in his eyes that she didn't understand.

"And we'd pretend all kinds of great adventures. . ." she said, less surely now. "That the rocks were booty. . .and we'd lug all that stuff back home. And then when we got home the rocks were never as great as we imagined at the quarry." She smiled at him, asking that he share in her memory.

But his face was sullen, and he didn't speak.

Something had changed in the air between them. She felt he was putting up barriers, daring her to cross them or ask why they were there. She would do neither, at least not today, and after a few more uncomfortable moments, she slapped her hands on her legs with a gesture of finality and stood up, saying that she would be downstairs if he wanted company. As she opened the door she remembered her mother's request and said, "By the way, you might try coming downstairs for awhile."

"Yeah. *Sure,*" he said, so insolently that she felt the urge to slap him.

With a sense of relief, she closed the door behind her and walked across the attic floor. When she reached the attic window, she stopped and looked down at the yard below.

A five-foot stockade fence ran the length of one side, and toward its far end a mural had been painted. Though the drawing was crudely done and the colors had weathered, it was still possible to see that the mural represented a paradise of sorts. Sam had loved the painting and often remarked on its beauty and the great artistic talent of its creators, Jack and Sunny.

The mural had been the cause of considerable uproar at the time of its creation. Mo and Sylvia had gone to visit Sylvia's mother and father in Miami Beach for a week one summer, and Sunny, staring at the bare fence one day during a visit to Jack, had remarked that the unpainted wood was a perfect opportunity for them to express their artistic what-cha-ma-call-it. With the sense of great adventure that had characterized their relationship, they proceeded to create their masterpiece. Mo, upon returning home, had been furious. Like the house, the fence was still technically owned by the bank. If he decided to sell, the mural would be a liability and would have to be painted over, which would ruin even more the natural tones of the wood. Jack had been punished, and Sunny, no longer living at home, upbraided. The two of them had drawn more closely together, muttering about Our Father the Tyrant, plotting ways to subvert his authority, and laughing.

As they regarded Mo's censure as out of proportion to their act, so too they regarded Sam's praise. The painting had never been "good." The two support beams running across its length gave it an oddly distorted quality. And now, years later, from the vantage point of the attic, the faded paradise seemed to Sunny like something planned and created by a former self to whom she felt she bore no resemblance.

More than that, it reminded her of how things had changed between herself and Jack. Was it, as he'd inadvertently said, because he was now a man? Or was this his way of expressing grief. Or perhaps she had deluded herself. Perhaps they'd never been close. This made her uneasy, for it implied that she could not even trust her own feelings, her own memories. There was yet another possibility, another source for Jack's anger, but she did not explore it, telling herself rather peevishly that she had remembered enough for one day. She had grieved enough. Sunny frowned resolutely, and started down the stairs.

But motion was no escape from memory, for the stairway and the act of leaving made her think of Sam and the way he'd said good-bye.

For years when her family had lived out of town, they'd come in to Buffalo only to visit Sam and Rose. When their visits were over and it was time for them to leave, Sam always cried. He'd stand on the upstairs landing and lean over the wooden railing, watching Mo and Sylvia and the children troop down the stairs. "Get outta here, go on!" he'd call, wiping his eyes and coughing to hide the emotion. "You ate up all deh onions from my herring, get out!"

And always, as they filed out the front door, he'd call, "Good ribbons to bad rubbish! And don't come back no more!"

It wasn't until years later that she realized he was mispronouncing *riddance,* but by then the image was set: when she heard him call out "Good ribbons to bad rubbish," she imagined a wide, red bow tied around a garbage can, as though to indicate some redeeming quality within.

As a child, and even as a teenager, she'd laugh at him and scoff to her mother, "Grandpa's so sentimental!" She could never understand why partings were the cause of such emotional turmoil. Now she tried to think back to when she had seen him last, but the recent visits blurred together; the way she'd said good-bye seemed insultingly casual, and careless of the power that fate had to change their lives. She remembered the phone call with her father and her refusal to come here yesterday. She felt that somehow she was at fault, that if she had come, her presence would have made a difference, and she would not now be standing in this darkened stairwell on the verge, once again, of tears.

Chapter 3

Convergence

Kay had never met Sam, and his death was as abstract to her as his life had been. Sunny had not cried when she'd learned of his death, and by the time she'd returned home from the funeral, she'd recovered her composure. Though she seemed to be unusually preoccupied for a few days, by the end of the week, it was almost as if (it seemed to Kay) nothing had happened.

At first she assumed that Sunny had not been particularly close to her grandfather. Then, thinking back, she interpreted Sunny's behavior as a sign of her inner strength, her indomitable will, and her resolve to survive and overcome whatever tragedies life had placed in her path. This was an impression Kay had of Sunny from the very beginning, an impression that refused to be shaken.

The two women had met several years earlier when Kay was an undergraduate at the University, and Sunny a secretary in the History Department. Walking in one day to inquire about a course, Kay came upon the following scene: Sunny sitting at her desk in a pose of determined relaxation, her mouth firm, her eyes fixed on a man who stood before her—the Department Chairman. Later, when the two women became friends, Sunny told her the specifics of the situation. But the specifics were never as clear as that first mental image.

The following semester when Kay was assigned a work-study job in the English Department, she often stopped in at the History Department downstairs to chat with Sunny. Sunny's obvious disrespect of the Chairman, her assumption that his power was illegitimate, her recognition that it was power nonetheless, fascinated Kay. Sunny seemed straightforward, matter of fact, and irreverent. The two women came to enjoy a casual yet profound communication whereby with a single look they could recall a previous conversation and would smile, or shrug, or burst out laughing without having said a word.

Then one day Sunny disappeared. She was not at work that day, or the next, or the following week. Kay was bewildered. Suddenly insecure about what their friendship meant, what they'd really said with those silent glances, she felt she had no right to call Sunny at home. Eventually, she learned that Sunny's daughter had died. She wanted to comfort her, to offer solice. But she imagined Sunny being surrounded by a bulwark of friends and family, and she didn't want to intrude.

She didn't see Sunny again until several months later when, turning down an aisle in the supermarket, she saw a woman standing near the frozen food section. She thought it was Sunny but wasn't sure. This woman seemed older. She was haggard and appeared ill. Kay approached her and touched her arm, speaking her name. When Sunny looked up there was no recognition in her eyes, and when Kay reminded her of their acquaintance, Sunny's reaction seemed muffled and dazed. Yes, she said, she remembered Kay, she remembered their chats, but her eyes were blank.

The meeting disturbed Kay. She tried not to think about it, and when she did, she told herself she would probably never see Sunny again.

One day almost a year later, they met by chance at the downtown library. Sunny had started a new life. She'd left her husband, gotten her own apartment and a different job, and had a determined, almost aggressive look in her eyes. Immediately, Kay felt that this was the woman who had so impressed her once before—the woman in control of her life, the woman who faced adversity squarely and refused to be beaten. Kay saw no trace of the woman in the supermarket and gradually forgot her. She assumed Sunny had recovered.

The first thing that jarred this assumption was Sunny's neighborhood. Sunny lived on the West Side across the street from the Buffalo Armory, a massive stone structure that occupied an entire city block. It took several visits before Kay realized that on the other side of the Armory was the Niagara River, where downstream a half a mile or so toward the Falls, Sunny's daughter had drowned.

The river was not visible from the apartment. But it was there. Sunny's continual and forced proximity to the river, and the fact that she so rarely spoke of her daughter, unnerved Kay. Finally one day she asked, "Why did you get an apartment so close to the river?" and was again unnerved by the look on Sunny's face, almost as if she hadn't

been aware that there was a significance to the apartment's location.
Neither of them mentioned it again. Kay told herself she was respecting Sunny's privacy. In reality, she was unwilling to face the contradictions and complexities that might flourish behind Sunny's strong determined exterior.

In June, Kay graduated from the University with a B.A. in Political Science. She'd thought of applying to law school. The prospect had seemed frightening, however, and she'd put off applying until it was too late. Her parents had helped her financially with college, and she was grateful for their help, but after graduation, she didn't want to take any more money. She looked for work, but a B.A. in Political Science didn't qualify her for much. Her only work experience was waitressing. Finally, she got a job in a little diner a few blocks from Sunny's apartment. Kay, who lived way out on the edge of the city by the University, did not have a car, and the result was inevitable: though Kay did not formally move out of her own place, she was in fact living with Sunny.

They were both satisfied with the situation. They casually discussed a more permanent move, but neither wanted to take the step.

Then one day in mid-November, during Kay's lunch break, she happened to call her house and was informed by one of the women that the house was to be sold and that in all likelihood, she would have to find a new place to live.

Walking home from work that afternoon, Kay realized that her perception of the neighborhood was changing from that of a visitor to that of a prospective resident. She didn't like the change. What had seemed quaint now appeared shabby. She knew that when Sunny got home from work, after they'd had supper, or perhaps while they ate, she would tell her about the house and tell her in such a way that Sunny would offer her own home to share. She knew also that lacking financial resources and a car, as well as the energy to search out a new living situation, she would probably move in with Sunny. But she had her doubts. She cared for Sunny. They got along well. But she feared that living together might limit her options for the future, limit her consideration of law schools, and necessitate a possible future break rather than a gentle tearing away.

At the front door she turned once more before going in. No, she decided, she did not care for the neighborhood as much as she might want. She didn't know if she could think of it as her home. But it would have to do. At least for the time being, it would have to do. She unlocked the outside door and walked up the stairs to the apartment.

Kay was by nature a more cluttered person than Sunny, but tonight she made sure that the apartment was neat and that none of her things were lying around. She started supper, making macaroni and cheese (Sunny's current favorite), and by the time Sunny opened the front door, the apartment was filled with the warm cooking smells of home.

It was a pleasant evening. Kay told Sunny the news; Sunny, as Kay foresaw, offered her apartment. "Are you sure?" Kay asked, and was a bit taken aback when Sunny replied, "No, I'm not *sure,* but I think it's the most practical solution given the circumstances."

"Gee, you're so romantic," Kay murmured.

Sunny half smiled, pretending to be indignant. *"I* think I'm romantic. . ."

"Yeah, sure. You're romantic at *certain times,* but otherwise, forget it."

Sunny laughed. "Hey, I'm new to this kind of thing," she said, holding her arms out to indicate their life together. "You never told me there was a rule book."

After supper they cleaned the kitchen, Kay clearing the table and putting away the leftovers, Sunny washing the dishes. At one point Kay opened a plastic container she'd found in the refrigerator, and said, "You've got something *alive* in here. Whew! It stinks! What the hell is it?"

Sunny glanced over. "I'm not sure. Maybe it's those garbanzo beans I couldn't find."

Kay shook her head. "For such a neat-freak, you have terrible lapses."

Sunny shrugged and adjusted the water.

They had decided to watch an old detective movie on TV, but when the dishes were done and the kitchen cleaned, Kay decided to take a shower.

She was in the middle of lathering up the washcloth when Sunny knocked on the plastic curtain. Kay pulled the curtain open a crack and saw Sunny standing there. "Yes?" she asked in a slightly clipped voice, taking the hint from the formal knock and Sunny's stiff bearing. "What is it?"

Sunny glanced at her wrist as if it were a watch and said, "It's time to be romantic."

"Get the hell outta here," Kay laughed, and pulled the curtain back. But after a moment she glanced out and saw Sunny undressing. She smiled.

Sunny joined her, and they traded soap and water as one or the other lathered or stood under the water, washing each others' backs, kissing wetly, and laughing. At one point Sunny began to sing, "Tooo Young, to go Steadeee. . ." and Kay cried, "No! No! Anything but that! *Please* don't sing!" At the same moment they remembered Mr. and Mrs. Mancuso in the quiet apartment below, and they shushed one another, laughing.

Afterwards, they dried themselves. The bathroom was warm and steamy, but the hallway to the bedroom was cold. Barefoot and naked, they ran into the bedroom and got into bed, clinging together and shivering. They made love, and then lay in one another's arms, talking. Soon Kay remembered the detective movie, and they went in to the living room to watch the last of it. Turning on the television, they cuddled spoonfashion on the couch, joking about the film's complicated plot and groaning when Sunny's cat Whiskers joined them and balanced with precarious ease on Sunny's arm.

At eleven the news came on. Kay, who worked the breakfast shift, was by then half asleep. But she felt Sunny's body tense, heard her exclamations of anger and disgust. Finally, Sunny sat up, shaking her head and cursing.

"What is it?" Kay murmured.

"This goddamned world!" Sunny snapped, and turned off the television set.

In bed, Kay snuggled up to Sunny so that they occupied virtually the same amount of space they had on the couch. But Sunny seemed withdrawn. She lay there, gazing at Whiskers who lay on her chest, petting him slowly, drawing her hand over and over again across his fur. Kay was aware that her own body and attention were focused on Sunny, but that Sunny was focused on the cat. She was aware, too, that there was a bond between Sunny and the animal that had existed when she came into Sunny's life, a relationship from which she was excluded. She lay there thinking sourly, I can't believe I'm jealous of a *cat*. Of a stupid cat.

She was not fond of the cat. It had rejected her many affectionate overtures, and contemptuously, she called it *The Cat*. Whiskers— How she hated that name! It seemed so childish—was unaffectionate to anyone but Sunny whom it adored, playfully attacking her feet as she walked by, sitting on her lap or chest for contented hours on end, and giving squeaky petulant cries when she moved. To Kay's annoyance, when Sunny was not home Whiskers sometimes walked around the apartment crying plaintively. He was not particularly handsome or unusual, being a plain black cat with a white patch on his face and white whiskers, but Sunny's devotion to him was obvious. To Kay he was arrogant and disdainful as befitted his position as the favored one, and treated her like an interloper from whom he must be prepared to expect the worst. He did not leave the house. Sunny called him "my agoraphobic cat." Outside, where he had to venture for occasional traumatic visits to the vet, he seemed to go into shock, and once home again, he had to be petted and pampered back into his arrogant paranoid self. Kay thought it was all ridiculous, and Sunny's solicitation over the stupid animal baffled her.

When she could no longer endure the purring and petting of which she was not a part, she said, "Well *one* thing I can tell you about me moving in, I'm going to have to get used to living with that stupid cat. *Whiskers*," she said disdainfully, "Where'd you ever pick a dumb name like that?"

She realized as soon as the words were out of her mouth that she shouldn't have spoken them.

"I didn't pick the name," Sunny said. "Debbie did. As a matter of fact, Debbie was the one who found him. She saved his life. Didn't she, you old Whiskers-face, you. . ."

Whiskers opened his eyes and blinked lazily, then unfolded a paw, reached out, and touched Sunny's face.

"How did Debbie save his life?"

"Oh. . . it's a long story."

"I have time."

Sunny smiled, sighing. "Well, we used to live a couple doors down from a restaurant. You know the place I mean. And one day me and Debbie were walking back from the library, and when we passed the back of the restaurant, Debbie stopped. I remember, I was holding her hand, and I felt her. . . I felt her stop. So I said, 'What's the matter, baby?' and she said, 'Mommy, what's that?' So I said, 'What's what?' and she said, 'Listen.' So I did and I heard this sound. . . . I didn't know what it was. It sounded at first like a baby crying, an infant. And it frightened me. I don't know why, but I knew it was something I didn't want to see, I didn't want to know. I wanted to keep walking, to go home and forget I'd ever heard it, and maybe I would have except for Debbie. But I didn't want her to see me do something like that, so we went towards the sound."

Sunny's lip quivered. She sighed and went on. "It was coming from this old oil drum, one of those fifty-gallon drums, the kind they store toxic wastes in. But the restaurant used it to throw away old cooking grease. I could smell it. And when I looked in, I saw this *thing* coming out of the bottom of the grease. It looked. . . it looked horrible, like an abortion from some kind of monster, and I wanted to turn away and let it disappear under the grease. Then I saw that whatever it was, it was struggling to keep its head above the grease. Its claws were scratching at the side of the drum, but it couldn't get out. It was trapped, and it was exhausted. I could tell. It was standing on its hind legs and slipped down and went under. Right before it went under it opened its eyes and cried, and I knew it was a kitten. I could tell from the cry that it didn't have any strength left.

"It all happened in a minute. I heard Debbie say, 'Mommy,' and I reached in and grabbed the kitten, but it slipped out of my grasp. . . ."

Sunny was silent for so long that Kay wondered if she was finished. Kay was about to speak when Sunny went on. "I'd seen some newspapers on the ground, and I grabbed them and pulled out the cat. I put him on the ground, and he just stood there, quivering, all slicked with that horrible brown grease. I remember his legs were shaking, but he looked up at me and meowed, and Debbie said, 'He's thanking you....' " Sunny smiled, her eyes filling with tears. "We began to wipe away the grease with newspaper, and when Debbie saw what he looked like, she said, 'Whiskers!' When *I* saw... when *I* saw, I understood what had happened. On the way to the library I'd seen a bunch of boys carrying the kitten. They were walking toward the restaurant." She looked at Kay and the tears spilled down her face. "They threw it in the grease," she said, sounding angry and bewildered. "For fun. To watch it suffer. To watch it die." Her lips quivered and she began to cry, covering her face with her hands.

Kay gave Sunny comfort. She stroked her hair and murmured soothing words, for it pained her to see Sunny so unhappy. But long after Sunny had fallen asleep, Kay lay awake staring into space.

After a time she got up and went into the kitchen, intending to make a cup of warm milk. But something about the apartment disturbed her, and had been disturbing her, she realized, for some time. On the surface everything was neat and in its proper place, so much so that she'd taken to teasing Sunny about her compulsion for order, her need for control. But there was another world, a chaos of disorder that existed under the surface, in drawers and cupboards and closets, a confusion of things Sunny had saved long after it was a practical thing to do. Kay wandered around the apartment, uncomfortably aware of the contradiction between what she could see and what she knew was hidden.

As she was getting back into bed, Sunny made a sound of protest in her sleep and rolled over. The side of her face was flushed and perspired, and she was frowning at whatever it was she was unable to escape.

She even worries in her sleep, Kay thought with a mixture of affection and concern. On one occasion she'd said to Sunny, half teasing, "You worry too much," and had been unprepared for Sunny's reaction: "Maybe I worry because there are things to worry about! Maybe you *don't* worry because you don't know what the hell is going on! Maybe I have good *reason* to worry!" A week or so later, when they were laying in bed, Sunny had put down the novel she'd been reading and said, apropos of nothing in particular, "You know, I've been thinking. Maybe you're right. Maybe I *do* worry too much. Because really, it doesn't make too much sense, does it? Abstract worrying? I mean, if you're going to *do* something about a situation, that's different. If you're going to *change* things. But if you're just going to *worry* about it...." But a week or so after that, as they were sitting in a movie theater waiting for the feature to begin, Sunny remarked, "Listen, I've decided. I'm sticking to my original decision about worrying." Kay had burst out laughing. "What the hell is so funny?" Sunny asked. Shaking her head, Kay said, "I never met anybody like you before. All this time you're worrying about worrying."

"Well. . ." Sunny responded, failing to see the humor in the situation, or unwilling to admit it.

But it did not seem so funny to Kay anymore, either.

Somehow, seeing Sunny's anxieties from a distance was safer, more romantic, easier to dismiss. Now, these same anxieties were uncomfortably harsh and constricting. She saw that behind Sunny's strength there was fear; beyond her determination there was terror; and behind the independent woman was a woman so fearful of loss, she was almost unable to love.

But she loves *me,* Kay thought, and the thought was both flattering and frightening.

Sunny, too, was made uneasy by the depths of rage and frustration that surfaced that night.

A cat had been tortured. What did it mean. . . and why was *she* tortured by the thought of it? Her immediate defense was to try to turn away from the fact of it and the emotions it engendered. It was past, over; there was nothing she could do. She felt equally powerless about the future as she did the past. Life on earth was being poisoned, doomed to either a slow choking death or sudden nuclear annihilation, and there was nothing she could do. Her response was to try to forget, to focus on her own life, unconnected and uncommitted. It might be lonely, it might be an illusion, but at least she could pretend it was painless.

The next day she felt vulnerable and exposed. She was relieved when after she got to work, the memory of her own anguished tears and the almost reluctant look she'd glimpsed on Kay's face lost its sharp edges and began to fade.

Sunny worked at Imperial Dynamics, an international company whose Buffalo plant manufactured, in her words, "parts for parts." The image of Imperial Dynamics as chosen by the public relations people was of a young, creative, socially concerned company. It was all a sham, and she knew it. Once, in the library, she'd looked up some of the company's history since its incorporation in 1871. She found it to be riddled with deception, collusion with corrupt government officials, illegal but successful attempts to quash competition, and violent repression of labor, especially during one bloody strike in 1933 in what amounted to the murder of seven workers. It had all been for the sake of profit and power. In spite of the public relations propaganda, it was the silent language of money that had determined Imperial's past glories and was determining its present functionings and future campaigns.

Her duties were mainly secretarial, but her goal was to leave not only typing behind but also the video terminal to which she was more and more becoming an extension. It seemed to her that she was continually being retrained for increasingly complex machines. She hated it—the words and numbers that had no meaning to her, marching on the screen in glowing green formation. The only way out that she could see was through promotion. It was company policy to promote from within, and she tried to be optimistic about her future at Imperial. This was especially true since there were rumors of a lower managerial promotion in the works, and talk had it that she was one of the three likely candidates.

Sunny evaluated herself continually. What she evaluated was not her work, for she knew that was good, but her appearance. And it was her entire appearance that concerned her: her looks, her voice, the image she presented to the world. She continued to use her ex-husband's name, though they were legally divorced. She tried even more than ever to be the subdued, modulated woman she'd always longed to be. Her appearance had mattered less when she was working at the University; at Imperial, appearance was all.

She took great care with how she looked at work, but invariably something betrayed her—a missing button, a scuffed shoe, the colors somehow not right. Sunny envied Kay's ease with clothes, her ability to throw on any old thing and look stylish and comfortable. It was a combination impossible for Sunny who either looked nice and felt miserable, or felt comfortable and looked sloppy. She would have liked to be taller, thinner, less dark. Her work clothes never seemed quite right on her, perhaps because she bought them for the woman she thought she wanted to be and not herself.

Sunny had had some success in transforming her image in the past: she'd maintained a coolness, a distance that passed for subtlety and modulation. Though it had always been an effort, it was one she made without conscious thought or deliberation.

After Sam's death, however, she began to change. In time, the change affected her appearance, altered the woman she presented to the world. It was a process of which she was completely unaware. She didn't think, my grandfather died, and I'm going to change. Nevertheless, the process had begun.

An image kept coming to her mind, an image of herself on her deathbed, suffocated by regret, smothered by all the rage and passion she had never voiced. She thought of her pleasant relationship with her grandfather and of all the things she'd wanted to ask him, to tell him. She had never talked with him about the day Debbie died. If only, if only. . . it had kept her awake nights. But she'd never spoken to him, and now it was too late.

She became aware that her life was filled with deception, and that she was a liar. She was not a unique or extraordinary liar, not a cruel or compulsive liar, not a psychotic liar. She was just your average everyday-garden-variety liar. She began to hear herself, see herself, understand the way she lied about what she felt, what had happened, and most of all, what she was. Subtly but absolutely, she lied by denial and by silence.

The most obvious thing was that she was the mother of a child who had died. One reason she had changed jobs, she realized, was so she wouldn't have to face that truth daily. When she'd first come to work here, Mary Grace Catalano, the woman with whom she shared an office, had asked her the standard questions: Are you married? Do you have any kids? "Nope," she'd said. Though it might have been the literal truth, it was a lie.

The lying had bothered Sunny, and she'd tried to put it out of her mind. But of course she couldn't entirely because Grace (as she called herself) had children, and her assumption that Sunny had none kept drifting into the conversation. The lie stayed in Sunny's mind, filled her with guilt, and inhibited their relationship. She decided to tell the truth, but she was embarrassed. Finally, one day when Grace was talking to her about her daughter, Sunny blurted out, "Grace, I have to tell you something. You once asked me if I had any kids, and I wasn't quite honest with you. I *did* have a child. A little girl. But she drowned. In an accident," she felt compelled to say. "When you asked me. . . your question was so casual, I just didn't know how to say it. Then I felt funny about it."

After that incident, Sunny felt better. But there were other things.

She consistently lied about her relationship with Kay. "I took my grandmother out to the Flea Market on Sunday," she'd say at work, omitting the fact that Kay had been an important, even essential, part of the day. Sunny told people she lived "with a friend," and when referring to her called her "my roommate," as though they were college girls thrown together by chance. It made her feel dishonest. Then she argued with herself: My private life is nobody's business! I'm a private kind of person. Why should I have to *define* myself? she demanded rather self-righteously, knowing full well it wasn't her own definitions she feared.

The worst of all the lies were those of silence. Sunny lied (though she did not see it that way) about being Jewish. At work she kept Frank's name, calling herself Sunny Strickland even though she and Frank were legally divorced. She did not look like what people thought of as "the typical Jew," and when they assumed, as they usually did, that she was Christian, she kept silent. She was afraid that people's feelings, attitudes, and expectations would change if they knew she was Jewish. She'd seen it happen. A glance would shift, a thread of smile from eye to eye would be broken, and suddenly she became a stranger, without commonality, without connection.

It was a terrifying feeling, as though she were somewhere outside of the world, as though her pain did not matter. It felt like she could be erased, and no one would care.

Of course, there were parts of being Jewish that delighted her, tickled her, warmed her, made her think—and she was learning more about them all the time. But when she was with people who did not understand what it meant to be a Jew, she hid the fact that she was Jewish.

Her deliberate omission of her Jewishness soon became irrelevant, however, because after Sam's death something else began to happen. It had nothing to do with conscious reflection, deliberation, or decision. It just happened, and it came from some deep unconscious place she didn't know existed, from a past she thought she'd gratefully forgotten.

She began using Yiddish. She wasn't even aware that she was doing this at first, but old familiar words and phrases slipped gradually into her conversation. The fact that she was using Yiddish bothered her, made her feel exposed in some dangerous way. And it annoyed her. She thought, You'll never become a classy broad with all this Yiddish popping out of your mouth. You have to stop this.

But it wasn't that easy. The words and phrases kept coming to mind and pushing themselves through her lips. She found that sometimes she was unable to express herself in English, to find that exact word, that precise feeling. Was it a Jewish feeling? Was that the problem? Was she trying to translate a Jewish sentiment into a foreign language? Even when she managed to suppress specific words, there was still a lilt, a way the words were strung together, a melody. And when she was silent, there remained a certain shrug of the shoulders that betrayed her: beneath that fine choking dust of Strickland there lay a Rosenthal in full bloom. Ashamed, perhaps. Insecure and uncertain of its existence, but vibrant at the core.

At work, at a place like Imperial Dynamics, at a time when she was bucking for promotion, Sunny had to be careful about exposing anything that she was. But even before she was up the front stairs heading toward the door to her apartment, she was unbuttoning buttons and unzipping zippers. Sunny was half-disrobed by the time she was past the kitchen and heading toward the bedroom, her suit jacket draped over her arm, her shoes held by two fingers. "Freedom!" she'd cry, and Kay, comfortable and beautiful, would smile in affectionate tolerance.

She was glad to get home at night, for more than ever, home had become her refuge. It was like the quarry: the one place where she could (or so she told herself) turn away from all the troubles of the world. In those autumn months after Sam's death, Sunny burrowed more deeply into her relationship with Kay. She made a precious island of their home. Here was a place where nothing could touch them. Here was a place that was safe.

She'd had a special feeling about Kay from the first time Kay walked into the History Department and their eyes met. When Kay began working upstairs, Sunny looked forward to seeing her, thought about her when she wasn't there, looked for things to share with her. In the beginning, Sunny talked to Frank about her, though he was clearly disinterested.

Sunny didn't make friends easily, so even though their friendship was casual and defined by their jobs, Kay meant a lot to her. But she never questioned her feelings or analyzed them; she was largely unconscious of them. The times late at night when her mind wandered. . . she kept those times closed off and never admitted them into her daylight thoughts. They had absolutely no meaning, she was convinced, and were irrelevant to her life.

Then one day they were alone in the office. Sunny was at her desk by the far wall and Kay was standing at the window describing the beautiful spring day. Sunny had been looking at the bit of sky she could see from her desk when she noticed the line of Kay's body where her belt encircled her waist. She noticed how the material of her plaid shirt strained when she lifted her arm. She noticed the curve of her hip. She was gazing at that smooth line where her hip flared out when Kay turned around, and their eyes met.

Sunny blushed, pretending nothing had happened, that the air was not suddenly charged. The moment passed, however, and Sunny thought no more about it. Later, when they became lovers, Kay sometimes teased her. "What were you thinking?" she'd demand with a wicked smile, and Sunny would blush all over again.

Falling in love with a woman was something she never would have expected, and it had taken her by complete surprise. She hadn't yet adjusted or come to terms with what it meant. She knew only that being lovers seemed like a natural progression from being friends. They had been close; they'd become intimate. Sunny, who'd always been sexually discrete because she disliked sleeping with someone for the first time, was struck by how comfortable, how natural it felt to make love with Kay. It was as though this was where she was meant to be, in the arms of another woman.

After they made love that first time, Sunny had cried. They were tears not of remorse but release. Kay kissed her forehead and murmured soothing words of comfort. It seemed to Sunny, as they lay in one another's arms, that there was a closeness between them she had never before experienced. Kay touched something inside her, the hidden heartbreak that in trying to be strong she'd ignored.

There was something about Kay that attracted Sunny immensely, something in her eyes, in the way she moved, that made Sunny feel good about herself and about the two of them together. Kay had a passion for the moment, and at the same time, her presence was like a link with a past from which Sunny felt at times almost totally separate. She began to feel that her relationship with Kay was meant to be, that this woman had been fated to bring her back to life, to lead her back to an understanding of love.

Sunny was delighted Kay would be moving into her apartment; she believed it would bind them more closely together. And Kay's casual admonitions that living together was only a temporary arrangement subject to possible decisions from law school admissions boards hardly put a dent in Sunny's happiness.

One thing that did make her uneasy was the fact that Jack was back in town and had been back for some days. She learned this from her mother, who'd phoned one evening to invite Sunny and Kay to come celebrate the first night of Chanukah, several weeks hence. Sunny was so delighted that the invitation included the both of them that at first she didn't sense the strained quality to her mother's voice. "Is Grandma all right?" she finally asked. Yes, Sylvia answered, Rose was fine. "Then what's *wrong*?" Sunny pressed. Sylvia hesitated, and told her that Jack had returned to Buffalo.

He'd returned, but he hadn't phoned her. Her feelings were hurt. When Sylvia added quickly that Jack had been busy, Sunny made light of it and asked to speak to him. Their conversation, however, was like the one after Sam's funeral. Jack's sarcasm was just on the edge of insolence. He offered no excuse or apology for not having phoned. He said he was home to stay, or to stay until the spirit moved him.

Sunny forgave his neglect and his insolence. No one was perfect, after all, and who was she to stand in judgment. She loved Jack and didn't want to be angry with him or feel estranged. Before they hung up, she made it a point to invite him to dinner that Friday night. She wanted him to meet Kay, she told him. She wanted them to be friends. She wanted the three of them to be like her image of what family should be: close, supportive, warm, honest.

Jack came to dinner, but the evening was out of kilter, unbalanced. Jack acted as though he didn't like Kay. When she was speaking, he interrupted her to talk to Sunny. He brought up subjects from which she was excluded. He leaned forward, visually coming between her and Sunny.

Sunny at one point pushed him back, gently but firmly, and said, "Jack, get outta my way."

He turned to Kay. "She's picking on me. You see how she picks on me? I brave the snowstorm, the first snowstorm of the season, just to see my dearest sister, and look how she treats me. Is that justice?" he pleaded, and Kay smiled.

When Jack left, Sunny stood at the open door. She waited for Kay to walk into the back of the apartment and then she said, "Jack, what's your goddamned problem? Are you jealous of Kay?"

He didn't answer, merely smiled.

"You know my feelings for Kay have nothing to do with my feelings for you. You're my brother and I love you," she said, and was unprepared (but not totally unprepared) for the look he gave her. In a moment of insight, she sensed what was wrong. She ignored it, however, and asked, "Are you upset because I'm with a woman?"

He paused before answering, zipping up his jacket. "Hey, it's your life."

"Yes. I know it is."

Later she was in the bathroom brushing her teeth when Kay, clad in a bathrobe and leaning against the doorjamb, frowned thoughtfully and said, "You know what was strange? While you were in the bathroom before, Jack made it a point of telling me he was adopted."

Sunny's hand stopped. "What did he say," she asked carefully and recommenced brushing, but more slowly.

"Well. . . I don't remember exactly, but he made a point of it. As though he wanted to see whether or not I knew. It was more like he was probing rather than telling."

Sunny nodded. "So what did *you* say?"

"I told him right out that I knew. That you'd told me."

Sunny rinsed her toothbrush and hit it against the sink to knock off the excess water. "And what did he say to that?"

Kay thought for a moment. "He just looked at me and nodded. Your brother's a strange bird, let me tell you." She started out of the bathroom, then paused and said, "You know, I'd always meant to ask you. . . I didn't think Jews adopted children. I thought you had to be *born* a Jew."

"Are you asking me now?"

"No. I asked Jack," she said, and began to turn away.

"What did he say?"

She turned back. "He said that according to Jewish law, the child is the religion of the mother. He said he wasn't Jewish since he never formally converted or had a *bar mitzvah*. Is he right?"

"Oh, I don't know that much about Jewish law," she said rather evasively. After Kay left, she bent to wash her face.

In a moment of clarity, she'd seen her life as it was, understood that she had to let herself out in bits and pieces, never able to be wholly herself, to express completely what she knew and felt. Not with anyone. She was a woman shattered into fragments, visible only when someone was able to see one small part or another. But in herself, whole. . . she was that before no one. And Sunny was suddenly engulfed in a terrible loneliness, saddened by the complexity that she had become, or rather by the complexity that she seemed to be in a world that abhorred complexity. She straightened and reached for the towel. Whatever others saw when they looked at her, she saw now as she stood before the mirror, her face still wet, only the depths in her eyes. Surrounded by her changing face, her eyes expressed the essence of her nature and the sum of her experience. Ever changing, yet always the same. It's me, she thought, it's really just me. It was a shock of recognition, as though she'd seen unexpectedly into her soul. She was unprepared and looked away, drying her face. When she glanced back to experience once again that touchingly bittersweet communion, it was gone. She saw her eyes looking at her eyes, and nothing more.

Several weeks later, on the first night of *Chanukah,* the Rosenthal family that lived in Buffalo gathered at Mo and Sylvia's house. Sometimes called the Festival of Lights, *Chanukah* commemorates religious freedom and the rebellion of Judah Maccabeus. The celebration is simple: on eight successive nights, Jews light *Chanukah* candles. Children spin the *dreidel,* a top with Hebrew letters on each side, and people eat fried foods such as potato *latkes,* or pancakes, because of the significance of the oil.

Sylvia Rosenthal was not thinking about *Chanukah* or its significance. She had forgotten to buy *Chanukah* candles and was hoping she'd saved two candles from years past for just such an emergency. She did not want her husband to know she'd forgotten and decided that if she couldn't find the candles, she'd have to call Sunny or Meryl and ask one of them to stop on their way here, buy some, and not make a big deal about handing them over.

That reminded her of the blender. Her electric blender was broken, and she was anticipating with dread the necessity of grating by hand all the potatoes and onions. *Latkes* for eight people. . . figure five *latkes* per person. No, better make it seven. Mo couldn't stand not having enough, and if there were any left over, she could freeze them; Mo could always eat them later. So eight times seven. . . that would mean ten potatoes and two big onions? God, her fingers would be in shreds by then. Unless Sunny remembered to bring her blender. But they'd have to keep it out of Rose's sight. She wondered if Sunny would remember this by herself. No, she'd better call to remind her, and remind her to bring the damned blender in the first place. The recipe for potato *latkes* did not call for shredded human flesh, and if she had to use the hand grater. . . .

Did she have enough potatoes?

Luckily, she found several candles next to the *menorah* on the top shelf of the kitchen cupboard. She stuck in the main candle, the *shammes,* and the first one. Then she carried the *menorah* into the living room where Mo was watching the news and placed it on top of the TV.

"Hey! Was your mother an iceberg?" Mo snapped. She was blocking his view.

"Sah-ree," Sylvia drawled, and started out of the room when she heard him say, "Hey Ma, why don'cha go in the kitchen? Syl wants to make you a cup of tea."

"Don't do me any favors," Sylvia said to him with a glance at her mother-in-law.

Rose was leaning forward, only momentarily interrupted in her narration of The Saga of Rose the Unvanquished, as Meryl called it. The current tale concerned her day at the Jewish Center. She had just finished laughing to her son about having received hints of a marriage proposal and was about to commence telling him how she'd responded when Mrs. Sadetsky, an old friend of sorts, tried to cut ahead of her in the lunch line.

"*Vuss?*" she asked, looking from her son to her daughter-in-law.

"It's not like I have nothing to do," Sylvia appealed to her husband. He countered with, "Come on, I'm trying to watch the news," and since watching the news was an almost sacred ritual to him, she gave in. "Oh all right," she said. "Come on, Ma, I'll make you a cup of tea."

"Nuh! I don' vahn no tea."

"Come on, Ma. I got your favorite cookies. Oatmeal."

"Oytmeal?"

"Yeah. You'll help me with the *latkes*. Come on, your son wants to watch the news."

"You vatching dah news?" Rose inquired of her son, to which he replied, "Ma! for Christ's sake!"

She looked at him, then turned a bewildered and innocent face to her daughter-in-law. Shaking her head, as if his annoyance were incomprehensible, she stood up and followed Sylvia out of the room.

The house had an odd feeling about it. Everything was exactly in its proper place, and guests sometimes felt uncomfortable, as though their presence was disturbing the proscribed order of things. Rose, however, took delight in being contrary, at least where her daughter-in-law was concerned. She found defiant, almost spiteful pleasure in leaving a glass on the end table, or her shoes peeking out from under the sofa, or her sweater dumped on the seat of the easy chair, so that Sylvia had to follow her, constantly putting in order what Rose was determined to leave in chaos. At the same time, Rose pretended to notice dirt everywhere. When she prepared to sit down on a kitchen chair, for example, she went through an elaborate pantomime: she'd look with barely concealed distaste at the chair, then take a handkerchief and dust off the seat as one might a park bench. Once she went so far as to place the handkerchief down as though the seat were a public toilet and she was fearful of some unmentionable social disease.

All of this exasperated Sylvia, as Rose intended it to, but the younger woman tried to maintain a humorous perspective, mainly because she didn't want to give Rose the satisfaction of knowing she'd gotten to her. Sometimes she'd jerk a thumb toward Rose and comment to whoever was nearby, "This is the same woman, mind you, who leaves her false teeth soaking overnight in a jar on the kitchen table."

As Sylvia was filling the kettle with water, the front door opened, and Meryl and her husband Joe walked in. Mo, still engrossed in the news, barely said more than hello. Meryl took no notice of her father's preoccupation. She, like the other children, had been raised in an atmosphere of political awareness. The evening news was a time when their father was not to be disturbed, and he would sit and shake his head over Richard Nixon and Southeast Asia as he now shook his head over Ronald Reagan and Central America.

But this awareness, and the Rosenthals' basically Marxist attitude about the oppressive nature of capitalist society, was tempered (or even overshadowed) by an all too acute awareness of the risks one took in opposing any ruling class. Rose's older brother had died in Russia opposing the Czar, and her nephew had lost a leg fighting against the Franco regime in the Spanish Civil War. Harry's promising career had been destroyed in the fifties because in the thirties he'd joined the Communist Party for a time, hoping to build a better world.

Meryl knew little about this. She was too angry and frightened about the way the world was going to be concerned about the personal consequences of taking risks. She had some time ago become frustrated with writing letters to legislators and signing petitions, and was hungering for a more dramatic way to express her outrage over the continued preparation for nuclear war and her fear about the future of life on Earth.

She removed her coat. Meryl was seven months pregnant and wearing maternity blue jeans with one of Joe's old flannel shirts. Pinned to the front was a button: a drawing of a cockroach and the words, *Nuclear War Survivor.*

Mo grimaced. "What the hell is that?"

She looked at him, her face impassive. "What does it *look* like?"

"Well. . . take it off."

Her expression indicated that she had expected precisely that reaction from him and was unmoved. "I'm going in the kitchen to help Mom," she said, and departed.

During this interchange, Joe had seated himself on the couch and faced the television. When his wife left the room he looked at his father-in-law. The two men exchanged a shrugging glance. They were

41

outnumbered tonight, and there was little they could do but grin and bear it. "Where's Jack?" he asked.

"Upstairs. He should be down in awhile."

Joe nodded, and they turned their attention once more to the television.

In the kitchen, Sylvia was peeling potatoes and dropping them in a bowl of cold water so they would not discolor. Meryl had flung an arm around her grandmother, who was seated, and Rose was smoothing her hand over Meryl's belly, exclaiming on the progress of her pregnancy as shown in her belly and her breasts.

Rose was an absolute believer in breast-feeding and was proud that Meryl had decided to nurse her baby. The fact that Sylvia had breast-fed none of her children was something Rose had still not forgiven. Every time one of the three girls had gotten sick, Rose threw it up to her for having denied them mother's milk. Once, when Meryl fell off her bicycle and broke an arm, Sylvia said, "I know, Ma, I know. It happened because I didn't nurse her."

The kitchen was brightly lit. From the outside, the kitchen curtains—a yellow and orange print of spices and jars—seemed like glowing rectangles against the dark house. Through the closed windows, Rose's laughter could be heard.

Sunny and Kay were passing by underneath. "I know who *that* is," Kay said, and Sunny nodded.

The path to the back was unshoveled. Sunny lead the way, cursing humorously and struggling to keep her balance in the foot-high snow, while Kay made a half-serious game of walking in her footsteps. "You're pigeon-toed," she complained.

Sunny hesitated only a moment before muttering, as though to herself, "Bowlegged people are the most critical goddamned people I ever met in my life." Kay smiled.

They'd gone around the back so that Sunny could show Kay the fence, though half way down the path they realized simultaneously that it was a stupid idea: it was dark, and they would have to tramp to the end of the yard where the mural was painted. After hearing Rose's laughter, however, Sunny was just as glad they'd taken the back way. Of all the family, Kay had had the most contact with Rose.

It was not by chance. Sunny had rightly sensed that among her relatives, Rose would have been least concerned about their relationship. Kay was Sunny's friend. She was a nice girl, and that was that. Rose was too concerned about and involved in her own life to bother about judging other people's morality. Besides, she did not depict morality in sexual terms, but in economic ones. Working people who saved their money to make better lives for their children were high on her list. The scum at the bottom—the "bestids"—were the capitalists, and the politicians they owned who cared nothing for the welfare of the very people whose lives they controlled, but were interested only in their own greedy ends.

As Sunny and Kay opened the outside door and stamped the snow off their boots, Sunny heard Meryl's voice. She remembered the day in September, several weeks before Sam's death, when Meryl came to visit. On an impulse (though it was an impulse she'd been thinking about for months), Sunny told her sister that she and Kay were. . . *together* was the word she used. Meryl knew what Sunny meant, and she was shocked. Sunny could see it even though Meryl tried to cover up. She was polite, almost like a professor who believed in academic freedom and contended that in all fairness, every side of an argument should be heard, even the wrong one. But the air was different between them; Sunny understood that for her sister, she was not the same person.

When Meryl left, Sunny had walked her downstairs to the front steps. She'd felt anxious about the distance between them and wanting to bridge it, she began to talk, to reminisce about the family and the times they shared, as though to remind Meryl who she was. When it was time to say good-bye, Sunny reached out and gave Meryl a big hug, kissing her on the cheek. At that moment, the front door opened, and Mr. and Mrs. Mancuso walked out. Seeing them, Meryl pulled away and cried in a kind of panic-stricken cheer, "I'll tell Mom. . . you said hello."

Sunny was shaken. She wanted to say that they had not spoken of their mother; there had been no talk of helloes. Instead, she introduced Meryl to the Mancusos as her sister.

When Kay came home, Sunny didn't tell her what had happened. She didn't know what to say, for nothing had really "happened." Besides, she didn't want Kay to feel uncomfortable around Meryl. Perhaps Meryl would change.

Now, hearing Meryl's voice loudly reassuring Rose that she would nurse, Sunny felt a terrible sadness. She would have liked to hold her sister, to smooth her hand over Meryl's belly, to touch that living part of her sister that she once had and might never have again.

She remembered all of this in an instant and remembered, too, that the last time she had been here for *Chanukah,* she'd been here with Debbie. They'd spun the *dreidel,* as she had done when she was a child, and sung the *dreidel* song. She turned to Kay, who'd just closed the outside door, and sang softly:

> *Dreidel, dreidel, dreidel*
> I made it out of clay
> and when it's dry and ready
> then *dreidel* I shall play.

Kay sighed. "I don't know if I'm ready for this."

Sunny smiled. They had talked about their behavior, warning each other about pet names, casual-yet-familiar touching, quick looks across the room that said more than they should.

At the door, Sunny removed her boots and put on her slippers. Kay stood there. Sunny glanced at her. "Come on, courage!"

"I forgot my slippers."

"What? You knucklehead... well, take off your boots. My mother'll have another pair of slippers somewhere."

"Okay."

Sunny knocked on the door and opened it into the kitchen.

Rose was drinking dark tea from a glass, sipping it noisily through a sugar cube she held in her front teeth. Sylvia was peeling onions. Rose put down her tea and picked up the conversation where she'd left it. Pointing a finger at Meryl who was heading out of the kitchen, she declared, "She's gonna noiss!" It sounded like an accusation or an announcement of victory.

"Yeah, Ma, I know she's gonna nurse. I never said she *shouldn't* nurse. Hello girls. . . ."

Once inside, the two women were engulfed at least outwardly in the mood and rhythm of the family—a somewhat chaotic mood made more confused by the business with the blender. Sylvia didn't want Rose to see the blender. Since Rose did not leave the kitchen except for once to go to the bathroom (whereupon Sunny and her mother exchanged humorously harried glances, and Sylvia said that this was ridiculous, she had to get her blender repaired), it meant that either Sunny or her mother or Kay (who was pressed into service) had to block Rose's view. Several times Kay sent Sunny glances asking what the hell was going on, and Sunny responded with a sigh which said, I'll tell you later.

Kay had expected something more formal from *Chanukah,* something more somber, something more. . . Jewish. And she was a bit disappointed that all it meant was eating these potato pancakes. The *menorah,* she saw when she went into the living room to meet Sunny's father, sister, and brother-in-law, was a modern-looking candelabra, and the two candles—small, spiraled, and of different colors—looked like they belonged more to a birthday cake than a religious holiday. Rose lit the middle candle and said a prayer, then handed the candle to Meryl who lit the first night's candle.

When they returned to the kitchen, Jack had just come downstairs. He poked around a bit, hands in pockets. Then, his face pinched and sullen, he wandered towards the living room.

"What the hell's the matter with him?" Sunny asked after he'd gone. Sylvia shrugged. "You know Jack. He makes waves," she said, as if Jack were a huge destroyer, the U.S.S. Jack, and woebetide the rowboat caught in his wake.

Their attitude annoyed Kay. Of course he would harbor resentment; he was so obviously an outsider. When he walked out of the kitchen, she watched him go.

Sylvia had begun to fry the potato *latkes* on a long black griddle, draining them, crisp and brown, on paper towels, and putting them in the oven to keep warm. When a large batch was ready, everyone sat down at the kitchen table to eat: Mo at the head of the table, his back to the sink; Sunny to his left and Kay to his right; Rose next to Sunny, Jack next to Kay, and past them, Meryl and Joe. The end seat was empty, for during most of the meal Sylvia stood at the stove overseeing the food, her back to the table.

There were often several conversations going on at once, and to make oneself heard, it was necessary to push through the jostling personalities and tangle of words. Yet despite all the words flung out in annoyance or tossed out in jest, despite the words that supposedly came so easily, there was a silent undercurrent of tension. Not from all of them, not all the time. But it was there. They seemed to self-consciously dress themselves up in the costume of a bustling family with themselves as actor and audience. All the while there was something else, and Jack was the reminder, not only by his presence but by his actions. He seemed to stand in the wings, observing in judgment and cool disdain.

The critical expression in his eyes made its way to his mouth when they first sat down, and he found fault with the fact that they were seated at the kitchen rather than the dining room table. "I don't even know why we *have* a dining room table, we never *use* it."

From the griddle came a sizzle as Sylvia spooned the cold potato mixture onto the hot oil. Without pausing from her work or turning around, she said, "If you think I'm going to stand over a hot stove all alone. . . ." While she said this in a humorous grumble, as though she were overplaying a harried housewife, the rest came out a little sharper, "then you'd better think again. If *I* have to suffer, *you* have to suffer."

"Suffer-shmuffer, who's suffering," Mo muttered. Then, folding his hands before him and speaking somewhat formally, though the tone sounded out of place given his rough voice, he began inquiring about Kay—her family, the length of time she'd been in Buffalo, her plans for the future. Rose knew the answers to almost every question, and supplied them, leaving Kay to sit there with an amused look on her face.

Mo smiled at Kay and shook his head. He leaned forward like an interested scholar and said to his mother, "And tell me, Sherlock, what does her father do for a living and how much money does he have in the bank?"

Rose, knowing she was being teased, chortled out, "*Oy!*" and laughed, saying something in Yiddish.

Only Jack had not laughed at this exchange. Kay heard him mutter,

"Why do you always have to talk about money?" When Sylvia brought the platter of crisp potato *latkes* to the table, he complained, "Isn't there a serving spoon?"

Without a moment's hesitation, she turned back to the table and with a daintily contemptuous gesture, lifted a *latke* by her fingertips and plopped it on Jack's plate. "Home-style potatoes, be my guest."

Meanwhile, Mo was looking at the table, frowning. "Syl, where's the sour cream?"

At the stove, there was a silence. Sylvia's back seemed to have stiffened, and the only sound was the timid sizzle of frying food.

"Uh-oh," Meryl said.

Sylvia turned and faced her husband, her eyebrows raised and her lips pursed together like a penitent defendant before a powerful judge.

"Uh-oh," Sunny echoed.

Mo's mouth fell open. He sat before a plate of waiting *latkes*, a knife clutched in one fist and a fork in the other. "Don't tell me there's no sour cream. . . ." From her silence, he knew this was precisely what she was telling him. His head drooped, and his fists, still clutching the knife and fork (though with considerably less determination), slumped onto the table. "There's no sour cream. I don't believe there's no sour cream. How can I eat potato *latkes* without sour cream?"

Kay was observing the interactions with a bewildered smile. Sunny, trying to explain, said, "My mother forgot the sour cream."

Kay shrugged. "Is it so terrible to eat potato. . . um. . . without sour cream?"

Mo sighed and stared at his *latkes*. "I want a divorce," he said.

Sylvia picked up the jar of applesauce and plunked it down in front of him. "Here. Here's your divorce. Now shut up and eat. If I have to listen to you *kvetch* all through supper about the G.D. sour cream. . . ."

"Go ahead, Daddy," Meryl said, "eat 'em with applesauce. They're good that way."

He glanced at her. His voice was loud and deliberate, sounding for all its worth like the voice of patriarchy. "Are you still wearing that goddamned button?"

"Mo. . . please," Sylvia said.

"I'm not going to sit and eat potato *latkes* while I'm staring at a goddamned cockroach!"

Meryl spread applesauce over her *latkes* and looked at him, unmoved. "Listen, Daddy. It's a fact of life that we're all living under the threat of nuclear war. I'm sorry to remind this happy family gathering of that fact, but I think you *need* to be reminded. I think that if more happy family gatherings were reminded of that fact, they might get off their happy family butts and *do* something, and then maybe the future will hold *more* happy family gatherings. Now you might look with contempt on cockroaches, but the fact of the matter is that we wouldn't survive a nuclear war and they would."

"Meryl, please...." It was Sylvia. "Do we have to talk about this now?" She brought another plateful of *latkes* to the table. "This is dinner. Can we have some dinner conversation?"

But apparently no one knew how to create this so-called dinner conversation, and for a time there was silence. Then Mo held out his hands and appealed to Kay. "Everybody's pickin' on me. You see how they treat me? First my wife makes me eat *latkes* without sour cream, and then my daughter makes me look at pictures of bugs. You see that?" he appealed. "You see how they treat me?" She smiled.

The eating and the talking continued. Sylvia continued to labor at the stove, turning *latkes,* blotting the excess grease on paper towels, piling them, still hot, on the always emptying platter. People reached across the table with hurried excuses, stood up to get the milk or extra napkins, leaned on the table. But it seemed that for all the actual physical commotion, the jiggling and bumping of the table were really due to another force, as if some nagging persistent spirit of the family had settled underneath to communicate its troubled message.

Throughout the meal Rose had, for the most part, focused on her food with a serious air. To her, mealtime was for eating, not for talking, and she'd said little—other than to insist, all the while she was consuming a huge portion of *latkes,* that she was not hungry and could not eat another bite. When at last she was done, she wiped her mouth with her napkin and looked at Kay, who sat across the table. She examined the younger woman for a few minutes and finally pronounced judgment. "A luffly goil." Then she held out her hand, indicating Kay to Jack, and suggested, "Jackie, a *shayneh maideleh.*"

Jack had not been paying attention. "What did you say, Grandma?"

Rose once more indicated Kay, who by now was blushing, and shaking her head in good-humored embarrassment. "A nice goil. A *shayneh maideleh.*"

Sunny and Kay exchanged glances, and in spite of themselves, burst out laughing. Jack looked from one to the other, and he smiled.

"Hey Jack," Meryl's husband quipped, "I think Grandma's trying to fix you up!" Meryl looked embarrassed.

But the comment made Jack laugh, and Sylvia said to him, "Well, I'm glad to see you've finally joined the party."

He shook his head, still grinning as though at some private joke he chose not to share. "Oh I've joined the party all right," he said, and Sylvia shrugged and sat down at last to eat.

Everyone else had by then finished eating. Mo, sighing pleasurably, sat back with his hand on his stomach as if presenting the evidence of the good meal. Rose nodded in agreement with his stomach and declared, "It vas de-licious! *Geshmack!* Ah! Vhat *latkes!* Dey vas delicious *latkes*," she said to the table at large, as though they hadn't tasted them and might be prone to skepticism.

"I was here, Grandma. Remember?" Meryl asked, for Rose had looked at her. Rose laughed.

They sat for awhile and chatted. Then the men adjourned to the living room and the women stayed in the kitchen—to help clean up, or, like Kay, to stand in the doorway and offer help. It was obvious, though, that with Meryl and Sunny clearing the table, Sylvia washing the dishes, and Meryl and Sunny putting them away, there was no need for help. Rose sat at the table and awaited another cup of tea.

When everything was done, the floor swept, and the kitchen returned to its premeal order, the women sat at the table and talked.

Kay was curious about the people they mentioned and finally asked if she could look at some family pictures.

"I don't see why not," Sylvia said, and went to get an album. She placed it on the table and opened it for Kay to see. It was an old-fashioned album, the pages thick black paper, the photographs held in place by triangular black stickers. As Kay looked through the pictures, she would point to a person and ask a question. Sylvia would answer or tell an anecdote. But the narrative seemed disjointed, and there were gaps in the album where photographs were missing, so that turning a heavy page, they would come across small black triangles that cornered empty fields of dark where pictures should have been.

When they were midway through the book, Kay, who'd been up since early that morning, got tired of listening and went into the living room. Meryl and Joe were just leaving. Jack had long since gone upstairs. Kay sat on the couch, put her feet up, as Mo suggested, and after awhile fell asleep.

When she woke the room was dark, the TV was off, and she was covered with a blanket. She stood up. Rubbing her eyes and yawning, she walked toward the kitchen.

In the kitchen there was an argument going on. At Kay's hesitant appearance, however, there was a sudden silence, as though they were all lead by the same powerful conductor.

On the way home Kay wanted to ask about it. But she knew her feelings would be hurt if Sunny evaded an answer as she sometimes did when the subject came to Family. So instead, Kay asked about the blender. Why had they tried to hide it from Rose, she asked.

Sunny said that the blender was a wedding gift from one of Rose's brothers, and that they had some long-running feud between them. She said this with a smile, as though their feuds were amusing, and went on to say that if Rose saw the blender, Kay would hear a whole new vocabulary: Yiddish curses. All evening, because once Rose got on a subject, she didn't get off.

What was the origin of the feud, Kay asked. But Sunny said she did not know, and Kay knew she was not evading.

"You should find out," she suggested.

Sunny wasn't interested, commenting that she was not concerned about some old battle between Rose and her brother since it had no effect on her own life.

Chapter 4

The Catalyst

Kay was going to spend Christmas with her family in Massachusetts, leaving on the 23rd and returning on the 27th. Nevertheless, she suggested to Sunny that it would be nice if they had a tree. "Our first Christmas tree," she said.

"But you won't even *be* here for Christmas," Sunny objected. "What's the point?"

"The point," Kate explained, "is that Christmas is more than just a day. It's a season. Come on, it'll make the apartment cheery. You'll see."

Sunny made a face. "I don't know... I'm surrounded by that stuff all the time. I'd like my own house to be nondenominational at the least."

"It's only a holiday. You take it too seriously."

Sunny shrugged. She'd thought of her home as the only refuge uninvaded by the Christmas spirit, and the last thing she wanted was a Christmas tree. But Kay would soon be officially moved in, so she finally relented and agreed. After all, it would be Kay's home too, and she wanted to be fair.

This year, Christmas annoyed her excessively. It was not the religious aspects but all the commercial trappings: the interminable and unavoidable selling of products and cheer. Why was *she* supposed to be cheerful? It had nothing to do with *her*. It made her feel like a Scrooge, and this too annoyed her since the implication was that her outlook was an error that could be corrected by a softening of her hardened heart. It was not the birthday of *her* God. Why was it assumed that her desire to maintain emotional independence—*not* to be uplifted, cheered, or made soft of heart—was an insult, an offense that could not be tolerated.

The worst of it was at work. With an instinct she didn't even know she possessed, she'd begun avoiding Louise Deckert who worked in the adjacent office, and who was one of the two other women being considered for the promotion. But avoiding her completely was impossible. One day when Grace was upstairs in the mail room, Louise poked her head in the door. "Did you see my little friend?" she asked. "Isn't he cute? Bob gave him to me because I'm such a Christmas *nut!*" She laughed, peeked around for The Big Boss (or actually, The Medium Boss, The Big Boss being in Kenosha), and not seeing him, came in to show Sunny her gift.

It was a little *tsatske*. (For the life of her, Sunny could think of no other word.) On a piece of wood sat a walnut with tiny button eyes and a tiny red and white Santa Claus cap. Underneath was written: *Christmas Nut*.

Louise sat down on Grace's desk and began complaining in a grumblingly cheerful tone about the added pressures of the upcoming holiday season, the shopping, cleaning and cooking, all for the hordes of relatives who were depending on her to provide them with a joyous and memorable Christmas. "Have you finished your Christmas shopping yet?" she asked, ready to offer sympathy to another member of The Club. In truth, her sympathy was tinged with smugness, since she was a woman who began shopping for gifts, decorations, and wrappings in January for the following year, taking advantage of the post-Christmas sales.

"Not yet," Sunny mumbled. She was irritated, though whether more at Louise or herself she could not say. I should have just said *no,* she thought after Louise left, because that would have been less of a lie.

She imagined and immediately rejected the idea of saying, "No, I don't shop for Christmas. I'm Jewish." But Louise might not have understood even that, being the kind of person (the kind of *goy,* she found herself thinking against her will) who believed that everyone celebrated Christmas. Christmas wasn't just for Christians, it was a *universal* holiday, wasn't it? She would never have considered attempting to break through Louise's arrogance, and brushed her off as someone about whom she should not trouble herself further.

When Grace came back from the mail room, Sunny said, "You just missed Louise."

Grace, who was of late in the habit of imitating one of the TV evangelists, looked up and murmured, "Thank you, Jee-sus."

Sunny shook her head, smiling.

If it were not for the fact that she and Grace worked together, they would never have met, or meeting, would never have trusted one another. But as it was, they respected each other's work habits, trusted each other's loyalties, understood each other's need for privacy, and from nine to five they were friends.

Grace was not being considered for the promotion. She was married to a union steward in the adjacent plant, and the company did not want a person in management with firsthand knowledge about how managerial decisions affected the workers' lives. Grace herself was happy with her job. She was not looking for change. As she said, "At five o'clock, Imperial Dynamics can go. . ." and finished the sentence with an obscene gesture, slapping her forearm and raising her fist. She was disrespectful of the boundaries set up by salary and title and didn't give a damn who knew it, communicating with her eyes even when her mouth gave only a silent disdainful twitch. After working with her for two or three weeks, Sunny had pointed a finger into her face and snapped, "*You*. . . are gonna spoil all my plans to become a classy broad, you know that, Catalano? You're a *bad influence!*" Grace had cheered. She described herself as "a fallen Catholic," a state for which she remained breezily unrepentant. She believed all religion was a racket to make money and couldn't understand, she kept saying, why God allowed it.

Sunny had her own opinions about the subject but didn't voice them.

A few days before Christmas, Sunny and Kay went out and bought a tree. Some friends of Kay's were visiting from out of town. On the evening of the 22nd, they came over to decorate the tree.

It was fun stringing popcorn and cutting out strips from construction paper to make interlocking rings. Sunny enjoyed Kay's sugary Christmas cookies, but her emotions went through strange meanderings that lasted until late that night when she was in bed staring sleeplessly across the room.

The evening brought back memories of those Christmases she'd spent with Frank and his family where she'd felt like the poor abandoned orphan who, except for them, would forever be out in the cold, nose pressed pitifully against the window, the eternal outsider observing the saga of family love within. It aggravated the vague lingering sense that she did not belong, that she was a stranger, though to what she could not have said.

For a time when she was married to Frank, she'd felt a part of his friends and family. Gradually she'd come to realize that they tolerated her for Frank's sake. Behind the welcoming smiles of his family was a discomfort, a resentment—against her for being a stranger, against Frank for having brought her in.

Thinking back on the evening, Sunny realized she'd slipped back into the same feelings she'd had with Frank and his family—a gratitude that they'd deigned to share their holiday with her. Becoming conscious of this, her feelings followed swiftly on one another: annoyance, loneliness, depression, and finally, once again, annoyance. What a *shlemiel,* she thought to herself about herself, she trims a Christmas tree with *goyim* and then wonders why she feels like an outsider! She sighed, impatient with herself for being so dimwitted, so slow to see the obvious. If it was standing any closer it'd bite you, she told herself. She plumped her pillow, turned over, and closed her eyes, prepared to sleep. Sometimes you're so slow I can't believe it, she thought by way of ending the matter, if you were with Jews. . . .

Her eyes opened once again, for her assumption had stopped midway to its conclusion which was, she understood, erroneous.

The next day, Kay officially moved in. Afterward, Sunny drove her to the bus station.

When they'd left Kay's house, one of her housemates called, "Merry Christmas!" and wanting to include Sunny, said, "Merry Christmas to you, too!"

In the car, Sunny ranted and raved a bit to Kay as she'd done several times already. "I *hate* that! Christmas Spirit. . . God! You know?" she asked Kay, who shrugged. "It's like. . . it's like this big happy family, like whatever our individual differences, this is the one thing we share. *That's* Christmas spirit. No matter what happens all year, at Christmas we can put aside our differences and be united. Well I don't *want* to be united, not if I have to say 'Merry Christmas' to do it!"

"Bah. Humbug," Kay said dryly.

"I'm telling you, if one more person says Merry Christmas to me, I'm going to turn around and say 'Happy *Chanukah.*' I am. I swear to God I am. I almost said it to your friend," she said, and it sounded like a warning or a threat.

"Why shouldn't you say it to my friend? What's the big deal?" Kay asked. "Why are you so uptight about people knowing you're Jewish?"

Sunny stared straight ahead, her lips pressed together, an ever-so-faint burning in her stomach. She felt stupid to be so uptight, as Kay said, about being Jewish. Then she thought, Sure, listen to *Kay* about what it should feel like to be *Jewish.* For Kay was the one, having known so few Jews in her life, who asked Sunny with embarrassed hesitation one day, "The word *Jew.* . . is it okay. . . I mean, is it okay to say it like that? Or is it an insult?"

"No," Sunny had said, somewhat depressed that she knew exactly what Kay meant, "*Jew* is the word you say. I guess it all depends how you say it."

At the bus station the two women kissed good-bye, playing the game they sometimes did in public: calling each other Ethel and Edith, those two little old ladies, the passionate truth about whose spinster relationship was never imagined by the casual onlooker. "Good-bye, Dearie, have a Merry Christmas," Kay called as she boarded the bus, her voice heavily laced with irony.

Sunny had no quick-witted response but merely laughed and gave her a look that said she was trying to think of one and when she did, watch out. Kay laughed—it was not often she left Sunny speechless—and waggled her fingers good-bye.

By the time she got home, Sunny had decided to send Kay a telegram saying that poor Edith had been driven mad by one last dose of Christmas cheer and was in (to use Sylvia's favorite phrase) the rubber room at the funny farm. When Sunny got home, however, called Western Union and learned the cost of a telegram, she balked. A joke was a joke, but fifteen dollars was fifteen dollars. This concern (was it an obsession? she worried) about money bothered her. Don't be so goddamned money-grubbing, she told herself. But still... fifteen dollars for a joke? Besides, she realized that the arrival of a telegram might send Kay's family into something of a turmoil. And finally, what "good friend" spent fifteen dollars sending a telegram that was nothing but a private joke? No, the telegram was out. A letter perhaps? Yes. Composed on her word processor at work. She would type it on Imperial Dynamics stationery. We regret to inform you, she would write, that Edith Shmaltz, loyal employee for twenty-five years, has recently been institutionalized.

She wrote the letter the next day, keeping it ridiculously formal (except for the incongruous "rubber room at the funny farm") and making no reference to her own true identity in case, God forbid, the letter should for some reason be returned. But she didn't mail it, thinking that what with the holiday mail, it might not arrive until after Kay had left. Instead, she drew a stamp in the corner, the picture bearing vague resemblance to Whiskers, and tacked the letter to the refrigerator with a magnet.

Christmas was a gloomy day. In the afternoon Jack called and asked Sunny to a movie.

They had a fine time, and Sunny's guard was almost completely down. Nevertheless, there was a nagging sense in the back of her mind that he was only pretending it was like it used to be.

Kay being absent, Jack being jovial, Sunny was lead to the conclusion that Jack was in fact jealous of Kay, or disapproving of their relationship. She reassured herself with this. At the same time, there was a deeper knowledge she ignored. She knew it in the strange way people sometimes have of knowing things—knowing and not knowing, knowing in some secret part while all their actions presume ignorance.

The next day she returned to work. She chose her clothes carefully because it was rumored that B.R. Bullard, The Big Boss from General Office ("B.B. from G.O.," as Grace called him, "or B.O. for short,") was due in for a visit. But he never showed up, and all day long she complained ("I *knew* he wouldn't come in the day after Christmas! I should have followed my instinct.") until Grace finally said, "Will you quit your belly achin'? Jesus! I hope they give you that goddamned promotion just so you'll shut up."

"Well. If I'm not appreciated. . ."

"No. You're not," she said, and Sunny laughed.

In midafternoon, Grace went upstairs to help out in the mail room. Sunny was in the midst of typing when she noticed a movement and glanced up to see Louise come into the office.

Louise was a woman who judged and reacted to people according to a complex, absolute, and unquestioned set of strictures. She had a saccharine compassion for those above herself—those with more status, power, or wealth—and total contempt for those below. "Mr. Bullard's son was supposed to go to a special summer program at Harvard, but he broke his shoulder playing racketball and he'll have to make up school then instead," she'd say, and shake her head at the terrible injustice of it, her face pinched into sympathy at the Bullard boy's tragedy. To misery on a grand scale, however, to starvation or malnutrition, poverty, brutality, her shake of the head would express a very different judgment indeed. "It's their own fault," she'd mutter with a touch of self-righteous indignation. "Why don't they. . ." and she'd go on to espouse some ridiculously unrealistic solution that had nothing to do, as Sunny would later complain to Grace or Kay, "with the price of potatoes."

Her pert and pretty face was usually fixed into a blankly pleasant smile, a smile that had caused Grace to remark once, "You know how there's a pain threshold? I think there's a *pleasant threshold* too, and you can only tolerate so much. Well. . . guess what. I'm at the edge of mine, and if Louise flashes that goddamned sugary smile at me once more, I'm going to toss my cookies. Right on the floor. Either that or I'll poke her in the eye, and see if she smiles at *that* one."

As there was Louise's smiling face at one end of the extreme, so there were Louise's fingernails at the other. Her nails were bitten to the quick, the flesh surrounding them raw and swollen. Louise was painfully self-conscious about her hands, always curling her fingers into fists or hiding her hands behind her back. When she and Sunny were together before superiors, Sunny maximized Louise's defect by keeping her own hands clearly visible, gesturing (though not enough to appear ethnic), touching (though not enough to appear sexually aggressive), and in general employing her hands to foster an appearance of assertive confidence—an appearance, she quite well knew, unattainable for Louise while she stood with fists clenched behind her back.

Sunny was half ashamed to take such blatant advantage of Louise's weakness; she had decided her behavior was cruel and immature. This shame and these decisions, however, did not change her behavior.

Today, Louise looked smug and gleefully malicious, and Sunny knew she was about to impart a bit of gossip. She looked so smug and malicious that Sunny sensed the gossip was about LaSan, the third woman being considered for the promotion. Nothing delighted Louise more than someone else's misfortune, that is, someone who "deserved" it.

Sunny's response to this kind of thing was contradictory, complex, and changing. From a distance, she was repulsed. But Louise's smug conspiracy seemed to promise protection to those who entered in, and Sunny could not help but be attracted. Lately, however, she'd begun to realize that this protection did not apply and would never apply to her. She, in more ways than one, was "them," and it was only a matter of time before Louise found out.

"Well," Louise said, plopping herself down on Grace's chair and with a graceful swing turning sideways to face Sunny. "I predicted it. I knew it was bound to happen. As soon as we heard about the inventory, I said to myself. . . ."

The phone rang. Sunny answered it gratefully, taking longer with the call than was necessary, hoping Louise would leave. She sensed what was coming, sensed it by the mention of inventory, by the look on Louise's face and her tone of voice.

The moment she was done with the call, Louise was waiting, ready to pounce. "You know, she puts on this act that she's different. But she's not different. She went home *sick*. She *said*. The only thing *she's* sick of is *work*. As soon as we heard about the inventory, I said to myself, she's gonna come up with some pretend illness. And as soon as it's time for us to really get in swing with it, wham. And we won't see her until it's over. You mark my words," she said, pointing a finger at Sunny as though it were a lesson they could share.

Louise had once before muttered "lazy nigger" while complaining about LaSan, so there was no doubt as to what she meant now. There had been a time when Sunny had secretly welcomed, even encouraged, such an attitude in hopes that it would lead Louise to repeat that remark in overconfidence in front of Danvers, the head of personnel. Louise, Sunny thought, was stupid, and just might do such a stupid thing. Imperial Dynamics did not want someone tactless working in a managerial position, and the promotion had, in fact, been Sunny's main concern. In addition, when Louise remarked about LaSan she was offering Sunny a bond—the bond of "us against them." But what, Sunny wondered, *was* that bond? Whatever it had been (she didn't care to define it too closely), it was no longer comfortable.

Something had changed. When Louise said *nigger,* or even had that look in her eye that *meant* nigger, Sunny imagined *Jew,* imagined the remark twisted around to reflect the appropriate stereotypes, and she felt a stab of anxiety.

Louise was waiting for her to respond.

"Are you talking about LaSan?" she inquired somewhat haughtily, meaning to show disapproval but feeling foolish because of *course* Louise was talking about LaSan.

Louise giggled, misinterpreting Sunny's remark. *"La San,"* she pronounced, and shook her head with barely suppressed glee. "Oh God, what'll they think of next. Oh well, I gotta go back to work. Bye-ee!" she sang, and lifted her hand in cheery departure.

Sunny sat there and watched her go. "Jerk!" she muttered, and returned to work.

In the back of her mind, however, she continued to think about Louise's attitude, and about LaSan.

When Sunny had first come to Imperial, she'd noticed a black woman, the only black woman in the office. When she and Sunny passed in the hall, they nodded to one another. In the woman's eyes, Sunny saw a multitude of thoughts, all kept in check by a wariness that seemed much like her own.

She was curious about her and asked Grace, who told her that LaSan had two children and lived with her mother. She'd gotten pregnant in high school and dropped out. She was in her mid-thirties. Her husband had died in a holdup.

"Did he work in the store or did he own it?"

Grace smiled. "That's what *I* asked. He robbed it."

"Oh."

"That's what *I* said."

"But she looks so classy!"

"Yeah, I know. She's had a hard time of it, lemme tell ya. She had to go back to school, and get her high school equivalency, and take secretarial courses. . . ."

All of this information impressed Sunny since LaSan's attitude and appearance suggested none of it.

Later in the afternoon, however, long after Louise's visit, long after Sunny had stopped thinking about LaSan, she remembered that on the way into work that morning, she'd seen LaSan coming out of the Ladies Room, and she hadn't looked well.

Then she *was* ill, Sunny thought.

LaSan's troubled face, her inward-looking gaze, was worlds apart from Louise's attitude. It was an attitude that Sunny could not quite grasp, but it seemed to imply that LaSan had no existence outside of her relation to Louise. That even her being ill was only to spite poor Louise, who would possibly have to work on the inventory alone. There was something frightening about Louise's sneering attitude, as though Louise thought it was the truth.

She remembered one of Frank's brothers trying to discuss the Holocaust with her, leaning forward with a most sincere look on his face and offering the theory that some of the Jews deserved the Holocaust because some of them were very bad people. He'd waited for her response, his attitude being that it was something they both knew deep down inside them but that she would not admit. He looked at her as if to say, Come on now, tell the truth. It's what you thought all along.

She'd felt obliterated. She'd shrugged, as though not knowing the answer to this interesting academic theory, and ignored the burning in her stomach.

Even remembering, her stomach burned faintly, like embers from a flame that would not die. She stood up and walked to the window.

To the right, adjacent to the maintenance building, was the bosses' heated garage. Toward the left, was the factory. The parking lot was in front, the office workers' area separated from the factory workers' by virtue of being enclosed behind a ten-foot chain-link fence whose gate was always open.

Everything had been constructed with fine degrees of hierarchy in mind.

She worked in the Reese Street wing of the office building, on the first floor. On this side of the hall, the "walls" separating the space into cubicles were made on the top of thin plexiglass that did not reach the ceiling. There was a continual buzz of business, and she could see and be seen by the people from one end of the wing to the other, as well as anyone passing by outside.

Suddenly she became aware of how she was standing: hands clasped behind her back, head tilted thoughtfully to one side.

One Sunday that summer, she and Kay had gone to a church bazaar. This bazaar was in a Polish neighborhood on the East Side of town and the women of St. Aloysius had cooked up huge amounts of *pierogies, galumpkies,* duck's blood soup, and noodles and cabbage. Outside in the courtyard were games of chance: bingo, wheel of fortune, dice, and booths with raffles.

At one point in the afternoon, Kay went to the ladies room in the church basement, leaving Sunny to wander around outside. She was strolling casually, enjoying the colorful booths, the hot early summer day, the people, when she noticed a man watching her. He had a pleasant look on his face, and it was a friendly crowd, so she smiled. He smiled back and fell in step beside her, pacing himself to her pace. "You're Jewish, aren't you?"

The question rightly shocked her and made her feel threatened. It was as though it were another time and another place and he had the power to usher her, with that same pleasant smile, over to the side of the stone wall to be shot.

"Why do you ask?" she said, her tone wary.

A smug look appeared on his face, as though she'd answered his question. She hadn't understood then, but later Kay told her that she'd heard Jews always answered questions with questions, and she'd remembered that man's look.

He said, "Because you're walking like this," and imitated her. Sunny's hands were clasped behind her back, her head bent slightly in contemplation, her pace slow and deliberate.

"How come you know so much about Jews?" she asked, her tone still wary. Then, smiling she inquired, "Are you Jewish?" She was aware that her smile and tone had changed, for she was delighted that here, in this crowd of church people, was a *landsman* who'd seen her and recognized their commonality.

He shook his head. "I'm Greek."

Greek, she wondered, trying to identify the history (*was* there a history?) of Greeks and Jews. She searched his eyes but couldn't read them. She saw only a pleasant smile, smug because he'd found her out in the midst of all these people, learned her secret.

"Oh," she said. "Oh."

Standing in front of the window, she looked at herself. Under the smooth surface of skin, her jaw was tense. Behind the superficial Imperial Dynamics gaze was a certain depth of desperation.

That night Kay called. They chatted for awhile, and then Sunny remembered the letter about Edith Shmaltz in the funny farm. She said with studied casualness, "Oh, you got a letter."

"From who?"

"I don't know. Maybe it was just junk mail."

"Well, I'll see it when I get home. How's the tree?"

"Oh, the *tree*," Sunny complained. "The tree's a pain in the ass. It's dropped needles all over the place, and Whiskers keeps eyeing it from across the room. I feel responsible that somebody cut down the stupid thing just so we can have it sitting in our living room for two weeks. Every time I walk past it I think it's going to attack me with its last dying breath."

"Trees don't attack people. Where the hell did you get your information about forestry?"

"Hey, didn't you ever see any of those Walt Disney movies where somebody's walking through the woods and all of a sudden a tree reaches out and begins to throttle them?"

Kay laughed. "I miss you."

"I miss you too. I got used to you being around."

"What've you been doing since I've been gone?"

"Oh. . . same old thing. I went to the movies with Jack."

"Did you have a good time?"

Sunny hesitated. "It was all right. But he's. . . he's weird. You know? He plays these goddamned mind games."

"I don't know. Maybe you're just picking on him."

"*Picking* on him. Listen, my dear, that brother of mine has a chip on his shoulder that's putting his *head* out of joint."

"Well. . . anyway, I called to tell you my bus'll be in at seven tomorrow night."

"Okay," Sunny said. "I'll be there."

Later that evening before she went to bed, Sunny took a bath. She loved winter baths in that apartment. The remodeled attic of an old house, it was not insulated, and the warmth from the living room space heater never quite reached either the bathroom or the back bedroom. In the dead of winter the temperature in that end of the apartment stole up to 60° or so, but usually not higher, and last winter she'd bought a small electric heater.

As the tub filled with hot water, she warmed the room. By the time the old claw-foot tub was sufficiently filled, the room had lost its chill. She turned off the heater, removed her robe, and slowly eased her body into the hot water.

It was a sensual experience: the hot water, the steam rising in the air. She looked with pleasure at her submerged body, its color warm and rich against the white porcelain. The winter wind rattled at the steamy windows in the corners of which snow had gathered. She sighed and closed her eyes, wondering what could be more wonderful than a hot bath in an old tub on a cold winter night.

After a time the water chilled. She opened her eyes, sat up, and lathered the washcloth. As she washed the front of her body, she felt a small lump about the size of a pea under the nipple of her left breast.

At first she thought it was a bit of soap. It's nothing, she hastened to reassure herself, but with her fingertips she felt that whatever it was, it was under the flesh.

Her mind seemed to go blank. She hardly dared to think. She finished washing, got out of the tub, dried herself, put on her bathrobe, cleaned the tub.

She hardly slept at all that night. Her fingers kept returning to the spot beneath her left nipple. She prayed that her fingers would find only the smooth familiar flesh that was her own, but again and again they encountered that persistent lump existing despite her wishes to the contrary. When finally she fell asleep, her dreams were anxious, and once she woke startled, her pajamas wet and clammy at her collar and back where her body had broken out in a cold sweat. Automatically she touched the spot, this time with her other hand, thinking in a hopeful, groggy daze that the lump was not in her breast but on her fingertips.

The next morning when she walked into the kitchen, she saw the letter on the refrigerator and took it down. How stupid it now seemed. How immature. She considered but rejected the idea of staying home from work. At work she would have less time to think about her body. Illness had no place at Imperial Dynamics, where business as usual would be conducted whether or not Miss Strickland had. . . . Yes, she forced herself to think it: cancer.

Pushing the cancer out of her mind when it might exist in her body was a pressure that mounted hourly at work, behind her bland competent smiles and reliable controlled attitude. Her control was tenuous; she wanted to scream. She could hardly believe it. While she was going along with *her* life, as it were, her body was going along with its own.

Nothing seemed to matter. Grace annoyed her with her chatter. The work itself seemed empty. She felt more and more like a prisoner.

After work, she drove to the bus station. She saw the city through the eyes of one who no longer belonged. She saw it existing after her death with hardly a ripple of disruption to show that she'd passed through. She felt angry. Why me?! she demanded. Haven't I been through enough? And why *now*? It seemed that she had just begun to live, to understand what she was doing here, and it all might be snatched away. She felt a dull ache in her heart, as though by the existence of this one bit of matter, she had been separated from all life on earth.

Along another track in her mind ran a more reassuring thought process that went something like this: It's probably nothing. It's probably benign, and they'll remove it, and you'll have nothing to worry about. And even if it's cancerous, it doesn't mean you have to *die*. And even if you do die, well. . . we all have to die sometime. But she felt separated, too, from this voice and regarded it as the implanted ravings of a lunatic.

At the bus station she stared at every woman, seeing her from this new perspective. Had *she* ever had this? If she had, what then? Were those her real breasts? Every woman looked the same. There was no way to tell, no way to know, and she wished for x-ray vision to see beyond the deception of clothing and false forms to the naked truth that lay beneath. She needed desperately to reach out to someone who had felt what she felt now, to find advice, reassurance, and compassion. But the truth was hidden, and all she needed remained beyond her reach. As she waited alone in that room of shifting strangers, she grew despondent and became convinced of her approaching death, a death that seemed to hardly matter.

Kay returned home in a fine mood.

All her brothers and sisters had been home, and her nieces and nephews, but as her parents' youngest and the one who'd come the farthest, she'd been pampered and babied.

She'd talked about law school with her mother and father. Her father had been thrilled back in November when she'd told him that she anticipated a high score on the Law School Achievement Tests. Now he said that perhaps she would have a chance of getting accepted at Columbia. Her mother suggested she might live with her Uncle John and Aunt Dorothy in New Jersey and commute. When she told them she was considering staying in Buffalo and would probably apply to the law school there, they acted surprised and disappointed and tried to dissuade her. She argued that Buffalo was one of the top twenty law schools in the country, that it had excellent instructors. She didn't mention Sunny.

The argument about law school didn't have any resolution because it wasn't an argument about law school. For Kay, it was an argument about Sunny; for her parents, about her not having settled down and met a man in Buffalo, their private unspoken fears about her life, their desire for her to live with John and Dorothy, where her behavior could at least be monitored.

Without mentioning Sunny, her reasoning didn't stand up against the way her father intoned *Columbia!* Finally, she said yes. She would apply. Immediately it sounded like a wonderful idea. But when she spoke with Sunny on the phone, it seemed absurd to have ever entertained such a foolish thought as leaving. She was optimistic about law school, her career, and their relationship, and she returned home full of plans and in high spirits. She imagined what it would be like, the two of them together. She thought of all the things she wanted to tell Sunny. She smiled to herself when she imagined her homecoming—greeting Sunny in the bus station, the two of them embracing with cries of "Ethel!" and "Edith!"

But her arrival was nothing like she'd envisioned. She was met by a woman who was pallid, worried, and sick at heart.

When she learned the reason for Sunny's appearance, Kay was concerned and frightened. There in the bus station she held Sunny in her arms, kissing her cheek and murmuring words of reassurance and support. Holding her by the shoulders and looking into her eyes, Kay spoke practically about what they must now do and how Sunny was not to worry.

But as they drove home, she began to feel resentful. Did it never end? Was there always something else? Was this woman's life just one crisis after another?

Against her will, her wishes, and her better judgment, she began to withdraw emotionally from Sunny. Though her behavior continued to be supportive, she feared Sunny would see through what was, for her, an essentially hollow performance.

Sunny's focus remained telescoped on her own body. She hardly noticed anything else. She was involved in her own heightened emotions, her own increasing anxiety and depression, her own ways of coping.

The next day, she made a doctor's appointment. He saw her the day after that. Yes, he said upon examining her, it was definitely a lump. Since he didn't think it was a cyst, he wanted to put her in the hospital rather than do needle aspiration in the office. She nodded silently, frightened and trying to be calm. He phoned the surgeon as she sat there.

Five days later she was in the hospital.

She refused to sign papers permitting anything other than the biopsy itself. If the lump were malignant, she wanted to think about what to do next.

Throughout all of it, she was struck by the disparity between what she felt and how she acted. While inside she was terrified, on the surface she appeared calm—reassuring Kay and Sylvia, making arrangements, discussing whether or not Rose should be told. She even managed to banter with the nurses and the aides up until the moment they wheeled her into the operating room. Then she counted backwards, as the anesthesiologist told her, and was asleep.

The next thing she knew, a woman was calling, "Sonia, Sonia. . . ."

Sonia, she thought, who's Sonia? It was someone else, her mother's great-aunt who had died in Europe, killed by Hitler. Killed by Hitler. The phrase was familiar, and she remembered Rose saying it as Sunny pointed to a worn sepia photograph of family in Europe. "He was a lovely boy. He played deh violin. But he vas kilt by Hitler!" Rose would say, and follow this with a string of angry curses against the unpunished murderer.

But why was this woman calling Sonia? Sonia was dead and repeating her name would not evoke her spirit.

She opened her eyes and saw that she was in a large room filled with bodies from which came a discordant moaning. She heard voices saying, "John, don't spit the tube out, honey. Gordon, wake up, Gordon." In the corner, one nurse was telling another, "Well I put in mushrooms, but you have to cut them up fine, otherwise you've got these big chunks of mushrooms in your meat loaf."

She closed her eyes and heard, "Sonia, Sonia, do you know where you are, honey?"

Where am I . . . where *am* I. . . . She tried to concentrate, for it seemed an urgent philosophical question, one whose answer would settle an age-old debate as to the meaning of her presence on earth. Perhaps. . . she wondered if the question were of a factual rather than a philosophical nature, referring to her hospital room number, and she tried to lift up her wrist to indicate the plastic strap containing all such information. Her wrist would not move. "The number's written on my arm," she mumbled hoarsely.

"You're still half asleep, dear. You're in the recovery room."

She closed her eyes. The recovery room, she thought. That means I'm going to be all right.

The growth had been benign and the surgeon had removed it. But Sunny's relief about the operation's outcome was dampened by the waves of nausea that swept over her as she hovered on the edge of sleep. She lay in bed feeling miserable and moaning hoarsely.

Once when she opened her eyes, she saw Sylvia sitting beside the bed. As she'd done when Sunny was a child, she was smoothing the hair away from her forehead in a gesture that was infinitely soothing and comforting. Kay was standing with her hands clasped in front of her like a woman of old, keeping vigil by a sickbed.

"Your father says 'hello,' " she heard her mother say. "You know how he hates hospitals. How do you feel? We didn't tell your grandmother, we didn't want her to worry."

The nurse came in to give her a pill, and she fell asleep.

When she woke, Jack was sitting by the bed. His arms were folded across his chest, his head was cocked to one side, and he was watching her. Out of the corner of her eye she saw the patient in the next bed get up and leave the room.

"Jack?"

He smiled.

"How long have you been watching me?"

"Next Friday it'll be twenty-four years."

Though she felt less nauseous, she was still groggy from the medication and closed her eyes, trying to understand. "Oh. It's your birthday. I forgot." She tried to wake up. "They drugged me."

"Who, the enemy spies?"

She smiled. Espionage had been one of the games they used to play in which going to the store for a quart of milk had been an undercover mission, and they'd conspire in low voices about the other shoppers. "That's von Braun," Sunny would hiss. "Here, take this cucumber and shoot him." Jack, a big-eared little boy, might give a dimpled giggle, or disagree that no, it wasn't von Braun, it was Agent X24, *their* man. Sunny might agree, or say, no! It *was* von Braun! Look at his pants. Von Braun came from a region in Europe that flooded periodically, and this man's pants were so short it looked like he was expecting a flood. At this point they would dissolve into muffled laughter, averting their eyes from the spy in question who might be staring at them.

They'd try to straighten up, walk away, and get serious because it wasn't nice to talk about people behind their backs, especially if they could hear.

"They captured me," she mumbled, echoing one of their lines, "but I didn't divulge the secret."

He nodded. "I know. That's exactly the problem."

That line did not sound like one of those from the game, and something in his voice frightened her. She closed her eyes to collect her thoughts and saw a clear vision of herself naked beside the quarry pond, heard the thermos shattering down the steps as she stood at her locked door. . . . "Jack," she murmured, not knowing she was going to say it until the words were out of her mouth. "What happened with Grandpa in the yard?"

There was silence. The bed felt hard and lumpy under her body. Her throat was dry, and she was thirsty. She opened her eyes and saw that her water glass was empty. She wanted to ask Jack to pour some from the pitcher. "Jack?"

He was standing at the window. The face he turned to her was ugly, holding in it a festering anger, unexpressed.

She wanted to ask him why he'd changed. She thought she did ask him. She opened her mouth to speak, then closed her eyes. When she opened them, he was standing by the small potted plant that Kay had brought her.

He was reading the card, and his face expressed disgust. Not remembering what Kay had written, Sunny felt a moment of panic and distrust for her sense of discretion.

"I see your 'friend' was here."

"Yes. She was here awhile ago. With Mom."

He shook his head. That expression had not left his face. "I don't understand what the hell you're doing with your life. Why do you always have to be *different?*" he demanded.

Sunny explained to him that she wasn't with Kay to be different. She had seen her one day by the window, and she knew that there were feelings she'd had for a long time that she'd ignored or denied. And then, when she'd encountered her again that day in the library, she'd been so happy. She had not thought of being different. How other people would react to her feelings had never entered her mind. It was just, she explained to Jack, that she understood she could love a woman. It was very simple, really, she said. . . or *thought* she said. Because when she opened her eyes she saw that Jack, standing across the room, was still talking. And from the odd feeling in her jaw, she knew she hadn't said a word.

"What the hell is the matter with you?" he demanded, his voice accusing. "Don't you know the family's *ashamed?*"

She blinked, unable to comprehend. The Family?

"Just because you lost your kid and your husband, that doesn't mean you're a failure and you had to turn to another woman." He shook his head in disgust. "Jesus, don't you have any self-respect? Do you want people to think you're a *lesbian?*"

The word shocked her the way Jack said it, isolating it like a filthy outcast. She wanted to answer him but didn't know how, and she closed her eyes once more, trying to think.

Why had he called her that? If he had called her *queer,* it would not have mattered. That was a word she could brush off with a laugh or a shrug. She had always been an oddball, a nonconformist, a little weird. But *that* was something else entirely, connoting, as he said it, a certain depravity, a lust for the perverse, something diseased within herself that she must deny at all costs.

She remembered Meryl on the porch, the look in her eyes, the stiffness of her body and her smile.

She had yet to answer Jack's question. It seemed that only a moment had passed, but when she opened her eyes he was gone and the room was dark, and she could tell by the silence in the hallway that it was the middle of the night.

The sky was black, and the moon cast an icy light into the room. It felt too bright, too still, and she lay there quietly, listening. She was surrounded by sickness and death, pain and loneliness, all of it wrapped in the silence of the walls. As she closed her eyes, she felt that the room was a ship floating in space, linked by the lighted hallway to an earth she could not see, and whose messages she heard only faintly, disturbing but as yet undecipherable.

When she fell asleep, she dreamed that she had awoke and found herself driving down a dark road. She panicked because she knew she was lost.

The next day when Sunny got up, she could not shake the feeling that something was wrong. She went through the possibilities one by one and rejected them as they came to mind. It could not be her anxiety about her health because the lump had been benign. It could not be the medication because surely that would have left her system by now. She remembered little of Sylvia and Kay's visit; she'd been too groggy to register much of what was said. She couldn't be upset about her father's failure to visit because she knew he was deathly afraid of hospitals. And she didn't think she was upset about what Jack said because that was just foolishness—all that stuff about self-respect. She'd never judged herself by other people's opinions. She felt she'd always been independent, a rebel. She did what she wanted, and if people didn't like it, well. . . too bad.

Then what could it be? Maybe she was due to get her period. Or maybe it *was* the aftereffects of the medication. Or maybe. . . maybe it was some kind of generalized postoperative depression. Whatever it was, she was determined not to give in to it. Putting the nagging emotional malaise out of her mind, she set about being cheerful.

Her attempts made her seem a trifle frantic. When Kay came to pick her up she found a befuddled Sunny who couldn't find this and forgot that and who, on the way home, was alternately rigid and jumpy as she kept up a nervous monologue: "We're going to hit that car, I know we're going to hit it. *Slow down* please. Take it easy, there's a red light. Watch it, watch it! Jesus, we almost hit that... that *thing*. What the hell was it?"

"It was a paper bag lying in the middle of the road, Sunny. Relax, will you please? You're making me nervous."

As they neared the house, Kay mentioned that she and Jack had gone shopping the previous evening and bought food for a homecoming dinner for the three of them. But Sunny was not enthusiastic. She wrinkled her nose and shrugged. "I don't know...."

Kay shook her head. "I don't know either. Two seconds ago you were full of vinegar, and now all of a sudden..."

"Well, it's just one of those things," Sunny said rather glumly. "You know? One minute you're full of vinegar and the next... you're not. You know?"

"Not really, but I'll take your word for it."

"Let's just go home and be together. I feel like we haven't been together in a long time. Okay?"

"Sure," Kay said, and when she parked in front of the house and turned off the ignition, she placed her hand on Sunny's. "I love you," she said. "I'm glad you're okay. I was worried about you for a lot of reasons. But I'm glad you're all right." She smiled. "How about if we go upstairs and you get into bed, and I'll make you a nice cup of tea. All right? I'll call Jack, and I'll tell him that you don't feel all that well, and we'll make it for another time. How does that sound."

"It sounds okay," Sunny said, and hearing her voice, thought, All I ever am is trouble for her. And she's trying so hard.

In spite of her efforts to be enthusiastic, however, her spirits kept lagging. After Kay fell asleep that night, Sunny went into the living room and cried.

The next day she was bored and restless, as though there were something she should be doing but she didn't know what it was. She walked around the apartment, her hands clasped behind her back, a contemplative look on her face. Should she clean the cupboards? Was *that* it? No. Then what *was* it!

Towards late afternoon, she found herself sitting in the living room, looking at the door that led to the front porch. On an impulse, she walked to it and pulled it open.

The many-windowed front porch was unheated but protected. It was a windy day, and even as she stood there, the wind blocked the sun with a small cloud, and she shivered. She got an afghan, closed the door behind her, and sat on a wooden chair near the window.

The porch was like a balcony, and she could see the entire street. It had snowed yesterday. Everything was still covered with a clean white. But what drew her attention, what dominated her vision, was the Armory, its huge stones brown and roughcut, like petrified chunks of earth.

What was it Kay had asked? Why did she live here, so close to the river? And she answered now: "So I can see the river and not see it at the same time."

Her chest felt tight, and tears came to her eyes.

So, she thought, *that's* what I have to do today.

She got dressed in warm clothes, took her keys (glad for Kay's insistence on walking to work), and went out to the car. She started the motor, let the car warm while she cleaned off the snow, got back in, and drove down Niagara Street toward the Peace Bridge that crossed the shores from America to Canada.

It was the first time she had been on the bridge since that day, and it seemed odd that for everyone else it was just an average day, as that other day had been. It amazed her sometimes how suffering could exist side by side with complete ignorance of that suffering. Why were people not like schools of fish or flocks of birds in flight, knowing, by instinct, what they felt and what they should do.

She paid the toll, drove across the bridge, and answered the questions: Where was she born? What was her reason for coming here, her destination? What would the customs official think if she said, "I'm coming here to visit my daughter's grave." Her real grave. For though she'd buried her daughter in the children's section of the old Jewish cemetery outside of town, she'd always felt that somehow Debbie was here, in the river.

As she drove towards the spot, she became increasingly agitated and remembered how angry she'd been on that day.

It was unbelievable! She'd had to drop Frank off in the morning and then pick him up in the afternoon. Why did he refuse to get another car? It was ridiculous. Absolutely ridiculous. And why in the world did he have to cross the river to *Canada* to fish? Did he think the water was cleaner here? "Do you think the dioxyn and all that other crap gets halfway across and reaches the Canadian border and says, 'Uh-oh, time to stop. It's the American factories that put us here, so here we've got to stay.' I'm sure that's what they say, Frank. Well I'm telling you one thing: I'm not eating that fish and neither is Debbie. As far as *I'm* concerned, you can go ahead and get cancer, but she's not eating one bite."

It was ugly between them by then. She was unhappy and so was he. She'd thought about leaving him, had thought about it a lot.

She'd been so irritable. She had all this running around to do: shop for groceries, pick up her grandfather at the doctor's, pick up Frank.

At the last minute, she decided to pick up Frank first and bring him home since she might have to sit a long time waiting for Sam. That way, Frank could take care of Debbie, and she would not have to worry about anyone else being cranky in the crowded waiting room.

Debbie hadn't wanted to come. She'd been complaining all the way about leaving her friends and picking up her father. She wanted to go home.

Finally, after they crossed the bridge and Sunny had answered the questions at Customs, she snapped, "Will you pipe down? You're driving me crazy!"

Then there was a cold silence in the car; Debbie was being sulky and spiteful. Sunny knew she would have to coax her out of it or she'd be impossible all day. When they reached the spot where Frank was supposed to be waiting, she turned off the ignition and looked at Debbie, whose face was turned determindedly toward the window. "Do you want to drive your poor mother crazy?" she demanded, teasing. Debbie giggled. "Well you will if you don't pipe down," she said, and Debbie, not having said a word since Customs, protested, "Mommy!"

She beeped the horn once, twice, then cursed. "Okay, now listen. You stay here. I have to go get your Daddy. I'll be right back."

But Frank was not at his usual spot. She looked around, sighing, then saw him, way ahead, just standing there. "Frank!" she called, waving, wanting to get his attention so she could point up ahead to the road where she would pick him up. But he didn't hear. Cursing again, she returned to the car, drove to the spot, parked, and walked (getting more and more irritated) to the water.

But as she neared the trees that lined the bank, she glanced back and saw that Debbie had followed.

"What are you doing? I thought I told you to wait in the car!"

"You told me *last* time. . ."

"Oh for goodness' sakes." Sunny put her hands on her hips and sighed, looking at the distance from the car to the river. "All right," she said, reaching out and forgetting that this was not Frank's regular place. "But you've got to hold my hand."

As they walked down the path between the trees and the water to where Frank was standing, Sunny remembered suddenly that they were in a different place and realized that it had rained the night before. The path ahead might be slippery.

She decided to tell Debbie to go back, but as she did, Debbie complained, "I don't *want* to hold your hand, I'm a big girl now," and pulled her hand away.

Sunny turned, reaching out, and saw that Debbie had slipped. She saw her daughter's face: fear and shock, but also a tinge of a nervous giggle, as though she were thinking she was bad to have pulled away; she would fall, and her Mommy would be angry; but she had only slipped a *bit*. . . and she fell into the water and was gone.

The next thing Sunny remembered, she herself was in the water, choking, gasping for air, struggling with Frank, who was shouting that it was too late. She was gone!

Her daughter had been caught in a current, a current she could not find.

They found Debbie, her body, found it down river in a small inlet, and they told Sunny she'd drowned.

In daylight Sunny clung in desperation to that drowning, but her sleep was filled with nightmares of violent battering currents and killing rocks.

She'd banished dreams, and feeling too. It was the only way. Then her memory was pocketed with huge chunks of empty space. She felt groggy, as though she'd woken from a forgotten dream that still existed, still replayed itself in another realm. Her thoughts had no depth. Simple facts like what she was going to do skidded off the surface.

She would blink and sense that time had passed and still she had not silenced the demons that plagued her. If only she had gone to pick up Sam first so that he could have waited in the car with Debbie. If only she had made Debbie go back to the car. If only she had remembered sooner that they were in another place.

She stood and gazed now at the solid mass of rushing current, the irreversible icy flow that had defined her life. "I forgot where we were," she whispered. The wind was cold. She felt it all along one side, penetrating her clothes and chilling her flesh.

Sunny looked up, looked around, and sighed. It was not a peaceful place. Factories dotted the opposite shore. She would not drink this water or eat its fish. And she knew that if this were her daughter's grave, it was a grave defiled. She was angry and for a moment wished to be God, to have the power to put right everything in this world that was so terribly wrong.

She'd imagined herself, when in the past she'd pictured returning, as crouched by the river and sobbing. But she stood here, a woman at the edge of the water, dry-eyed, tormented, and silent.

Then she was angry at herself, as though she were a fool to have come here.

"Debbie," she murmured, saying it aloud, making herself say it. But Debbie was dead she reminded herself, as though in accusation, and calling her name would not evoke her spirit.

She turned away, not seeing the comfort in the call itself, and walked, eyes downcast, to the car.

Back across the bridge she drove toward home. There was snow on the houses, on the porch railings and steps. Yet the houses seemed more dominant now than in the summer when lush green bushes cradled them, graceful leafy trees touched their roofs and porches. As she got out of the car, she thought she sensed a whiff of summer in the air, but the instant she tried to catch it, it vanished.

She stared toward the houses and quite unexpectedly remembered a certain summer day, a hot blue afternoon when she, a pretty young woman in a pale yellow smock, sat on the porch glider and drank iced tea while she watched her daughter sitting on a blanket, kicking her feet enthusiastically in the sun. The ice cubes in her glass had melted down, and on a whim she placed a rounded bit of ice on the blanket. Debbie reached for the small shining object but it was slippery, and it took some effort before she could pick it up. Then, before she could bring it to her mouth, it popped out of her grasp. She yelled out, her face angry.

Sunny had laughed and said, "Go ahead, sweetheart, you tell the world, tell them all about it," and Debbie yelled again, answering, showing off, knowing she was the center of her mother's attention and wanting to stay there.

The sun was hot on her bare arms and legs. Sunny had stretched, looking off at the strip of blue sky that was bordered by the awning's scalloped edge and the rooftops across the street.

It had seemed nothing more than a pleasant moment until now when her chest suddenly ached with grief, and she knew that she was about to cry.

Oh God, she thought, not now. She quickened her pace, pressing her lips together and telling herself: No. You can't break down here, not walking down the street. Not in the middle of the day.

Her shoulders were hunched and she was staring at the sidewalk with a frightened angry intensity. She felt like one of the crazy people she'd seen in the street, the people who talk to themselves because no one else will listen, the people who have never recovered from heartbreak, injustice, abuse. But I've *got* to recover, she vowed, I've got to! She wiped her eyes and strode toward home, her body rigid with determination.

Chapter 5

The Turning Point

It was Jack's birthday, and when Sunny got home, he was there, waiting.

He was sitting at the kitchen table, leaning back. Kay was sitting across from him, leaning forward, and talking about Columbia versus Buffalo.

When Sunny opened the door and saw him, she gave Kay a look that said, What is *he* doing here?

Kay looked at Sunny, who appeared so bedraggled and damp, and responded with a silent, You *invited* him! Don't you remember?

Sunny nodded, as if to say, Oh. I invited him. Okay. . . .

Kay sighed impatiently and did not turn as Sunny walked toward the hallway that lead to the bathroom, the bedroom, and the small spare room where Sunny stored things out of season, old things, and Debbie's things.

During dinner, Sunny seemed dispirited. Kay tried to include her in the fun, but Sunny needed so much prodding. Looking into those eyes with their faraway expression made Kay angry and impatient.

She'd made Jack a cake, and the two of them laughed because the top layer had slid over to one side. Sunny smiled sadly at the lopsided cake. Jack gave Kay a look that said, What's with her? to which Kay's glance responded, Who the hell knows.

Later, they went to the movies, to an old theater that showed second-run films for two dollars. The seats were hard and lumpy, and the building smelled of mildew. Sunny sat between Jack and Kay. She was unresponsive to their comments or questions about the movie, saying, "What?" or answering in monosyllables. Eventually, they leaned forward and talked to each other.

It was snowing when they left the theater. Jack and Kay were arguing about the movie, making fun of each other's opinions and having a fine time.

Sunny walked to the side. Her hands in her pockets, she gazed past the white flakes rushing down against the dark sky. "I didn't like the movie," she said thoughtfully. "I thought parts were anti-Semitic."

Jack looked at Kay as if Sunny were a madwoman they should humor. Then he leaned toward her and asked, "Did you hear anybody use the word *kike*?!"

He'd yelled that word in her ear, and she blinked, as if she'd been slapped.

"Then it's not anti-Semitic," he said, and held his hands out as if glad of having proved his point.

Kay was shaking her head in disapproval. "Jack" she said.

Jack looked at her with a sheepish kind of self-righteousness, as if to say, Yes, he knew she was right, but he couldn't help it.

When they got home, Sunny said she was tired and went to bed. Jack and Kay decided to play cards. The kitchen was drafty, and Kay set up the space heater under the table. After they played a few games (Kay was winning and didn't let Jack forget it) she said, "Would you like a cup of tea?"

"Sure," he said. "Sounds good to me."

"Good. I'd like a cup too. The tea bags are in the cupboard."

He laughed. "You got me," he said, and stood up to get the kettle. "But wait," he added, pointing a finger at her. "The game's not over yet."

She shuffled the cards like a cardsharp, flipping them back into place with a snap. "We'll see," she murmured. "We'll see."

They continued the game and the conversation. Their conversation was competitive, as though they were friendly enemies. But underneath all the good-humored joshing and teasing, Kay was vaguely uncomfortable. She wondered whether it was her imagination, or was there a certain tone in Jack's voice, a certain attitude? He made her uneasy in a way she could not define. She knew only that she kept referring to Sunny, since Sunny was their common bond. Every time she did, he got a look on his face—as though he were bored; as though Sunny were irrelevant or unimportant; as though he didn't care about her, and if *she* were smart, she wouldn't care either.

Whiskers had been in the bedroom with Sunny and came out to eat. The corner near the refrigerator was his. Sunny had even attached a small poster of Morris the Cat to the wall where he could see it. On the floor, on a section of newspaper, was a double bowl for water and dry cat food. Whiskers did not always like dry cat food. Sometimes he preferred to give himself a special treat: he'd stick his paw in the bowl of food and flip the small dry chunks over into the water, sit and wait until they softened (watching them float around as they did) and then with his paw retrieve the softened bits and eat them.

He was doing it now. Kay thought the display was highly comical, and she loved to watch Whiskers' intensely serious expression. But Jack was not amused. He said, "Look at that stupid poster. She spoils that cat rotten. I can't understand why the hell she's so attached to it, it's unnatural."

Kay wanted to say that first of all, the poster was not so much for Whiskers' benefit since he obviously didn't appreciate it, but was merely something cute that Sunny had done on the spur of the moment. And second of all, the cat *really* wasn't spoiled rotten. But more important than saying any of this was explaining to him (how could he not know it?) Whiskers' origins and significance in Sunny's life.

She began to tell him, and he gave her a look that said she was a fool. "Don't tell me you believe that story about saving its life?"

She nodded. He shrugged, as though he knew something she didn't but didn't think he should tell her. "Isn't it true?" she asked.

"Who knows? *I* was under the impression that she got the cat at the S.P.C.A. But hey, I don't want to spoil your illusions about my *sister*."

She put down the cards. "Don't you like her?"

"It doesn't have anything to do with liking her. It has to do. . . with *trusting* her."

"Don't you trust her?"

He shrugged. "She's secretive."

"Secretive!"

"Yeah."

"I think she's the opposite."

"Well. . . maybe you don't know her as well as I do. Gin," he said, and laid out his cards.

The card game and the discussion continued. In a way, Kay felt disloyal talking about Sunny, but she reminded herself that Jack was, after all, Sunny's brother.

She was still chilly and went into the bedroom for a sweater. She didn't turn on the light, not wanting to disturb Sunny, but when she opened the drawer, Sunny looked up.

"Are you awake?" Kay whispered.

"Yeah. I can't sleep."

She sounded as though she'd been crying. Kay looked at her. "Have you been crying?"

"No," Sunny said, but Kay did not believe her. She returned to the game. The stakes were up. They were playing five hundred now, not for empty points but for favors. It was a rousing game, and the air was filled with threats, cries of victory, and vows of revenge.

The next day Kay and Sunny argued. It was a foolish argument whose origin neither of them understood. Although by the end of the day they apologized, a cool feeling remained.

On Monday, Sunny returned to work.

Right before lunch, in the midst of a conversation, without a second thought as if it were the most natural thing in the world, her friend Grace used the phrase "Jew me down" and went on talking.

Sunny was stunned. Not at the phrase. She had heard it before; Frank had used it all the time. But at the realization that the phrase did not consist of empty meaningless words that were pulled from the sky. They meant something, something she did not like at all, and she knew she had to say something. But she did not know how to explain why that phrase was so offensive. *Was* it an offensive phrase?

She argued with herself, using the arguments she thought Grace might use, and backed herself into a silent corner. The moment passed. She imagined the bewildered, perhaps slightly bemused expression on Grace's face if she said, "When you said 'Jew me down' five minutes ago. . . ." In the end, she said nothing.

When Grace left for lunch, Sunny leaned back in her chair and sighed. She glanced up at the ceiling and complained: what *is* this? Am I *Job* or somebody? Come on! *Cooperate*! I mean I've heard I'm *chosen*, but what I want to know is what the hell am I chosen *for*?

This humor, however, was not something she could maintain. When Grace returned after lunch, Sunny couldn't help but feel hurt. She told herself, It's just a phrase, but all day long she thought about that phrase. To *Jew someone down*. What did it imply? A clever, conniving sneak. That was how Jews got ahead. They were all cheats, using unfair advantage, wringing greedy hands over stolen gold. . . or so the stereotype went.

She thought of her grandmother and remembered the day she and Kay had taken Rose to the Flea Market.

For a long time, her mother had told her about Rose's mind for business. "Ma has a mind like a steel trap," she'd say. "She would have been a financial genius, but she was born too soon. She was a woman, and Pa wore the pants as far as money was concerned. He was insecure. He had to save every nickel. Do you know that in the twenties, before the Depression, she had a chance to buy a piece of land on Delaware Avenue? *Dirt cheap*. But Pa wouldn't let her. Do you know how much that land is worth today?"

Sunny had heard this so often that the frequency of the hearing had robbed it of its meaning. Besides, she thought her mother to be something of a dreamer, seeing the world as she wanted it to be and not as it was. She discounted the story about Rose the financial genius and what would have happened had she been allowed to control the family purse strings. Discounted it, that is, until the Flea Market.

At the Flea Market, Sunny saw that Rose's mind was more like a calculator than a steel trap: she added, subtracted, multiplied, and divided faster than Sunny or Kay could follow. The two women stood back in admiration as she pointed out the shoddiness of what seemed to them to be perfectly good merchandise, made lower offers based either on these flaws or on the possibility of her making multiple purchases, and played on the dealer's sympathy that she was a poor frail old lady. Rose would approach a booth, walking in the posture of this alleged old lady, her face expressing a kind of pitiful yearning for sympathy. She would involve the dealer in a conversation somewhere in the midst of which she'd slip in the difficulties of living on social security and the uncaring attitude of one's children and grandchildren (one of whom stood nearby, smiling in awe). By the time she was finished, the dealer would be about ready to give her an item for free. Sometimes the dealers were sharp, but even so, she was sharper. She was the little old lady con artist then, and it was all a big game (a game that they, too, enjoyed), but she *still* managed to come away on the winning end.

When they left the Flea Market loaded with purchases, Rose returned to herself: her expression shrewd, her posture proud and erect, her gait strong and determined. Sunny was filled with respect but she said, "Grandma, what the hell are you going to do with all this junk?" To this, Rose merely smiled.

Now, she wondered, was that what Rose had been doing? That charming display that had so awed and delighted her—was Rose "Jewing them down?" Because her eighty-some-odd-year-old grandmother got a used dish drainer for fifty cents, should she now be feared, envied, and despised? Sunny thought of her own complete financial ineptitude, her total lack of all business sense. She was an intelligent woman. Was she purposefully helpless in this one area just out of fear, out of her own desire to say, I'm not *that*.

During supper that night, Sunny told Kay what Grace had said and waited for her reaction.

Kay nodded thoughtfully, then said, "Jack thinks you're too hung up about being a Jew."

"Oh really? And how do *you* know what Jack thinks?"

Kay glanced at her. "He told me."

"Oh, did he? And when did he tell you this?"

"Why are you getting so uptight?"

"I'm *uptight* because I don't understand what the hell *Jack* knows about being a *Jew*. The last time *I* looked, he was trying his damndest to be everything *but!*"

"Jesus! Sorry I mentioned it."

"Yes. I am too," Sunny said, pronouncing the words distinctly.

The next day they apologized again. Again, it was form without substance.

Within a few days, Sunny had forgotten about the whole scene. She had other things to think about.

At work, the promotion was once more in the wind. Several months ago it had died down completely, even though for the previous six months Danvers had repeatedly alluded to it. He was alluding to it once again. "What *is* this?" Sunny said to Grace. "Every time inventory comes around they start talking about promotions?"

At the end of the week she went to the doctor's office to have her sutures removed. When she got home, Kay said that Frank had called.

"What?"

"Frank. Your exhusband. He wants you to call him back. He left this number."

"Oh. Okay," she said, took the slip of paper, and phoned Frank. They said hello, and he told her that he'd been transferred back to Buffalo and wanted to know if they could get together for a cup of coffee.

"Sure," she said, and looked at Kay. "When?"

"Any time convenient," he said.

"Now?" she asked, and he agreed. Now. "Frank wants me to meet him for coffee," she said to Kay.

"What for?"

"I don't know." She went to get her coat. "I'm going to meet him at that bar on Elmwood."

"I thought you said coffee."

"What. . .?" She couldn't find her keys. "Have you seen my keys?"

"No."

"Oh, here they are. What did you say?"

"Never mind."

"Okay. See you later," she said, gave Kay a peck on the cheek, and was out the door.

Frank was at the bar, and when he saw her walk in, he moved to a table. She suppressed a comment about old times and ordered a drink.

They chatted awhile. He asked what she was doing, and she told him briefly. She asked him, and he said his new wife was pregnant with their first child. They were staying with his mother until they found their own place. Sunny said to say hello. He nodded and told her his mother had written him that she'd read about Sam's death in the newspaper, and he was sorry. He'd always liked Sam.

She nodded.

They ordered another round of drinks. Then he took a deep breath, cleared his throat, folded his hands together and looked at the thick wood slab that was the table. "I want to tell you something," he said.

"I always blamed myself for not being where I should have been that day. I thought about it and thought about it." He looked at her and continued, "I was pissed at you. We'd been fighting. I wanted... I wanted you to come looking for me," he said, as though it were a confession. "I know you blamed yourself. And I didn't help any. I know I said some pretty rotten things to you."

"Yes."

"I guess what I'm trying to say to you," he said almost defensively, "is that... I'm sorry."

She looked at him. "Thank you, Frank," she said, and he nodded.

There seemed little else to say. After they finished their drinks, they put on their coats and left. Outside the bar they said good-bye. They gave regards to each other's families. She thanked him again, and they parted.

In spite of the fact that several times during their conversation Sunny had been on the verge of tears, when she was driving home she felt elated. By the time she walked up the stairs and opened the front door, she was grinning. "I had a wonderful time!" she announced even before Kay asked. "I feel like I've lost twenty pounds of misery."

"Oh really?" Kay said dryly, then added, "Wait. You can tell me as soon as this commercial is over. I *love* this commercial, it's so *cute*."

Sunny walked into the kitchen and made a cup of tea. Then she took a bath.

In bed that night, Sunny snuggled up to Kay, but Kay was unresponsive. They had not made love since before Kay left to visit her family and Sunny, who found it difficult to be sexually assertive, got a bad case of hurt feelings.

After Kay was asleep, she lay in bed worrying. Maybe it *is* wrong, she thought. Is the family really ashamed like Jack said?

She worried about this awhile, then thought, Oh well, if they're ashamed, that's their problem. She closed her eyes and soon was asleep.

Kay had come back from her Christmas visit anxious to tell Sunny about the Columbia versus Buffalo conversations: what they had all said and what they hadn't said but meant.

Sunny had a physical problem. Kay understood that. But afterwards, after she came home from the hospital, she continued to be so infuriatingly glum! She wanted to be alone; she seemed to take offense at everything; and worst of all, she just wasn't there. Kay tried to talk about her Christmas visit, her father and mother, her feelings about Columbia. If she stayed in Buffalo and went to law school here, she and Sunny would have to talk about it. But Sunny didn't seem interested.

Kay was used to Sunny's joking manner. But *this*, this gloomy abstractness, as though she were always somewhere else. It was only a biopsy! What was the big deal? "Are you worried about cancer?" she asked the night of Jack's birthday after he had gone and Sunny had come out for a drink of water.

Sunny had looked at her, a vague, unfocused expression in her eyes, almost as if. . . .

With a slight lurching feeling, Kay remembered that woman in the supermarket, standing by the frozen foods, her eyes empty.

"Cancer," Sunny repeated, trying to focus. "Do you mean because of the fish?"

"Fish? What are you *talking* about?"

Sunny looked at her, frowning. "Oh, I thought you meant. . . never mind, I thought you meant something else."

Then suddenly Frank came to town. They went out for a drink, *not* coffee, and Sunny came home once more, Kay thought wryly, full of vinegar. She'd lost twenty pounds of misery. She hadn't even looked at Kay in weeks, and all of a sudden, after seeing her exhusband, she wanted to make love.

The next day, Kay filled out her application to Columbia.

She didn't tell Sunny for several weeks. When she finally mentioned it one Sunday afternoon, Sunny frowned and said, "You know it'll mean you'll have to leave Buffalo if you go to Columbia."

"*I* know *that!*" Kay snapped sarcastically.

"Oh." Sunny looked at her. "Is something wrong? You seem so crabby lately."

"Nothing's wrong," she muttered and turned away.

"Don't say that. Don't tell me nothing's wrong. I *know* something's wrong."

Kay turned back. "Are you calling me a liar?"

"I'm not calling you anything. I'm trying to talk to you. I mean. . . hey, we haven't slept together for over a month. Doesn't that mean something?"

"Maybe it means sex isn't that important to me anymore."

"Oh. Okay," Sunny said, nodding. "Fine. Great. Wonderful. Then I guess I'll just have to. . . do whatever I have to do." And she shrugged in annoyed acceptance of Kay's decision and turned away.

By that evening they were speaking. They even, after a few days, made love. But it was not the same as before.

Then Sunny began working overtime. She would come home at eight or nine o'clock, sometimes ten. One Friday night, having gone for a drink after work with "the girls," she came home at eleven. She would trudge upstairs exhausted, take a shower, get into her pajamas, eat a quick supper, and sometimes fall asleep while watching TV. Kay asked her about inventory: what it was like, what they did, who was there. But Sunny would wave her hand and say, "I'm stuck in that goddamned place all day and half the night. I sure as hell don't want to talk about it when I get home."

"Oh." Kay nodded. "Have you see Frank lately?"

"Frank. . . what are you, kidding? If he doesn't work at Imperial Dynamics, I haven't seen him."

"*Does* he work at Imperial Dynamics?"

Sunny turned her head away from the television and gazed at Kay tiredly. "Kathryn, are you having a mild case of the insanities? Is it the old P.M.I.'s, the pre-menstrual insanities? Or is it just happening all by itself. I mean, am I going to have to call up and reserve a rubber room at the funny farm for you?" She paused, then sighed, smiling. She'd just remembered with sad fondness that lovely old couple, those romantic spinsters, Ethel and Edith. "I wrote you a letter," she said. "But it doesn't seem important anymore."

"Was it about Frank?"

Sunny groaned and stood up. "Good night nurse. I'm going to bed. Come on, Whiskers," she said, and left Kay sitting alone in the living room.

One evening the following week, when Sunny was working overtime, Jack called. He asked for Sunny and sounded surprised when Kay said she wasn't there. He'd called, he said, because he'd wanted to ask Sunny if she wanted to go to the movies. He seemed disappointed. Then he asked, did *she* want to go? Kay said yes.

Sunny continued working overtime. But late one afternoon of the week after Jack and Kay went to the movies, she called home. She'd just found out that she was getting out on time. Did Kay want to go out for dinner? she asked.

Kay agreed and hung up the phone. Jack was watching her. "Who was that?" he asked, knowing full well who it was.

"Your sister."

"She's not *my* sister," he said, shaking his head like it was all a big joke.

"Come on, Jack. Don't be like that. Sunny *loves* you."

He nodded. "Sure," he said, as if the two words, *Sunny* and *love*, should not be used in the same sentence.

Kay sat at the table and looked at the makings for bologna sandwiches. Jack was working first shift at a local factory, and he'd picked Kay up at the diner after work. They'd been talking about when—they'd already solved whether or not—Jack should return to school.

"Sunny wants to go out to dinner," she said, and they exchanged looks. It struck her then (why hadn't she noticed it before?) that she felt an alliance with Jack that she had once felt with Sunny. An alliance she *should* feel with Sunny. But as soon as this thought touched her, it left. Jack said, "Well, have a good time." Just the way he said it, she knew he thought she wouldn't.

When Sunny picked her up, the car kept backfiring and stalling and giving Sunny trouble, and it focused their attention on that. When it quieted, they drove in silence. It wasn't an unpleasant silence, however, and Kay began to relax. The night was beautiful: the sky very black, the new fallen snow still white and untouched.

Then Sunny said, "I went to the river the other day."

"What?"

"I went to the river. To the spot where Debbie. . . where she. . . fell in."

There was a silence.

"When did you go?"

"A couple of weeks ago. One day after I got home from the hospital."

Kay nodded. "Why didn't you tell me *then*?"

They were stopped at a red light, and Sunny glanced at her. "What do you mean, why didn't I tell you then. What the hell does *that* have to do with anything?"

"Because I want to know why you waited to tell me."

The light changed and Sunny pulled away, not speaking. When they reached the restaurant and Sunny parked the car, she shut off the ignition and said, "Why does my telling you have to be the focus? Why do *you* have to be the center of everything?"

I don't have to be the center of *everything,* Kay found herself thinking, I just want to be the center of *you*. "I don't have to be the center," she pouted. "I just resent your being so secretive about everything."

"Secretive! I go down to visit my daughter's grave. . ."

"I thought you said you went to the river."

"I *did* go to the river. Oh for Christ's sake. I *can* say for Christ's sake, can't I? I mean, everything *else* I say, you jump down my throat."

Kay had a petulant expression on her face. "I don't give a shit *what* you say, because *most* of what you say is bullshit. You're either changing your mind, or lying, or keeping things secret. . ."

"Lying! When the hell did I ever lie to you!"

When you told me you loved me, Kay thought. She said, "You said move in, and I moved in, and it's been downhill ever since."

Sunny pointed a finger at her. "Hey. I never asked you to move in. You came to me, and you said your house was breaking up, and I knew you needed a place to stay. Now don't shit me. Let's get the facts straight. We *both* know what happened. You needed a place to stay. And I offered it."

"So that's all I am? Your roommate?"

"That's the way *you* want it, not me. As far as *I'm* concerned, you're nothing but a fucking pressure to me. I was happier before you moved in. At least I could be miserable in peace."

Kay's eyes filled with tears, and she blinked them away rapidly. "Are you saying you want me to move out?"

Sunny looked at Kay, her expression one of impatience and annoyance. "Did I say that? Why don't you try to *listen* to me for a change. Your problem is you don't know how to listen to me."

"I'd listen to you if you *ever said* anything! You never say a goddamned thing!" Tears spilled out of her eyes, and she pulled off a mitten, wiping her face angrily. "You come upstairs looking like it's the end of the world, and when I ask you what's the matter, you say 'Nothing.'" Her *nothing* sounded like a cruelly sarcastic version of Sunny's gloom. "I might be a pressure, but to tell you the truth, Sunny, you're a real drag. You know that? You're no goddamned fun anymore."

"Well if you're so miserable living with me, you know where the door is."

Kay glared at her. "Yeah, I know where the door is. And believe me, I'd walk right out that door in a minute if I could."

"Well what's stopping you?"

"What's stopping me is I don't have any *money*," she said, and her tone was nasty.

"Hey, if money is all that's keeping you with me, you can leave tomorrow. I'll lend you the goddamned money to find yourself another place."

Kay's mouth was hard. "Gee, thanks," she said. "You gonna charge me interest?"

Sunny's mouth fell open. She stared at Kay whose face was pouting and sullen because she was ashamed of having made the remark and didn't want to admit it. "You know," she said, her voice cool and distant, "I was just thinking about money. In the back of my mind, I was just thinking that I could've stayed at work and been perfectly comfortable and gotten paid for it. Instead, I'm going to go in there, all full of aggravation, and pay somebody so I can get an ulcer. It's pretty ironic, isn't it?"

Kay didn't answer. She was looking at her mittened hands lying in her lap. The car was chilled, and she shivered.

"Well. . . I'm going to go eat. You can come in with me or stay here. I personally don't care." She got out of the car and closed the door behind her.

Kay sat in the cold, dark, silent car. She was thinking, God. . . I don't believe I said that to her. I don't believe I said it.

She got out of the car and joined Sunny in the restaurant. It was dim. Between them, a candle glowed from within a thick, red glass. They ordered drinks. Kay said, "Sunny, I'm sorry I said that to you."

Sunny nodded. "I'm sorry you said it, too."

Kay wanted to say, I'm angry because you've changed and you don't love me anymore, but she said nothing. They looked at the menus, ordered their food, and sat in silence.

After awhile, however, after the mellow mood of the place and the drinks had their affect, they felt more friendly with one another. They chatted casually about casual things. They even let out tentative laughs. Then it all changed back. Kay wasn't sure how it happened. She'd asked a question about Jack, and Sunny had gone off into a long, abstract, boring monologue that was more like a speech, an oblique lecture about lies and honesty and the damages done by deceptions. It seemed almost as if she were speaking to herself. Kay, who'd lost track of what she'd been saying and had stopped listening, thought, What the hell is she talking about? She pretended to listen, thinking of something that had been on her mind. When Sunny was finished, she said, "By the way, I wanted to ask, where did you get Whiskers?"

Sunny had been frowning in thought, still wrapped up in what she'd been saying, and at Kay's words, her eyes widened in shock. "What the hell are you talking about? You know how I found Whiskers."

"Oh." Kay flushed, realizing how her question had sounded. "Yeah, I know, but. . . I don't know, I was just wondering. I mean, if you knew where he came from before that."

"No. I don't know," Sunny said, and went on eating.

The evening was a failure. There was no topic around which they could comfortably meet. In the end, they fell back on talking about other people—Ichabod, Sunny's old boss, and Mrs. Mancuso, their landlady—for it was only in agreeing about others that they could feel closer to one another.

By the time they finished dinner and went outside, a light snow was falling. Sunny, wanting to avoid the forecasted storm, pulled out without sufficiently warming up the car. All the way home it kept coughing and backfiring. She alternately pleaded with and threatened the car, as though it were a capricious donkey while Kay muttered, "I *told* you it wasn't warmed up enough. I told you."

When they got home, Sunny turned off the ignition and sighed. She looked at Kay. "Listen. Let's just be friends, all right?"

To Sunny, the *just* meant, Tonight, if we can do nothing else, let's be kind to one another. But to Kay, it sounded like a new definition of their relationship, like the beginning of farewell.

Sunny reached over and placed her hand on Kay's. Her touch was different; her hand did not rest firmly on Kay's, confident of its welcome. It was wary and seemed, as soon as making contact, to want an excuse to depart.

Kay's hand was unresponsive. After a moment or two, she slipped it away under the pretext of unbuttoning her jacket.

Everything had fallen into place for Kay. All the pieces fit into one neat, ugly package: Sunny's withdrawal, her change of spirit after seeing Frank, her overtime, her talk of lies, her talk of friendship. Kay forced herself to face the painfully unavoidable conclusion.

They had in the past talked in circles about monogamy versus nonmonogamy, each of them debating one side and then the other, but they'd come to no decision. Or they'd come to so many decisions that the whole topic had turned into something of a private joke. They did promise to be honest and tell each other if a sexual attraction were felt or an affair contemplated. But Kay had been lied to in the past by men and women, friends and lovers, about a variety of subjects, and she had little faith in the constancy of human emotions.

The fact that Sunny had no time for this alleged affair and was at home except for easily verifiable chunks of time was an irrelevancy of logic. Kay's suspicions, her jealousy and distrust, needed no physical evidence. She sensed that Sunny had secrets about which she did not speak.

Once the conclusion was planted in her brain, it was not easily dislodged. It found its own reasons for being, justified its own growth, fed on simple misunderstandings when, inflated by its own malevolent force, it convinced her not to question, not to clarify, not to unravel. You see? it would demand, You see?, as if everything in their relationship from the first moment of their meeting to the very last incident were proof that Sunny did not care about her. She doesn't care about me, the monster pouted, having triumphed in her mind. She doesn't care about me at all. But it doesn't matter. Because I don't care about her, either. Right?

She was angry and defensive. It doesn't matter, she thought, it's just that she should have told me. If that's how she wants to play it, I'm game, but she ought to let me know she changed the rules. Her feelings were hurt, and she felt betrayed. Beginning to realize that she was more in love with Sunny than she had thought, she became increasingly hurt and angry.

She was awaiting her LSAT scores which were due to arrive in late February. Every day she walked home from work with great anticipation. She'd round the corner of the Armory, head down, and at the last moment, look up to see the house and the tip of the mailbox. Her eyes on the mailbox, she'd hurry the last halfblock, run up the stairs, flip open the mailbox hood, and until the first Saturday in March, she found nothing relevant to her life or her future. Anticipating her test scores assumed great importance in her mind. She was glad that at the last moment she'd taken her father's advice and applied to Columbia. Sometimes she thought back in wonder to a time when her entire future seemed settled in this city with this woman. Now, feeling as she did, mistrustful and defensive, she would have been relieved—or so she thought—to have gotten accepted anywhere but Buffalo.

Then, she and Sunny argued again. For Kay, it seemed not so much an argument as a declaration of intention.

In the beginning of March, Sunny's sister Meryl gave birth to a healthy baby girl.

Sunny had mixed feelings. She felt resentment and sorrow as well as something else she couldn't define. But she felt it welling up in her heart, and it made her want to cry.

Friday night she worked late, went out with "the girls," and got drunk. She didn't realize she was drunk until she walked into the apartment and Kay said, "You're drunk." They had an argument she didn't even know the point of, and she went to bed.

Sunny spent a restless night. She woke and slept, dreamed and woke up thirsty. Finally, toward dawn, she fell into a deep sleep and had a dream.

She dreamed she was searching for Debbie and Sam. She was in a city, and she walked from street to street, looking. Every time she saw them up ahead, they turned a corner and disappeared. She called out, "Grandpa! Debbie!" but they were like statues, moving slowly but inexorably toward their destination.

They didn't even look back, and that frightened her the most. I have to reach them! she thought, but it was difficult for her to move. She felt as though she were moving in slow motion, or through deep water. She saw them going up a hill. She followed, although she was tired. They turned a corner at the top, and just as she was about to make a last burst of effort to reach them, something made her look back, and she saw them at the bottom of the hill.

They were sitting in an old-fashioned car, like something that might have been popular when Sam first came to America. They were sitting in the back seat, facing forward, hands folded in their laps. It looked like a picture. *Sunday Drive.* Except everything was so terribly gray, awash with gray, a gray that made her feel chilled and lonely. The car drove away, and she knew even as she reached out, about to call, that she would never see them again. She woke with her hand clasped over her open mouth and tears in her eyes.

She sat up, as though to get away, then burst into sudden tears. And she sat and cried, and cried, and cried.

When Kay came home from work, Sunny was in the kitchen making something to eat. Neither of them spoke. Sunny remembered the night before only vaguely: the angry accusations and scornful denials, Kay's tears and declarations, and her own annoyance and withdrawal. She remembered the words they said as though they were strangers, the looks that made them seem like enemies.

Sunny thought, I should talk to her, but this seemed like such a waste of energy that she let it go. Forget it, she said to herself. If that's what she thinks of me, the hell with it. It's not worth it. She ate her food, did the dishes, and left.

Today was the day she was going to take Rose to visit Meryl in the hospital.

It was a beautiful day, unseasonably warm, and the snow was melting fast. Sunny went to the bank and to the supermarket. She drove downtown to the main branch of the library, browsed around a bit, and checked out some books.

At three, she drove up Elmwood Avenue to the side street and the gray-shingled house.

When she arrived, Rose was about to take a shower. Sunny knocked on the open bathroom door. "I've come to keep you company while you take a shower. You mind?"

"*I* don' mind, not me!"

Of course not. Rose loved to be naked and was completely un-self-conscious about her body. She believed that one's skin had to breathe, and it could not breathe properly when constricted by burdensome clothing.

Steam was coming from behind the curtain and drifting out the open door. Rose was singing, and though Sunny couldn't recognize the words, she recognized the tune and the chorus of "yum-tiddy-tum-tum-tum." The curtain was open slightly. Sunny, sitting on the toilet lid, glanced inside. Rose's flesh was soft and settled with age, the skin wrinkled and sagging. But underneath there was a firmness of muscle that came from her love of the out-of-doors, the delight she took in walking, and her general determination to live as long as possible. Her legs were strong and her posture erect; her arms and shoulders were dotted with freckles from an old tan.

Sunny watched as Rose lifted her breasts and washed the midriff underneath.

She realized that she was looking at the body of an old woman—at her own future, perhaps—and it did not displease her. Rose saw her observing and grinned. "Gotta vash and be clean!"

Sunny smiled in return. "By the way, Grandma," she inquired, "how's you arm? Does it hurt anymore?"

"Vell," Rose called over the sound of the running water, "I'm gonna tell you. Deh ahr-rum dat I broke, it took avay a half of my strengt'. I 'aven't got no strengt' now. I make myself to do deh voik. But listen, agains' dese vimmen, vhat dey are, tvunny years younger den vhat I am, I feel much stronger den dey are. Dey are cripple—dey push a liddle vagon, dey can't valk all alone, dey don't have deh strengt'!"

"Who's that?"

"Vimmen in Center."

"Oh."

"So. . . I can't complain. Take dis an' vash my back."

"What?"

"My *back.*"

Sunny opened the curtain half way and scrubbed Rose's back, listening to the rest of the broken arm story.

"Deh ahr-rum took avay alotteh strengt'. But deh docteh said, it's a miracle dat in my age, it knits. After seventy years old, it don't *knit,* a bone."

"Seventy?" Sunny teased. "Is that how old you are?"

But Rose, as she'd foreseen, ignored the question. She held out her hand for the washcloth and pulled the curtain shut. "An' dis," she continued, "dis knits. It knits betteh den a boy sixteen years old. He broke it deh same time dot I did. But mine knits, because I vasn't lazy. Ve strong people. *Strong*! An' *you* strong. You alvays been strong." She turned off the water.

"Have I?" Sunny asked, handing Rose a towel.

Rose stepped out of the tub and began drying herself. Apparently, however, she thought of something, for she paused and sat down at the edge of the tub. With her hands on her knees, her body leaning forward, she said, "Vun time, you vas sick. You 'ad di-rhee vhen you vas about tvelve days old. You almost died fum dot di-rhee. You muddaih, she diden 'ave no milk. She vas noivus because you faddaih vas outta voik."

"I didn't know my father was out of work when I was born. . ."

"So deh milk it dry. I vould 'ave given you *my* milk, but I diden 'ave no milk neideh. No milk dat all. So, vun time she 'ad to go on a vedding."

"Whose wedding?"

"Whose vedding. . ." she repeated, frowning. "Vay. I'm gonna t'ink. Oh! Deh sisteh's vedding."

"Her sister? The one who. . ."

"You vas twelve days old, an' you 'ad tehr-ble di-rhee. All deh kids vas dyin' fum dot. Dey diden know vhat to do! So ve called up dis docteh, a *voman* docteh she vas, an' she said, 'All deh kids is dyin' fum dot.' Dyin'!"

"The children were dying from diarrhea?" she asked skeptically, and at Rose's emphatic nod, she thought, Well, I'm going to have to ask Mom about *that* one.

"But I vudden give up on you!" Rose went on, and Sunny realized she was hearing another episode in *The Saga of Rose the Unvanquished*. She smiled, but nevertheless listened, because she knew that there would be a kernel of truth here somewhere.

"So me an' Pa star-et to t'ink vhat to do. Vell. . . ve vent an' ve bought oytmeal. And I put it in a double boiler, and I cooked it, and I put skim milk, and cooked it in skim milk. Vell, you vas very 'ongry because ev'vyt'ing used to come ahlt from you. You vas just *dot close* to dyin', dot's all. Vell, you ate it up 'ef a cuppie, an' you vent to sleep. And I come and vatched you," she said, and Sunny pictured Rose as a younger woman watching a sleeping child.

"And I vas afraid you gonna get cold, so I vent to bed, and I put you like dot," she said, and encircled her arms around an imaginary baby strapped to her front. "And I see, suddenly you vaked up. You looked vondehful! An' in two hours you moved you bowels. An' it vas long pieces like dot, *solid*. I called up deh docteh an' told her dot you gonna live. An' she says, 'Now ve gonna know how to save dose kids. It neveh came on my mind. Now all deh kids is gonna be saved. T'ank you Meeses Rosent'al." She nodded in emphasis so her sometimes thick-headed granddaughter would not miss the point that she had been thanked by a *doctor*.

"Oytmeal!" she went on. "Dot vas it. Oytmeal. I saved you life, me an' Pa. An' you lived. You did, you lived. An' ev'vybody vas so suprise. Dey look on you and dey said, 'T'ank God. T'ank God she's vell.' But it vasn't God dot made you vell." She shook her head. "It vas me. *I* vas you God. You should t'ank *me*."

Sunny smiled. "Thank you, Grandma."

"You velcome," she said formally, accepting the gratitude that was long overdue. Then she stood up and continued rubbing her body with the towel. When she was almost done she paused, apparently having thought of something. She looked at her granddaughter and pointing her finger said, "You gotta remember dot. You strong. You had ter'ble trouble. *Tsuris*, deh Jewish people call dot. *Tsuris*. You had a lot. But you still a luffly goil. And you strong. Don' fuhget!"

Sunny smiled and nodded. "Okay, Grandma. I won't forget."

"Okey-dokey. On deh go, kid!" she said, and continued drying herself.

Just as she finished, the doorbell rang. "*Oy, a choleria!*" she cursed, annoyed. "Who's dot! Give me my teet'!"

Sunny complied, handing Rose the cup in which her false teeth were soaking. Rose, slipping them into her mouth, walked into the kitchen, heading toward the living room, the towel thrown carelessly over her shoulder.

"Uh, Grandma, now that you have your teeth in, does that mean you're fully dressed?"

"*Vuss?*" Rose inquired. Looking down at her naked body, she laughed.

Sunny laughed along with her. "You want me to get it?"

"Nuh! It's my 'ouse. Give me deh *shmatte*," she said. When she was covered, she went into the living room and lifted the window.

By the time Sunny and Rose got to the hospital, it was almost six. She left Rose with her friend Mrs. Sadetsky, who was awaiting a gall bladder operation in another wing, and headed toward the maternity ward. Sunny had phoned Kay several times from Rose's. Walking to Meryl's room, she passed one phone, and another, and when she reached Meryl's door, her thoughts were still focused on the last phone she'd passed. When she opened the door and saw her sister, however, all such thoughts fled her mind.

Meryl lay facing the wall, the covers pulled up around her shoulders. Something was wrong. Something about the way she lay there hunched and unresponsive disturbed Sunny. "Meryl?" she said softly, walking to the bed.

Meryl seemed to rouse herself into forced sociability, sighing as if in annoyance at the necessity to perform. But seeing it was Sunny, she said, "Oh. It's you," and seemed to sink once more into herself. "I wish everybody would go away," she muttered.

This was so unlike the reaction that Sunny had expected that she stopped midway in pulling a chair over to the bed. She realized that when she was thinking of coming to see Meryl, she'd imagined a stereotyped new mother: joyous, rosy-cheeked, glowing with love.

"Do you want me to leave?" Sunny asked.

"No." Meryl sat up awkwardly. "Not *you*. Just *everybody*. Did you see Rachel?"

"No, I. . . ." Sunny was ashamed to tell her sister why she hadn't yet seen the baby. Sitting beside this pitiful, bedraggled creature, she felt foolish to have been jealous. "I haven't yet. I will after I visit with you awhile."

Meryl made a sour grimace. "Visit. I'm not much up for visiting. I'm not much up for anything."

"I can tell *that*."

Meryl sighed. "I mean. . . what's the point? You know? I had a baby. So what's the point? What right do I have to bring a baby into this world? Oh. . . ." She shook her head. "Never mind. I don't even want to talk about it."

Sunny had by this time pulled the chair closer to the bed. "Maybe you should talk about it. Maybe it will make you feel better."

"Feel better! Oh. . . I get it. You think this is some kind of postnatal blues. The poor postpartum nutsies. That if I feel better, it will make all the difference in the world. Unfortunately, the problem isn't my *feelings*, the problem is the *world*."

She sighed. "Before she was born, in the last months, I thought, Oh God, I wish she wouldn't be born. I wish I could keep her, safe, protected, like I'm protecting her now. Because once she leaves my body. . . ." Her lips quivered, and tears spilled out of her eyes and rolled down her face. She glanced at Sunny, and seeing that she only partly understood, she wiped her eyes angrily with the back of her hand and said in a voice that was tight with her attempt at control, "Do you know that some scientists predict that if over a thousand missiles go off, it will change the weather so drastically that it will be the end of life on earth? The end of life on earth. That's inconceivable. That's not a war, or an isolated catastrophe. That's the end. No seeds growing. Anywhere. *Ever*. Nothing. And right now between the U.S. and Russia there's over fifty thousand missiles in existence. And that's not counting France and Britain. I mean. . . how many times can we kill ourselves? How many times can we kill the Earth?" She gave an abrupt bitter laugh. "And Mom comes and tells me I have postnatal blues, that every woman goes through this, that every woman has felt this way since the beginning of time." She shook her head. "I doubt it. I doubt it very much."

She looked at the blanket and was silent. She gave a despondent sigh. "I wake up in the middle of the night, and I think, What have we done to this planet?" She looked at Sunny, shaking her head. "I can't believe it. I think it must be a nightmare. But then I know it's not. I think, This is the real world. The world I brought my baby into. I think, I gave life to a child in a world that hates Life." Her face looked stunned and bewildered, for she was unable to understand this central point of her existence.

"I want to *tell* people. But how do you say to people, 'Wake up and save the Earth.' How do you get them to *listen*? I want to walk through the halls, and tell people. . . ." She leaned forward, putting her hand gently on Sunny's arm. "I want to say, 'Don't you know that we have to save the Earth?' "

For an instant she held Sunny's gaze with her own insistent eyes. Then she sat back, a knowing glint replacing that intensity. "Do you know what people would think if I actually did that? Do you know what they'd do? They'd probably try to reason with me, and if I didn't stop trying to *tell* people, they'd lock me up." Her face got a sullen look about it, and she said, "They've done that before. Lock up people who tell the truth. They do it all the time."

She shook her head slowly. "Mom tells me that it can't happen. They won't blow up the world. It's too crazy, too terrible." She gave a strange mirthless laugh. "I told her, I said, 'I can't believe you said that. You're Jewish, and you're telling me that something won't happen because it's too terrible to happen?' "

"I sit here and I watch TV. I watch the news, and I can't believe what they show. I *know* what's important. I know. And I'm sitting here, and I just had a baby. . . and what do *I* know, right? I sit here and watch TV, and it's all such a lie that it drives me crazy. So Mom says, she tells me, 'Don't watch TV.' "

She looked at Sunny and Sunny nodded. Yes, that was Sylvia.

Meryl shook her head and leaned back against the pillow, turning her face to the window. "Did Mom tell you I have no milk?"

"No. She didn't."

Meryl nodded. "You know that I wanted to nurse."

"Yes."

"But. . . I can't." She gave a helpless little shrug. "No milk."

She took a deep breath to calm herself. "I *always* thought I'd nurse. I remember. . . one day at Grandma's and Grandpa's. You were in Grandpa's room nursing Debbie. Everybody else was in the living room, and I went in to ask you something. You were sitting in the chair by the window, and you were holding Debbie in your arms. You were smiling at her, looking into her eyes. She was looking back. There was all this noise from the living room, but you and Debbie, you were looking at each other. . . with such love. . . ." Her lips began to quiver, and she shook her head to refuse admittance to the rising emotion. "I thought, *I* want that. *I* want it. But I have no milk. No milk at all. I'm so angry and frustrated. Look what it's done to me. Look what it's done to my baby."

She covered her face with her hands. "Maybe I *am* crazy. It would be a relief to think so." The tension went out of her body, but the energy was gone too. She seemed completely depressed. Meryl put her arms down at her sides, shook her head, and began to cry weakly.

Sunny sat there motionless, not knowing what to do, what to say. She would have liked to offer the comfort of her arms, to soothe her sister with a warm embrace, to stroke her hair like a mother would a child, to murmur words that gave her courage, strength, and sustenance. But she feared that Meryl would misunderstand and recoil. And feeling as if she, too, would cry, she reached out and grasped her sister's hand in her own, holding it tight, as though they were frightened lifelines to one another.

Chapter 6

The Web

When Sunny saw the baby, red-faced and crying, she felt again that welling in her heart. But now, she knew what it was.

She put her arm around Rose and said, "Hey, Rosie, how do you like your great-granddaughter?"

"*Oy gevalt!* Such a *shayneh maideleh, kineahora.*"

Sunny smiled, for that was what Rose had said about Debbie. They left the hospital, and Sunny drove Rose back to the gray-shingled house. Then she drove home.

On the way she thought about Kay and how bad it had been between them. She resolved that when she got home she would sit Kay down and say, "Listen. Let's talk."

But when she rounded the corner of the Armory and saw Kay standing on the porch, coatless and shivering, she knew something was wrong. Her heart lurched.

She parked the car and walked quickly across the street, saying, "What is it? What happened?"

Kay met her eyes. Even from midway across the street, even in the night, Sunny saw something in her eyes.

Kay looked away quickly; almost, Sunny thought, as if she were pretending it *hadn't* been quick. As if she'd turned away to look for something. "Whiskers got out," she said, and turned back to wait for Sunny's reaction.

"What! What happened? How did he get out?"

"I. . . I called him and called him, and he won't come. I was going to look for him. I was just going to go in and get my coat."

"How long ago did he get out?"

"About. . . ." Kay hesitated, then confessed, "I don't know." She was close to tears. "I just realized he was gone."

"Well, how do you know he's outside? Maybe he's just hiding in the house."

"No. I looked for him and looked for him. Then I remembered I'd seen a cat on the porch before, and it looked like Whiskers, but I didn't *think*. . ."

"You'd seen a cat on the porch before *when?*" Kay didn't answer right away, and Sunny shook her head. "Never mind about that now. The important thing is to find him."

"I'll help you, I'll go get. . ."

"No. I think I'll have better luck alone. You go on inside before you catch pneumonia."

"All right. Sunny, I'm sorry."

"Okay, it wasn't your fault. Go on inside."

"But I want to. . ."

Sunny waited, and when Kay did not go on, she said with a kind of gentle brusqueness, "I have to find Whiskers. Go inside. We'll talk later."

Kay nodded and turned away.

Sunny searched up and down the block, poking her head in the back yard, looking across the street at the base of the Armory, behind bushes and trees. Finally, she walked all around the block, down the driveways or pathways of the houses whose back yards bordered hers.

She looked until she got tired of fighting despair. Then she returned to the porch. She stood there a long time. After awhile, she began to sense that if she were Whiskers, confronted by that huge and unknown world that loomed beyond the doorstep, she would not go far from home. She stepped off the porch once more and walked into the back yard.

She'd never been in the yard in wintertime, and like the human solipsist that she was, had given no thought to the yard's existence when she was not present to admire it—as though her presence gave it life, or gave its life meaning. Now she saw that the yard had its own existence, even in winter when everything was asleep to her perception.

"Whiskers!" she called softly. "Whiskers. . . ."

The night was painfully beautiful. She looked up and saw the sky. It was a city view, obscured by what the weathermen euphemistically called "ground clutter." But she saw the Milky Way and the North Star, the Big Dipper, the Little Dipper. She saw stars she didn't know, stars whose placement might suggest animals or myths of long ago.

These stars, she realized, had shone before her birth and would shine long after she was gone. She was intensely aware of the frozen ground beneath her feet, and overhead, the immense enveloping sky. At that moment she yearned for the impossible: for life to be as it was before it had been so carelessly damaged, for the days and nights and seasons to pass in their own rhythmical succession for billions of years to come as they had in the past. This was her home, this Earth. Here she lived and here she would be buried, under this sky, under these stars. She was no visitor here. She could not pack her bags and move to another place. This was her home.

The air was still and crisp. Her breath, coming out in steam, seemed to hover for an instant before disappearing. That evening, while she was in the hospital, a quiet snow had fallen, and flake upon flake lay over the most precarious of surfaces—the cables running overhead, the twigs of the forsythia, the tree next door, even the wire mesh of fence separating this yard from the next. For an instant she imagined no fences, no cables, no boundaries, no houses, but only the forest that must have once been here.

"Whiskers!" she called with insistent softness, "Whiskers!" There was no sound, but she did not leave. She felt sure that the cat was here, and her eyes searched for a sign or a movement.

It was a good-sized yard. Her landlord had shaped it to his conception of beauty. On summer evenings, he, cigarette in hand (for his wife did not allow him to smoke in the house), had pointed out the results of his pruning, weeding, mowing, and uprooting, while she, knowing her welcome was due to her being an admiring audience, duly admired.

Along one border he'd planted evergreen shrubs. Each morning when he came out to hose down the yard, he hosed away the webs that had accumulated on the shrubs since the last hosing. She had always thought of those webs as junk. Or annoyances. Unsightly things that *should* be hosed away. But one morning when her landlord was away, she'd investigated the evergreens and seen that the webs were made by spiders.

These spiders were shy creatures, for when she blew gently, the large ferocious-looking things would scurry inside the funnel shaped webs, unlike other spiders (she learned) who clung obstinantly to the centers of their concentric webs no matter what kind of gale came from her mouth. It amazed her and made her feel very humble to know that all of this variation of life existed in her own back yard, and she had never known or cared to see it.

The next day when Mr. Mancuso came out, hose in hand, she wanted to stop him, to tell him that the spiders had as much right to live there as he. But he had paid the mortgage to the bank for this property, and it was therefore his right, according to the law, to destroy the webs. "You know, those are spiders' webs," she told him. He nodded and hosed them away.

The webs were gone now, the evergreens covered with snow. What happened to the spiders in the winter, she wondered. Did they burrow underground beneath the frozen soil?

"Whiskers!" she called softly. "I know you're here. Please be here." This time she heard a questioning meow. Turning, she saw now, where before she'd seen nothing, a face peeking around the corner of the shed, a white patch and those round yellow eyes.

"Hello, you funny looking thing," she said, and knelt down. "Where did you go, you bad kitty?" As she spoke, he approached her tentatively.

"I've been looking all over for you," she murmured. When he brushed against her, she smoothed the fur on his back, smiling at the purring meow that sounded like a chirp. "I thought you were lost. How did you get out?" she asked. Picking him up, she stood and closed her eyes, pressing her face against his fur.

For a moment, nothing else seemed to exist. Only her cheek pressed against this animal's fur underneath which she could feel the warm purring vibrations.

She opened her eyes and saw the snow-covered evergreens. Where *did* those spiders go in the winter, she wondered. Looking around one last time, she understood that the yard, though set in the city, was a part of the earth and all its natural cycles.

Whiskers meowed, as if to remind her that *he* should be the center of her attention.

"What a cat you are," she said to him, smiling, and he blinked lazily in response. "Come on," she said, "I'll treat you like royalty. I'll give you *milk*. I'll dry off your *fur*. How does that sound, Whiskers? You gorgeous cat, you. Would you like that?"

And holding him in firm protection, she headed toward the path that lead around to the front of the house.

Upstairs, Kay was in bed, wrapped mummylike in the blankets and shivering. Eyes closed, she wished for sleep, wished perhaps for oblivion. When Sunny carried Whiskers in loving triumph into the bedroom, she smiled weakly and offered congratulations that sounded more like an apology.

"Well what *happened*?" Sunny demanded, but she was smiling when she said it.

"I. . . I. . . I. . . ."

Sunny laughed and plopped down at the edge of the bed. "Ay-ay-ay? That's some answer! Is that an example of your defense techniques?"

"What?" Kay looked at her, trying to decipher her meaning.

"Whiskers!" Sunny complained, for the cat had struggled out of her arms and jumped down, where he began cleaning himself.

"What do you mean, *defense techniques?*"

"When you become a lawyer."

"Oh."

"Listen," Sunny said. "Let's talk."

Kay's heart began to pound. Sunny reached out and placed her hand gently on Kay's arm, or rather on the mound of blankets under which Kay was holding her body tight to keep from shaking. Sunny's touch did no good, and Kay's body gave a kind of exaggerated shiver.

"You're cold," Sunny said, and she sounded concerned.

Kay nodded, aware that she was looking for sympathy and feeling ashamed.

Sunny rubbed her arm and shoulder. "You must've gotten a chill. Listen, now that the tragedy is past and Whiskers is safe and sound—though obviously ungrateful that I saved him, from the looks of it—I think we should talk. Or maybe it would be better to say, *I* should talk."

Sunny began to talk, but Kay hardly heard. She heard bits and pieces but not the whole. She heard Sunny say, "I think my problem was that I was walking around trying to pretend nothing was wrong. In a way you were right: I *was* selfish. I should have talked to you." And Kay heard her say, "Just because my brother's fucked up doesn't mean it should spoil *my* sex life. Right?"

Kay completely missed her meaning. "What?" she asked, hoping the question would not betray her.

"I mean I should have *known* he's nothing but an ungrateful little bastard—just like Meryl said!"

"When did Meryl say that?"

"What? Oh, I don't know. Anyway," she rubbed her eyes, sighing, and dropped her hand to her lap, "it hasn't been an easy year for me, Kay. Maybe that's all I'm trying to say. Do you understand?"

The room was dark and quiet. Whiskers had jumped up and was sitting at the foot of the bed, washing himself with noisy pleasure.

"Sunny," Kay began, but the words weren't there. Or if they were there, she couldn't seem to propel them out of her mouth.

"Is something wrong?" Sunny asked, for Kay had spoken her name with such urgency, and then had fallen silent. "Are you okay?" She paused. "Did you stop loving me?"

"No."

"Okay, *that's* good," she said, and cocked her head as if to say, Then what *is* it?

Kay sighed. "Maybe I'm tired. I think I don't feel good." She closed her eyes and murmured vague answers to Sunny's attempts to pinpoint her ailment, agreeing that she needed sleep and should be left alone. But when she saw Sunny's silhouette, her back dark against the frame of lighted hallway, she called, "Sunny!"

"Yes?"

"I have to ask you a question. You weren't having an affair, were you?"

"What?" Sunny smiled quizzically. Kay could see her face, dark and smiling. "Kay, I have enough trouble being with *you*. What makes you think I have energy for somebody else? Did you really *think* I was having an affair?"

Kay opened her mouth.

"You did."

"I . . . I wasn't sure."

Sunny shook her head, still smiling at the absurdity of it. "What a knucklehead you are. God! I'd *never* do anything like that behind your back." She laughed. "I might have an *affair,* but I'd *tell* you about it. Come on, smile. I was only joking."

Kay nodded. Forcing herself to smile, she watched Sunny leave.

She lay in bed listening to Sunny in the shower, in the kitchen. When Sunny came to bed, Kay pretended to be asleep and listened to the silence.

Or she would have liked there to be silence. She would have liked to silence the thoughts that spun raucously in her mind. More than anything, she would have liked to forget what had happened, but there was no escaping the facts, though she tried to excuse them, to explain them away.

When Jack had phoned that afternoon, she'd felt a certain spiteful satisfaction hearing his voice. When he asked what was wrong (she sounded annoyed and glum so he *would* ask), she complained vaguely about Sunny, saying that she was beginning to think he was right. He asked what she was doing, and she replied in bored tones that invited a suggestion. He suggested the movies. "Sure, why not," she'd replied flippantly, knowing full well what was in both their minds and exactly where it would lead.

They'd gone to the movies and come back to the apartment. They were cold—though not so cold as they pretended—and sat on the rug in front of the space heater. They drank some wine, smoked some grass.

Afterward, she'd seen a glimpse of something in his eyes: he'd gotten exactly what he wanted from her, and he had no use for her anymore. She'd felt ill. She wanted him to leave. She couldn't look at him, couldn't bear to see a confirmation of what she'd recognized before. They parted with brusque embarrassed bantering. She was so intent on having him leave quickly that she didn't notice that Whiskers was in the hall and must have been there the whole time, didn't notice until he ran out the open front door, hesitated a moment on the porch, and was gone.

She sighed and turned over, trying to find comfort. But comfort eluded her.

It's not such a terrible thing, she told herself. You've slept with men before.

But she knew that sleeping with a man wasn't quite the point. Her face burned, and she pressed her hand over her eyes. Go to sleep! she told herself. What's the matter with you? You did it and nothing's going to change that. You weren't to blame. You were angry. You thought she was having an affair.

But even as she said it, she wondered how she could have been under such an illusion. Sunny would never have lied about something like that, and she had known it from the very beginning. Then why had she slept with Jack? It was very easy to say she got caught up in the passion of the moment, but the point was that she'd created the possibility for that moment to happen. She sighed and tried once again to close her eyes. It doesn't matter, she thought. I'll tell her and she'll forgive me. Or she'll never find out. I'll call Jack tomorrow and make him promise not to tell her. But she didn't trust Jack and knew she wouldn't call him. She'll never find out, she thought with less conviction. Or if she finds out, she'll understand.

But all of this was poor comfort, for she kept coming back to the same question: how could she have done it? How could she have hurt Sunny? For that the end of all of this would be Sunny's pain was an unavoidable conclusion.

She had betrayed someone she was supposed to love. Sunny had trusted her, and she had repaid that trust with betrayal. The fact that this was Sunny's first relationship with a woman made what she'd done all the more cruel. How could you have *done* it?! she asked herself. Kay looked over quickly at Sunny, for her thoughts had been so loud she thought Sunny might have heard.

Sunny slept soundly, and her sound sleep seemed like an accusation. How could you have done it? she asked once more, and defended, Well, it wasn't just me. Jack had something to do with it too.

What about Jack? Why had *he* done it? The passion of the moment... yes, yes, yes, but *why*? Why had he betrayed Sunny? She thought back to all those conversations, conversations where Jack had twisted things around.

In a moment, seeing those conversations in a linear way and seeing their cumulative effect, it struck her that Jack had set out to turn her against Sunny. But this was something she could not bear to face for long. She would rather have been actively guilty than have been a passive instrument, manipulated, as she now suspected.

Oh, God, she thought, and got out of bed. Every room was like a cage. In the bedroom was Sunny, in the bathroom the mirror. In the kitchen they had sat and played their foolish games, and in the living room.... She sat, nevertheless, curled up on the easy chair, and forced herself to think.

What was she going to do?

What was she going to *do*? I have to tell her, she decided. I can't not tell her. I have to tell her and that's all there is to it. That was the only solution. Tomorrow, she thought. They would have the whole day together.

Back in bed she still could not sleep. Finally she snuggled up to Sunny, who lay in a curve around Whiskers.

Sunny half woke and turned to Kay, smiling. "Hello," she murmured. "It can't be morning."

"No, it's still night. Go back to sleep."

"I love you," Sunny said softly and closed her eyes. But Kay lay there, wide awake, staring into the dark. I have to tell her, she decided again. Tomorrow. I'll tell her tomorrow. I made a mistake, that's all. A mistake. I'll tell her and it'll all be over.

The next day, however, the temptation to turn her back on that mistake was too great. She tried several times but imagined the look on Sunny's face. She thought about it all day, planning how to tell her. But the right words never came to her. Then she decided it was better to wait and tell her on an impulse. Certainly the right moment would come.

Even as she thought this, she knew that there would be no impulse, that no right moment would come. By her silence she had lied, and her lie was now entrenched in their lives.

For a week or so, Kay continued to act odd, but Sunny was determined to be patient. Soon things seemed to return to normal. They were no longer arguing, and that snappish tension was gone.

The only thing marring all of this was the fact that Kay began to have stomach problems. Nothing seemed to sit right with her. After eating she'd get a lump in her throat that felt, she said, as though she hadn't swallowed properly. The food was just sitting there. She began to experience dizzy spells and vertigo. Once, in the supermarket, she almost fell down while they were standing in line and had to grab Sunny's arm.

She shrugged it off. But Sunny was concerned. She wanted Kay to get a physical. Kay refused. Finally, Sunny called the doctor and told him about her friend who had stomach trouble and dizzy spells. "Could it be emotional stress?" she asked, and the doctor said, "Could be." That night she asked Kay, "What's wrong? Are you under emotional stress?"

Kay admitted that she was worried about law school. She should be hearing soon, she said. The U.B. Law School began to notify students at the beginning of April. And Columbia, soon after.

Sunny nodded. She understood at last that Kay's choice about law school might very well determine the course of their relationship. Or, conversely, their relationshp would determine Kay's career choices. It was not a simple matter. She could well comprehend that Kay's emotional stress would cause her physical illness. Sunny tried to make sure that Kay ate right. She urged her to get enough sleep.

Sunny reassured her. Things would calm down, this stressful period would pass, and everything would be smooth at home again.

Her overtime had stopped, and she was glad they had time to spend together. She realized how very much she'd missed her when they'd been estranged, realized how much she needed Kay's affection, their laughter and their talks.

Their talks. She had to talk to someone: she had to decide what to do about Grace.

Things had changed at work. Sunny realized that Grace's friendship had been the only thing that made her day at Imperial Dynamics bearable. Gone was the easy bantering, the atmosphere in which she or Grace could say the most outrageous things and the other would understand. She hadn't wanted things to change, but they had changed nevertheless. She couldn't help that she'd grown cool, and Grace, after perceiving that this cooling was not a matter of Sunny having gotten up on the wrong side of the bed one morning, had grown careful. Sunny felt badly, especially because she knew Grace wondered why she'd changed. But she could not imagine herself saying, "By the way, I never told you in the year or so we've known each other, but I'm Jewish. And you really pissed me off when you made that crack."

No. If she'd done it right away, it would have been different. After all this time, however, it would seem like she was dwelling on it. Which she was.

Grace was supposed to be her friend. But if they'd lived in another time, another place, what would that friendship have meant? Sunny thought, Scratch a *goy* and you find an anti-Semite. Who had said that? Her father? Yes. When she'd heard it, she'd scoffed, annoyed at his cynicism, judging it to be indicative of the outmoded thought patterns of his generation. Now she wondered, Was it true? And if it were true, what did it mean?

One morning, an incident occurred that made her reevaluate the statement—or rather, expand it.

She had her period and felt miserable. Her breasts were sore, and she was worried. Her breasts had been sore twelve times a year almost every year since she was eleven, but now this soreness had taken on a different meaning.

In mid-morning she went to the Ladies Room. She changed her tampon, washed her hands, and walked out to the foyer. Against one wall of the foyer was a formica counter, and over this, a wall-sized mirror. On the other side of the foyer was a small alcove into which a hard vinyl couch fit. The couch was supposedly for the benefit of the female employees of Imperial Dynamics, but until that day she'd never seen anyone using it.

She stood in front of the mirror. Seeing her reflection, she sighed despondently. God, you look like shit, she thought to herself. Everything seemed wrong. She wasn't young enough or thin enough. She tried to put on a bright look to widen her eyes and appear more alert and enthused, but the expression was obviously a mask and nothing more.

She felt suddenly peevish and angry because she remembered herself at the quarry. At the quarry, her face was beautiful. Though it might be tired or harrassed or worried, it was beautiful because it was herself. At the quarry she was confident enough to stand naked under the sky.

But this was not the quarry. Standing there, quite still, she examined herself critically. So lost was she in this harsh, disappointed inspection, in trying to see herself through Imperial eyes, that she failed to notice she was not alone in the room.

Then she heard a sigh and turned to see LaSan in the alcove. She'd been laying back on the hard couch.

Something went through Sunny's mind, too fast for her to grasp it.

But when their eyes met in the mirror, she knew that LaSan had gotten it. Perhaps because she'd seen it before in other eyes. She shot out a challenging, almost resentful glare that somehow reminded Sunny that Imperial Dynamics employees were by State Law entitled to fifteen-minute breaks in the morning and afternoon, that LaSan was on such a break, and therefore had a right to be doing exactly what she was doing—nothing.

But past that look, Sunny saw that LaSan was in trouble. Her face was drawn and haggard, and it had taken some effort for her to sit up. She seemed to have little strength. One hand was pressed to her stomach, just below her rib cage.

"LaSan... are you all right?"

She looked at Sunny but did not answer.

"Do you want me to get somebody?"

She shook her head.

"Are you sure? You don't look good at all."

LaSan glanced at her watch, sighed, and stood up. She looked in the mirror to check her appearance, and something about her changed. It was something that happened in her eyes. An armor seemed to go up, a defense to hide whatever others would perceive as weakness.

She headed toward the door. As she pulled it open, she paused and murmured "Thank you."

Sunny nodded, and in the mirror watched her go.

In the hallway, on the way back to her office, she wondered what LaSan had seen in her eyes.

She didn't have to wonder for long because she remembered what had crossed her mind when she first spotted LaSan on the couch.

She'd seen LaSan lying on the couch as confirmation of Louise's judgment. She hadn't seen, in that one instant, that LaSan was ill. She hadn't seen a woman in trouble. She'd seen what Louise saw.

Back at her desk, she thought about LaSan and how the office in general perceived her. LaSan had the reputation of having a sharp tongue. The implication was that it had less to do with wit, intelligence, or courage, however, and more to do with the fact that though she might *look* like a classy black, she was really nothing but.... The rest was left for the white imagination to supply: a brazen nigger, a sassy bitch. In reality, her sharp tongue was probably one of the skills she'd honed to ensure her survival in an often overtly hostile white environment. To Louise, of course, she was and always would be "that lazy nigger."

She held up the phrase for examination: *lazy nigger*. Where had it come from? Who had said it first? Why had they said it? She was alone in the office. Sunny stood up, stretched, and went to the window. It was one of those dreary late winter days, the sky dark with lowering clouds that were filled with the tension of a rain not yet ready to fall. It would be a treacherous rain, hitting the frozen ground to turn to ice.

She looked at the window and saw her reflection against the gray day. For the first time, she understood what it was her Imperial eyes were always searching for; understood that in spite of her blue eyes, it was her strong features and dark, curly hair that defined her. She might have called her looks "exotic," but those who knew saw through her self-deception to what she really was. Automatically, she comforted herself with her "alias" and her silence. But she felt ashamed, trapped by the lie that she herself had created. It struck her that the distance between Sunny Rosenthal and Miss Strickland might grow, and if she were not careful, someday she might return home to find that Sunny Rosenthal had vanished.

Out of the corner of her eye she saw Louise walking down the hall. Automatically, without a conscious thought or decision, she kept her eyes averted. Gazing into the glass, she looked into her eyes. Is that it? If they don't know what *you* are, you won't have to confront them with what *they* are? Is *that* it? That you're a coward?

She returned to work, but as she typed and filed and answered the phone, in the back of her mind she kept thinking. She came finally to the conclusion that she did not want people at work to know she was a Jew because what that meant was already branded in their minds. It was a definition anchored firmly in their deepest prejudices about human behavior, and everything she had ever done or would do would be seen in this context.

It was the same thing with LaSan. If LaSan were sick on the couch, it was proof that she was a "lazy nigger." If LaSan worked hard, Louise's attitude was, I see the *lazy nigger's* finally getting off her ass— what is she trying to prove?

Now she thought in answer to Louise: She's trying to prove she's not a "lazy nigger," you moron.

Toward quitting time, Grace came down to tell her that LaSan had vomited blood in the Ladies Room. "I think it's bleeding ulcers," she said. "My uncle had it."

Alone again, Sunny could not concentrate on her work. She kept thinking about LaSan and the fact that she might have bleeding ulcers. As she'd isolated that other phrase, so, too, did she isolate this one: *bleeding ulcers.*

Bleeding ulcers. It would not leave her mind. Why had LaSan gotten bleeding ulcers? What was she carrying around inside herself that she would not let go? *Could* not let go. Or perhaps was not allowed to let go. Was it that sometimes the simplest word, or even the quickest glance, carried with it the weight of history? Hundreds of years of attitudes.

Yes, she thought, I know all about *that.*

At the end of March, Sunny turned thirty. She was not one for birthdays. If it were up to her, in fact, the day would have passed by with little notice. Kay, however, surprised her with a birthday cake on which was written, *Happy Birthday Sony.*

"Happy Birthday *Sony?"* Sunny asked. "What happened? Did I turn into a Japanese tape recorder factory on my thirtieth birthday?"

"They spelled it wrong. I'm sorry. But I thought you'd like it. It's an ice cream cake."

"An ice cream cake! Let me at it."

The nicest thing, however, was the gift Kay gave her: a small gold *chai* on a chain. Seeing it, Sunny's eyes filled with tears.

"I thought you'd like it," Kay said. "The lady at the store said it means *life.* I thought it would remind you of our life together."

"Oh, how sweet."

"Sunny... you know, sometimes people make mistakes. And sometimes they do stupid things, *really* stupid things, and then later they're sorry. But it doesn't mean that their feelings are any different. Do you know what I mean?"

Sunny frowned. "Not really."

Kay hesitated, and when Sunny took her hand, she smiled as though it were only a joke. She blurted, "I'm sorry your cake said *Happy Birthday Sony."*

Sunny smiled, a bit unsurely, since she'd thought Kay was being serious. "I love you," she said, "and I love your gift."

That night when they made love, Kay cried in Sunny's arms. It was the first time this had ever happened, and Sunny at first thought that Kay's tears were like her own had been. But she sensed that they weren't, and though she tried her best to be comforting, she was puzzled.

Later, they lay in bed talking. Eventually the conversation got around to Grace. Kay said, "You can't hold back if you want to be friends. You've got to tell her."

Sunny regarded her with a smile. "Where'd you get this sensible streak," she commented. "It's a new you."

"Yes, I guess it is a new me. Maybe I'm growing up. Do you like the change?"

"Yeah. It's pretty nice."

"I know it's hard," Kay went on after a thoughtful pause. "It's not easy to tell somebody something you should have told them right away. It's like. . . now you're caught. If you tell her, maybe she won't understand. And if you *don't* tell her, it's deceitful. I mean, you having all these feelings and not letting her know. You know?"

"Mmm."

"But if you don't tell her and she finds out, then on top of everything, she'll think you're a liar."

"Well, I wouldn't go *that* far. I don't even think she'd remember the incident. It wasn't that big of a deal. Anyhow," she smiled, "maybe I'll just invite Grace to the *Seder* in April. Or I won't even have to do that. Now that I have my *chai*, she'll see it. Of course she'll probably think it's Japanese."

Later that week, Kay was accepted at the U.B. Law School.

She was delighted. She and Sunny sat at the kitchen table making plans, some of them borne more of enthusiasm than rational thinking.

The following day, Kay's enthusiasm still high, she suggested they drive out to the Amherst Campus so she could visit the law library. Sunny agreed. Once they got there, however, she was bored with the law library, the people, and Kay's enthusiasm. Finally she said, "I'm going over to the main library. I'll meet you out front in an hour, okay?"

Outside the building, she passed a park bench, considered sitting, but changed her mind. I can always come back, she thought, went into the building and walked upstairs.

Glass display cases stood in the large entranceway. Sunny walked over out of curiosity. When she was too close to turn away, she saw that the title of the display was "Anti-Semitism in History." She thought, Oh no, I *really* don't want to look at *this*. But it was too late for her to turn away.

She looked through thick glass at old books, the edges frayed, the paper brittle. Some were in different languages; some had pictures.

One picture was a fifteenth-century woodcut: a long-nosed, long-fingered Jew sticking his long tongue into the ass of a pig. The caption was translated: "The horned Jewish devil urges the Jews to drink the sow's milk and eat its excrement 'since they are, after all, your best delicacies.' "

It made her feel ill. *Dirty Jew,* she thought sadly. That's a *Dirty Jew.* No wonder it had hurt so much when she'd been called that. That phrase had the weight of history behind it.

She moved to the next book, the next table. As she did she became self-conscious. She was the only one at the display. Several people walked by, one or two stopping to glance, and keep walking. No one seemed interested. Or perhaps they didn't have the time or didn't want to stop and be exposed like she was.

She pictured herself, hands clasped behind her back, leaning over slightly. A Jew looking at the history of Jew-hating, she thought with some irony. But the irony hurt, and she became defensive. I don't care how self-conscious I get, she told herself. I'm going to stay here. She read on.

Finally she got to the history and function of anti-Semitism in Nazi Germany. This was not something she'd been taught at school. From her childhood, the Holocaust had been treated like a shameful secret, the humiliating memory of her own people who had no will, no strength, no courage, but passively dug their own graves and passively went to their deaths. It was only later that she learned the truth: the resistance that came too late against an all-powerful state and the complicity of the world.

In one of the books she found a document from the concentration camp museum at Dachau. It was a drawing showing the various insignias the inmates wore on their sleeves: red triangles for political prisoners, black triangles for anti-socials, purple for Jehovah's Witnesses, blue for immigrants, and pink for homosexuals. These were some of the people that were murdered. The Jews, of course, had their own special insignia, the yellow Star of David. But if a Jew were something else, the Nazis had another system of identification: that person's marking was a yellow triangle, and over it, one that was red, or black—or pink.

She'd known these facts, but not so specifically. She knew that the Nazi's victims comprised a wide range of humanity, but how wide she had never realized. She'd seen the documentaries with mountainous tangles of skeletal arms and legs; haunted eyes staring from behind barbed wire, the self inside having gone into a realm beyond her comprehension. But she'd always reassured herself with the distance between herself and them, the distance of time and geography.

Now there was no distance. Now, for some reason, standing there in the library, it was suddenly real. When she turned to the next book and saw a photograph of faces staring out at her, she felt a pain she'd never known, because it was not *them* who'd been humiliated, and terrorized, and tortured, and murdered. It was herself. She saw herself in those pages, in those pictures, in those triangles. Herself and her family. It was as if time and geography had changed, and she'd been moved body and soul into that history. Or as if she and history had come together with a sudden explosion in her mind.

She stood there, stunned.

At the end of the display was a book refuting all that had come before, telling her it was a hoax.

This, she disregarded. She walked out of the library, on the way remembering a joke one of Frank's brothers had told. Question: What's the difference between a Jew and a pizza? Answer: A Jew screams when you put it in the oven. Then, seeing that she'd been within earshot, he'd apologized. "Oh, I'm sorry, Sunny. I didn't see you."

105

It was a curious apology. Not, I'm sorry I said it, or, I'm sorry I feel that way, but, I'm sorry you heard.

And what had been her response. She didn't remember. She knew she hadn't yelled, or cried, or expressed any of the things she'd felt. Perhaps she'd just walked away. That's all right. Go ahead and joke. I won't get in the way. I won't make you feel badly by letting you know you hurt my feelings when you joked about the murder of my family.

Outside, she walked to the bench and sat down. She breathed deeply. It was such a beautiful day. How could it be such a beautiful day?

After awhile she saw Kay coming out the door of the law library building. Kay saw her and waved, grinning. Sunny waved back. As Kay approached, she thought about telling her what she'd seen but decided against it.

She knew Kay wouldn't understand—not immediately and not with her heart. And she didn't want to explain. Not now. She didn't want to have to prove anything.

Kay was excited. She chatted all the way home about the school, the library, and how wonderful their future together would be. Sunny nodded and kept driving.

When Kay looked in the mirror, she was likely to encounter, at different times, two different women. Sometimes she could not look into her own eyes, and her mirror glances were quick and for the sole purpose of checking her appearance. Did she look presentable? Yes? Good, then that was all she wanted to see. Other times she held her own gaze—defensive, defiant, as though it were a test of strength. She alternated between a deep, pained remorse and a self-righteous posturing. In neither was she able to think clearly.

A hundred times in that first week she'd tried to tell Sunny, to touch her on the shoulder and say, "Sunny, there's something I have to tell you." But each time she caught herself, stopping on the verge of touch, on the verge of speech.

She was ashamed and, more than anything, wanted to forget. The memory of that night made her face burn with humiliation, not because of the sex itself, but because of her own spiteful motivations and the look she'd seen in Jack's eyes—the look of smug satisfaction and victory.

Then, too, she'd seen something in herself that she'd never encountered before, and she didn't like it. She knew now that she was capable of betrayal. She was capable, she saw, of lying, her thoughts skipping ahead so that she lay in wait, as it were, for Sunny's questions. Some of what Sunny had said in the restaurant came back to her: the way a lie grew, one lie covering up another, and another, so that the liar stepped continually backward into a sticky web of deceit. She hadn't thought she'd been listening. She hadn't known she'd heard.

Jack didn't phone. He didn't try to see her. He offered nothing—no apologies or explanations. He had turned his back on her completely. He had used her, she saw more and more, as a weapon to hurt his sister. Would he also use her to hurt his family? She had been intrigued by and sympathetic to his alienation from his family. Now it threatened her. She imagined a scene: all of them gathered around a table and Jack standing there, shouting to Sunny, "That's how much your girlfriend loves you! That's how much she cares!" Would Sunny ever be able to face her family after that?

As the days passed, the implications of what she had done became more and more terrible.

She phoned Jack once, but he was not home, and Kay panicked when his mother asked if there was any message. Not having thought the move through carefully, she lied and identified herself as a "friend." And what if Mrs. Rosenthal recognized her voice? She imagined another dinner scene: Mrs. Rosenthal saying, "You know, your voice sounds so familiar. I know. Weren't you the girl who called last week? Why ever did you identify yourself as a friend?" What, her voice would imply (and everyone would know it), do you have to hide?

Her worst fears and imaginings centered around this dinner scene, and the dinner itself was not imagination. In the third week of April, she and Sunny (and undoubtedly Jack) would meet over the table at Passover. She tried to think of a plausible excuse to stay away, but nothing sounded real. She knew that there was no way to avoid it.

Kay recognized that before the *Seder*, she had to make a decision and take a stand. Sunny had come to her with an open heart and open arms, and she must either tell her the truth and be done with it, or try to forget and hope that Sunny would never discover what had happened.

In the end, her own indecision was itself the decision. Looking into Sunny's face, she could not bear to think of telling her. And then the time for telling had passed. It was too late. She'd made a choice and had to follow through. This decided, she felt better.

Her vertigo lessened. Her depression let up a bit. She began to sleep. She was no longer acting with Sunny. She felt better, in fact. After all, she told herself, many couples had little flings, little peccadilloes, little secrets from one another. Perhaps in years to come she would even smile sheepishly at Sunny and confess: "You know, about. . . oh, six or seven years ago, I'm sure you won't even remember. . . we had this big fight. It was a couple of weeks before I'd gotten accepted at U.B."

Sunny would frown quizzically. "U.B.," she'd say, because by then Kay would have been a practicing attorney for some time.

"Well, your brother came over that day," she'd go on, and Sunny would once more frown quizzically. "My brother. . ." she'd say, because he would have by then passed out of their lives, having gone to

Denver or Seattle or beyond.

Beyond—that's what she would have liked. She would have liked him to get hit by a bus. That way there would be no danger of ever being discovered. She didn't trust Jack at all. She feared he would tell Sunny, and tell her in such a way so as to make her look as bad as possible. She felt she'd been a fool, and she prayed to get accepted at Columbia so that she and Sunny could move to New York and start a new life.

"What would you think about moving to New York?" she asked her.

"New York? Why would I want to move to New York?"

Kay shrugged. "I don't know. I thought it might be nice."

"Nice?" Sunny laughed, shaking her head. "What would I do in New York?"

"Doesn't Imperial have an office there?"

"Yes, but why would I want to leave Buffalo? It's my home. You're funny," she said, and laughed again.

Kay laughed too. Things seemed so much better between them, almost as if it had never happened. Or as if Sunny knew and had forgiven her. In one of her fantasies when she, in six or seven years, said to Sunny, "Well, your brother came over that day," Sunny would smile, give her a big kiss and say, "You silly thing, I knew all about it. I knew it wasn't important and that it wouldn't affect our relationship. I didn't want you to feel bad, so I never let on I knew." That was Kay's favorite fantasy because if Sunny knew, there was no need to tell her.

Kay ricocheted among all the possible variations she'd set out in her mind: it was a foolish mistake but didn't mean a thing; Jack would leave and none of it would ever come to light; they would move from Buffalo and never look back; and Sunny knew and understood.

The one possibility Kay did not entertain was that Sunny did not know, and that when she found out, she would be devastated.

Pesach, or Passover, is the Festival of Freedom and celebrates the liberation of Jews from slavery in Egypt over three thousand years ago. The *Seder*, the Passover ceremony, is held on the first and sometimes the second nights of Passover and consists of saying prayers and eating ritual foods that tell the story of Moses, the Pharaoh, the ten plagues, and the flight across the desert. In following the ceremony, a small booklet called a *Haggadah* is read. While there have always been a variety of *Haggadahs*, the Rosenthals had used the same *Haggadah* for over twenty years.

In recent years, mainly due to the influence of feminism, some alternative *Haggadahs* have tried to expand the meanings of slavery and freedom. Some remind the reader about more contemporary struggles, such as the revolt of the Warsaw Ghetto freedom fighters against the Nazis which began on the first night of Passover in 1943.

Norma, the oldest daughter, had phoned from Boston to ask if she could bring an alternative *Haggadah* that one of her students had shown her, and if so, how many copies they would need. Sylvia, speaking on the phone in the living room, said, "Alternative *Haggadah*. . . don't see why not," but Mo's resounding "No!" could be heard from the kitchen where he'd gone to poke around in the refrigerator. They would use the traditional *Haggadah* he said upon returning, the one they had always used.

Sunny, learning of this decision on the phone one evening before the *Seder*, said, "Daddy, the *Haggadah* we use was printed by the Chase and Sanborn coffee company. What the hell kind of tradition is that? I mean, I really don't think that we 'always' used it, do you? I mean, do you think Moses drank Chase and Sanborn instant coffee out in the desert? How would he boil the water? Where would he get a pot? They left in a hurry, remember? I can just imagine: 'Hey, Miriam!' " she said in a faint Yiddish accent, " 'I know we're in a hurry, but but don't forget the pot! I gotta have my Chase and Sanborn instant coffee!' I mean, I don't even think they had metal in those days."

"That's enough," he said. "Don't get smart. What are you, getting like your sister Meryl? A fresh mouth? I don't want to hear anymore about it. When you have a *Seder* at *your* house, you use a hippie *Haggadah*. This *Seder* is at *my* house, and we're using this one."

Since this was the final word, Sunny was left with only two choices as far as she could see. She could either refuse to attend the *Seder*, which was out of the question, or she could do what she did, which was to murmur, "Yes, Daddy Dear," hang up the phone, and mutter to Kay about her father.

Kay had never been to a *Seder*, and beyond her anxieties about her own personal situation, she was immensely curious. "Why do you call it Passover?" she asked.

"Why do we call it Passover? Because the last plague was that the Angel of Death *passed over* the Jewish houses when he slew the first born sons of the Egyptians."

"Oh. Why don't you eat bread?"

"Because the Jews left in such a hurry that they didn't have time to let their bread rise, so they ate unleavened bread. Although I don't know why they didn't have time to let their bread rise," she said dryly, "they had time to bring pots for their Chase and Sanborn instant coffee. . . . Am I being sacrilegious? Wait, what the hell am I asking *you* for?"

"I don't know. But listen, why did they. . ."

"Hold on. I'll tell you what. I'll give you a *Haggadah* to read, and it'll answer all your questions. All right?"

But Sunny forgot to tell Kay that the book read from right to left rather than left to right; and Kay, glancing through the *Haggadah*, found the story disjointed and confusing.

As the *Seder* was changing now, so too had it changed in the previous generation. The *Seders* held by the generation that had come over from the old country, at least those dominated by fiercely religious men such as Rose's father Mordecai, were very different indeed.

When Rose's father was alive, *Pesach* had meant elaborate preparations and a lengthy ceremony, or ceremonies. Being an Orthodox Jew, he insisted on *Seders* on both the first two and last two nights of *Pesach*.

The preparations began weeks before. They were carried out by Rifke, Rose's mother, and after her death by Rose, with whom Mordecai lived when he came over from the old country.

The entire house was given a thorough cleaning. All the dishes, utensils, pots and pans, were removed and put in storage, as well as the *chometz*, all food that was not *kosher* for Passover: the flour and flour foods, the grains and cereals, the rice and beans. Once Mordecai, during one of the eight days of Passover, caught Harry walking in the house with a piece of pepperoni from the grocery store across the street hidden in his hand. Pepperoni! Pepperoni was *traif*, un*kosher* any time of the year, but at *Pesach* it was unthinkable. Mordecai had taken his fist and smashed it down on Harry's head, as though to pound him into the ground. Harry ran and hid in the cellar of a friend's house and didn't come home until the next day, at which time he still got a beating.

After the *chometz* was removed from the house, the cupboards were scrubbed, then the walls and the floors. The night before the first day of Passover, the whole family would go around and check the cupboards for *chometz*, peering into the recesses with a candle. Rifke—or later, Rose—would have purposely placed a scrap of bread there so that the family could discover it. Mordecai, who the family eventually came to call Zadie with the Cane, would brush the scrap of bread onto an old wooden spoon with a piece of rag and tie the rag around it with a bit of spring. All of this—the bread, the rag, the spoon, and the string—was burned as an avowal that the house was clean and *kosher* and ready for Passover.

Ready for Passover. Ready for the Passover plates, utensils, pots and pans to be taken from a separate storage place, washed and dried, and put away in clean cupboards. Rose disliked Passover intensely, disliked all the labor and ceremony that interfered with her life, her independence, her time. But in this, as in all things, she obeyed her father.

The *Seder* itself began at sundown and lasted sometimes until midnight. Because the participants are supposed to sit reclining, Sam's easy chair was carried out to the kitchen, and Mordecai sat propped up by pillows. But there was only one easy chair, and not many pillows, and not much room, so Sam and Rose and the children sat in regular kitchen chairs. For the children—Harry, Morris, and Eva, or *Heschel, Moishe,* and *Chava* as they were called in Hebrew—the hours of droning in Hebrew was interminable. The wine was sweet and good, and they were always hungry. After four glasses of wine, they sometimes dozed off; and when the boys did this, they were ignored. But Eva, the youngest, never learned the knack of holding the *Haggadah* in her lap and cat-napping as she pretended to read. She always fell asleep outright, and for this she earned a sharp rap on the head from Zadie. He made her sit beside him and was always vigilant, always ready to strike if she transgressed.

Though the current preparation and ceremony was not nearly so elaborate as it had once been, there was still a lot of work. Sylvia had to clean the house, find the recipes and figure out how much food to make, do the shopping, and prepare the special food. There was the *charoses*, a mixture of grated apples, nuts, cinnamon, and sweet kosher wine, used in the *Seder*. There were the special *Pesachdeke* desserts using potato starch and *matzo* meal. There was the kosher turkey with special *matzo* stuffing.

By the time everything was complete and the table was laid, by the time Mo and Harry left to pick up Rose and Sylvia was alone in the house, she was quite exhausted. But beholding the *Seder* table, she felt that it was worth it, and she was looking forward to the family gathering. Everyone would be here. Harry, Rose, Mo, and herself. Meryl and Joe and the baby. Jack. Sunny and her friend. And Norma was coming from Boston with her husband and their two children. Then Jack came home, took one look at the table, announced that he would not be taking part in the *Seder,* and continued on his way upstairs.

Sylvia stood there, dumbfounded. Being a person who disliked conflict and tended to look for the easy way out, she told herself that Jack was only joking, or that he would change his mind. Accordingly, she said nothing to her husband. Unfortunately, this course of action (or more accurately, nonaction) caused great anxiety on her part, since if in fact Jack was not joking or did not change his mind, her husband would demand to know why the hell she hadn't told him sooner!

When it was almost time to sit down for the *Seder*, Sylvia walked through the dining room and stood at the doorway of the living room where Meryl and her father were having an argument. Sylvia preferred to call it a discussion.

Harry stood in the corner, listening to them. He was there because he had no place else to go, his young wife having taken their child and left him for a younger man. He was depressed but putting up a good front. He glanced from his brother to his niece as they spoke.

Meryl had been talking about the Seneca Army Depot. The Depot, two hours from Buffalo, was a long-time storage site for nuclear weapons and the current storage site for the Cruise II and Pershing missiles that were to be deployed at, among other sites, the Greenham Commons Air Force Base in England and the Comiso Air Force Base in Sicily. Women's peace encampments had started at both European places—the one at Greenham Commons was two years old—and a group of women were planning a peace encampment near the Seneca Army Depot.

Meryl had been saying that she and her friend Francis were planning on attending a vigil outside the main Depot gate later that weekend, when Mo interrupted with, "Do we have to talk about this now?"

Meryl looked at him. She'd just put the baby down on the double bed and was sitting at the edge of the sofa, not so much because she expected Rachel to cry, but because edges felt like a normal place to her these days in general. There was still some strain around her eyes—she hadn't been sleeping through the night—but she looked and felt much better than when Sunny had visited her in the hospital. She was not so consumed by despair about what was going to happen because she was too busy trying to figure out what to do. Now she said to her father, "Maybe if *your* generation had educated yourselves and tried to understand and maybe stop all this when it began, *I* wouldn't have to be doing it now!"

"No one's telling you to do it," he said blandly, reaching out to the bowl of peanuts on the coffee table.

"My conscience is, and yours would be too if you knew the facts."

Mo popped the peanuts into his mouth and turned his gaze back to the television, where it had been when Meryl had interrupted him. As he began chewing, his expression was tantamount to a disinterested shrug. "Listen," he said, "it's going to happen, and there's nothing we can do about it."

This infuriated her, and she was about to speak when Harry interrupted. "I resent your saying that no one did anything. We knew what was going on, at least *some* of it, the beginnings of it, though we certainly never could have foreseen how horrible it would be. But you don't know what it was like after the war. The Cold War mentality, McCarthy, the persecution of radicals. At the same time that they were creating all these new kinds of chemicals and building all these new kinds of weapons, they were hounding radicals. All you had to do was to stand up and protest the atom bomb and all of a sudden you were a Communist. A Russian spy. In league with the Kremlin. A traitor. You don't know what it was like. Didn't you ever hear of the *Rosenbergs*? The Rosenbergs were *executed*! Don't you think that was meant to be a lesson to the rest of us?" He paused and looked at her. She was silent. "*I* wish I'd done something too. It breaks my heart to see you like this. You should be happy. You just had a *baby*, for Christ's sakes, you should be thinking about *Life*, and here you are thinking about the end of the world. You don't have to blame me. I blame myself enough."

He stopped, embarrassed. He cleared his throat, and with a self-conscious comment to the effect that he had spent enough time bawling out one niece and was going into the kitchen to find Norma, he headed out of the living room. Meryl followed. She put her arms around him and spoke to him, though none of them in the living room could hear what she was saying.

Sylvia had been waiting for just such a lull, but the door opened and Sunny and Kay walked in. It wasn't until after all the hellos were said, and coats were put away, and weather was remarked upon, that Sylvia had a chance to tell her husband what Jack had said when he'd come home.

Mo didn't want to start any arguments in front of Kay because she was company rather than family. "Well, we'll see what happens," he said, and let the matter drop.

Kay, overhearing that there was a possibility that Jack would not be there, brightened immediately. She accepted the glass of peppermint *shnaps* that Rose offered and proceeded to get slightly drunk. Perhaps it was the *shnaps,* but the spread on the dining room table seemed one of the most beautiful and warm she'd ever seen. Everything radiated a dull gleam, like old polished brass. The deep burgundy bottles of wine, the clear, sparkling glasses, even the tablecloth on whose creamy white background a white pattern shimmered—everything caught and gave off light.

Sylvia and her oldest daughter, Norma, stood near the kitchen doorway watching the others enter the dining room, some of them pausing to admire the table. "Nice, huh?" Sylvia asked.

"Beautiful," Harry said, "just beautiful," and he sounded sad, as though it were already a memory in his mind.

Mo took his place at the head of the table, telling Kay that as the guest, she should sit at his right. She did so, feeling intimidated by the approaching ritual, though she felt more relieved when Sunny sat down next to her, and Meryl and Joe sat opposite. When everyone was settled but Jack still had not appeared, Mo instructed his wife: "Go upstairs and tell him we're going to start the *Seder.*"

She hesitated, then said: "Let him be. He'll come down when he's good and ready." What she meant was that *she* was not ready for the added turmoil that Jack, feeling as he did, would bring to the table.

Mo sighed, but for the sake of peace, he agreed. He cleared his throat and leaned forward, very much the head of the family. "Now Kay," he said solemnly, "this is a *Seder.*" Sunny and Meryl sighed audibly. He let his mouth drop open, then said to Sunny, "Well have *you* told her anything about it?"

"Yes, as a matter of fact I did. I even gave her a *Haggadah* to read."

"I can imagine," he said, his thoughts still on the "hippie *Haggadah*" that Norma had brought and insisted he see.

"Go ahead, Dad," Sunny prompted. "Now Kay, this is a *Seder*. . . ."

Sylvia had been handing out the *Haggadahs*. Manufactured in the fifties, they were titled *Haggadah for the American Family*. The cover showed a photograph of a table much like this one, though because they were old and worn, the pictures were dull in comparison. Some lacked covers altogether, and Kay's was torn and repaired with tape.

There had not been enough of them to go around, which necessitated some amount of discussion and debate about who would share, and passing of *Haggadahs* across the table. When everyone was settled and silent and had turned to the first page, Mo cleared his throat and began to read: " 'We are now about to begin the celebration of Passover, the most ancient of all Jewish festivals, which celebrates Israel's redemption from bondage in Europe.' "

There was some scattered laughter. "He does that every year," Norma commented to the table at large, and Meryl corrected, "Egypt, Daddy, Egypt. You do that every year."

His face had reddened, and he said, "Excuse me, my mistake. 'Israel's redemption from bondage in Egypt.' "

The *Seder* commenced, each of the people gathered reading a section. But when they reached the "Four Questions" which signaled the telling of the story of Passover, Mo called a halt to the proceedings. By tradition, the youngest son usually read the "Four Questions." Though Norma's youngest was prepared to read, Mo was reminded of Jack's absence since as the youngest in that generation, he had done the reading in the past. "Go upstairs and get him," he directed his wife.

She looked at him; he looked at her. She sighed and got up. When she returned and sat down Mo demanded, "Well?" She hesitated, sighed again, and said, "He says he isn't Jewish so he isn't coming to the *Seder*."

"What?!"

Meryl shook her head and muttered, "He's nothing but a goddamned ungrateful little bastard." As soon as the words were out of her mouth, Mo picked up his fork, reached over, and jabbed her lightly but firmly in the elbow.

"Ow!"

Sunny murmured to Kay, "Remember I told you about the Fork in the Elbow School of Child Rearing? Well, this guy's the main practitioner."

"No swearing at the table," Mo said. "Well, let's get on with it then, with or without him."

And that is what they did. They continued with the *Seder*, telling the story of Passover. They dipped their spoons into their wine glasses ten times and let ten drops fall on their plates, reciting the ten plagues. They sang *dayenu*, drank the second glass of wine, and washed their hands with a washcloth Sylvia had brought from the kitchen. They ate the *moror* and *charoses*, the *matzo* and *moror*. Then it was time for dinner.

Sylvia, Norma, and Sunny made an assembly line, Sylvia ladling the chicken soup into bowls, her daughters carrying it into the dining room and coming back with orders: "Joe wants two *matzo* balls and a piece of carrot," or criticisms, "Daddy says you got a piece of carrot in his soup," at which Sylvia shook her head and muttered, "It's not going to *poison* him."

After the soup, the daughters cleared the dishes while Sylvia carved the turkey and spooned out the accompanying food, which the girls set upon the table.

By the time they sat down, the food was being passed, and everyone began to eat. First there was no talk; everyone was hungry. But soon, conversation began. Harry said to Mo, "You know, when you poked your poor daughter there, it reminded me of Zadie with the Cane. Remember how he used to smack Evie when she fell asleep during the *Seder*? Remember how we used to laugh? When I grew up and thought about those times, I felt sorry for her. Even *you* always picked on her."

Mo flushed and, with an annoyed, determined air, slid his fork under the potatoes and went on eating.

"She had it rough," Harry said. "Zadie never liked her. Why didn't Zadie like her?" he asked Rose.

Rose leaned forward. "Vell," she said, "I'm gonna tell you."

"Ma! Don't talk with your mouth full!" Mo snapped.

She ignored him and went on. "My muddaih," she said, "vas a sick voman."

"Ma, he didn't ask you about your mother, he asked you about your daughter."

"Eh?" she asked, not having heard him.

"Pass the potatoes," he said.

"Here's the potatoes," Meryl said. "I'll trade you for a hunk of turkey. No, not white meat. I *hate* white meat. No, not *that*. That's too big."

Mo sighed and looked to his son-in-law for support.

"There, that one. Okay, thank you. This is a good turkey, Ma."

"It is," Mo agreed. "Where'd you get it?"

"At K-Mart," she said. "In Ladies Wear. Where do you *think* I got it? I got it at the supermarket."

"All right, all right," he said, holding up his hands in momentary surrender. "I was only asking."

"Everytime we have turkey, he 'only asks,'" she complained to Norma. "I can't figure out what he expects me to say."

"Hey Dad," Norma asked. "What'd you think of my *Haggadah*?"

He made a grimace of distaste. "Looked like a hippie *Haggadah* to me. Look at the drawing on the front. If that doesn't look like hippies. . ."

"Daddy Dearest," Norma said, with a wry glance at her husband, "I think the drawing is supposed to represent Sephardic Jews."

"Well, they look like hippies to me."

"You're so ethnocentric," Norma complained to him. He pointed his finger at her and warned, "Don't call me names during the *Seder*." But he meant it with a touch of humor, for he looked at his fork and warned, "It's still here."

"Well *I* thought it was a nice *Haggadah*," Sunny offered. "I think we should use it next year."

Mo cleared his throat. It meant, I'll ignore that for now.

"Really," Sunny went on. "I think we should. What do you think, Mom?"

Sylvia shook her head indicating "no comment" and went on eating.

"*I* think it would be a wonderful idea," Meryl put in. Mo glanced at her and said, "*You*, I'm surprised you're not wearing *bugs* to the table."

There was a lull in the conversation, and the only noises were those of people eating. Rachel woke and began to cry. Meryl went to give her a bottle. "Do you want me to take care of her?" Joe asked, but she shook her head.

"Who was Zadie with the Cane?" Kay asked.

"Why," Mo said, "who was talking about Zadie with the Cane?"

"I was," Harry said, and answered Kay, "Zadie with the Cane was Ma's father. He was a very learned man. He used to give Hebrew lessons. And if you didn't pay attention, wham! With his cane."

"Is that why you called him. . ."

"Yes. Now if *he* was here tonight, this *Seder* would go on for hours. In Hebrew. Oh, he was Ultra-Orthodox. He ruled all of us, even Pa. Right, Ma?"

Rose nodded and speared the piece of cooked carrot that Mo had passed to Sunny to put on Rose's plate.

"The whole house. And his whole life revolved around his religion. His whole world. And if you disturbed that world. . . ." He shook his head. "There was no going back. He never forgave. Never."

"I remember him," Norma said. "Not very well. But I do remember him. I think I must've been eight or nine when he died. But I remember those *Seders*! They were so long," she said to her husband. "You know I remember one *Seder*. . . do you remember the time you got so angry, Grandma?" she asked with a smile.

"I remember," Harry said. "That was when Zadie brought. . ."

"Please pass the potatoes," Mo interrupted.

Harry looked at him and said to the table at large: "You know when my brother dies, his tombstone is going to read," and he gestured with his finger as though reading line by line, "Morris Rosenthal—Rest in Peace, but first Pass the Potatoes."

Mo glanced at his older brother who ate (as far as *he* was concerned) like a pig, but remained damnably slim. "All right, Harrison," he said, and Harry, hearing his *goyishe* stage name, flushed.

"Anyhow, as I was saying before I was so rudely interrupted," Harry went on. Addressing his remarks to Kay, he said, "I was telling you about how religious Zadie was, how he followed tradition to the letter of the law. Well, according to tradition, Passover is a time when Jewish families open up their homes and share their meal. One year the first night of *Pesach* fell on a Saturday. That's our Sabbath. And that morning, Zadie went to *shul*—the synagogue—and he met this poor homeless man." He smiled, enjoying the narration, unaware that his brother was frowning and seemed in discomfort. "So. . . what could he do? It was *tradition*. He *had* to bring him home. So he brought him home, and he stayed, and he stayed, and he stayed."

"How long did he stay?" Kay asked.

"A mont' he stayt, a mont'!" Rose put in, and as she spoke, a bit of food flew out of her mouth.

"Jesus Christ, Ma," Mo complained.

She ignored him and went on. "He vas a *shnorrer*."

"What's that?"

"A freeloader," Sunny explained.

"Ma, he was no *shnorrer* and you know it," Harry said. "He was a poor homeless man who'd worked for Cook County and lost his job when he wouldn't testify in front of HUAC. The House Un-American Activities Committee," he translated automatically to Kay, "and the FBI kept following him so he couldn't hold a job."

Mo was shaking his head. "He just told you that song and dance to sucker you in. The guy was a *shnorrer*. He knew a sucker when he saw one, and he knew what line to hand every one of them. And Zadie—God rest his soul—was not a very smart man when it came to the People Department. We all know that. So this *shnorrer* tells *you* he's a card carrying member on the run from the FBI, and he tells Zadie he's an Orthodox Jew without a home, and he tells my poor sister. . . ." Here he stopped and cleared his throat. "Believe me," he said, "the guy was no good. That was proven, wasn't it? Now I think we ought to have some nice dinner conversation and. . . change the subject."

The subject was duly changed, though the nice dinner conversation never did come about.

Sunny had been quiet during the *Seder*. Ever since Sylvia had relayed Jack's message, she'd been thinking.

And now, hearing the talk of the *shnorrer* from Chicago, hearing the discomfort in Mo's voice, the meaning behind his words, the way the subject was dropped and not brought up again, her thoughts had begun to crystallize with sudden clarity. She thought, Jack knows. And he knows *we* know. He knows *I* know.

After dinner, after the conversation and cleanup and the dessert and cleanup, when everyone had scattered here and there in separate conversations, Sunny headed toward the back stairs.

Kay was coming out of the bathroom. "Where are you going?"

"Upstairs. I want to talk to Jack."

"Oh. Well... I was just going to ask you... if we could go home soon. I have a splitting headache. I think I drank too much wine."

"Oh."

"Do you think you could talk to him another time?"

"I suppose so. Maybe now's not the right time anyway. Do you want to leave now?"

"Um... yeah, I think so."

"All right then. Let's make our farewells."

In the car, they were quiet. Sunny asked about Kay's headache, and she replied that it was worse. When they got home and opened the downstairs door, Kay went upstairs immediately, but Sunny paused to pick up her mail. As she stood there, Mrs. Mancuso opened her door and looked out. "Oh, hello dear," she said. "How are you?"

"I'm fine, Mrs. Mancuso. How are you?"

"Oh, I'm fine. I wanted to let you know that we're going to Jamestown to visit Vincent and his wife this weekend."

She'd said this with a smile of modest pride that invited response, and Sunny responded appropriately: "Oh, that's nice."

"Yes. He's been wanting me to come and visit for I don't know how long." There was a rattle of newspaper from within the apartment, but Mrs. Mancuso ignored it and continued. "He's been telling me, 'Mama, you gotta come out and visit the kids. When are you coming out?' But I couldn't, *you* know," she said, and with a meaningful raise of her eyebrows, gestured with her head toward the other side of the door where presumably her husband sat behind his newspaper. "His *back*," she whispered.

"You don't have to whisper," her husband called. "I *hear* you!"

She gave Sunny a shrugging look that said, My Husband.... To him she called, "Luigi, *veni ca*, come and tell Sunny about your back."

"I hurt my back!" called a voice from inside the apartment.

"Well come and *tell* her."

There was another rattle of newspaper. "I don't *want* to come tell her. I don't want to get *up*. I hurt my back, remember?"

Mrs. Mancuso sighed, indicating that her husband was being difficult. "*I* could tell you, but it wouldn't be the same. It's *his back*."

"That's okay," Sunny said, and called, "I hope your back is better, Mr. M."

"*Thank* you!" he said, and there was the sound of the newspaper being snapped upright.

"The reason I'm telling you," his wife went on, "is that we'll be leaving on Saturday and we'll be gone until Sunday night, and I wanted to know if you'll be home. Will you be home?"

"Sure, I'll be home."

"Good. Well. . . I hope you have a Happy Easter, and I'll see you next week."

Sunny was already on her way up the stairs. "Thank you," she said. "But it's Passover."

"What?"

"Passover. I celebrate Passover," she added when it seemed that her landlady did not comprehend. Still seeing no comprehension in her eyes, she explained, "I'm Jewish."

Mrs. Mancuso's jaw dropped slightly and her eyebrows knit in concern. "Oh! *I'm* sorry," she said. She did sound genuinely sorry, but whether it was for her own blunder or the misfortune of being Jewish, Sunny did not know.

In either case, she smiled. "I'm not," Sunny said, and continued on her way up the stairs.

Just as she was at her door, she heard Mrs. Mancuso call. "Oh, did you ever find your cat?"

Sunny poked her head around the landing. "Yes, I did. Thank you."

"Your girlfriend was so worried. And her friend."

Sunny had started to turn back to the door, but at this she paused. "Who?"

"Your girlfriend's friend. I don't know if it's her boyfriend or not. . . the handsome one with the brown curly hair and the dimple in his chin."

"Oh. That's my brother."

"Oh! Your brother? Oh. . . ."She shrugged and said good night.

Sunny thought, I didn't know Jack was here that night. I wonder why Kay didn't tell me. I'll have to ask her. But she had so much on her mind that the thought passed quickly, and even as she opened the door and called out Kay's name, she forgot.

Chapter 7

The Quarry II

For the first time in her life, Sunny did not eat bread during Passover week. She didn't know why; she just didn't feel like it. She could do without bread for a week, she decided. Besides, the *matzo* tasted good.

Matzo sandwiches were a bit awkward and crumbly, and sitting at her desk eating egg salad or tuna fish salad on *matzo*, she felt self-conscious and somewhat defensive. Nevertheless, she took *matzo* sandwiches to work just as she'd taken bread sandwiches.

She was most concerned, of course, about Louise. One day Louise came back from lunch early, peeked in to smile hello as Sunny sat there, and hardly glanced at the *matzo*. Her eyes registered nothing. Sunny thought, Could she not know what it is? and she answered, She doesn't know.

That weekend, on Saturday morning, she phoned Jack. She'd been thinking about him all week, thinking about what to do, what to say. But she'd come only to a decision about where to take him.

She would take him, she'd decided, to the cemetery. Even if there was no other link between them, Sam still was. There at the cemetery, she felt sure, the right words would come to her.

It was brilliant. She was proud of herself. She said to Kay, "I'm going to talk some sense into that brother of mine if it's the last thing I do," and she was so enthusiastic, so confident in her enthusiasm, that she hardly noticed Kay's uncertain smile.

Waiting for Jack to come to the phone, she was assured by the simplicity of it all. He was her brother, and their bond was their years of shared experience: all their laughter and their serious talks; their blustery conspiracies as though they were freedom fighters against the authority of the family; the times he'd come to her for advice, and she'd played, enjoyably, the role of older sister—telling him, advising him, about life. They were bound by all those years of trust. When she said hello, her voice was softened by the memory of those years.

But his response was sullen, and she understood that his memories must not be the same as hers. Their conversation was foolish and disturbing. They argued about how long it had been since they'd seen one another, since they'd seen one another alone; how long it had been since they'd talked, since they'd *really* talked; and finally, what was the purpose of talk, of communciation. It was one of those convoluted conversations in which the main point is the fact of disagreement itself. "What's the *point* of it all?" he'd demanded finally and waited for her answer.

In his silence she knew that whatever she said would be wrong. He would find a flaw in logic or tone, and the reason she'd called would be pushed further and further into the background. But she had to try. "The point of it all is that I want to go someplace this afternoon and I don't want to go alone. Come on, don't be such an old fart." Slipping into this frivolous coaxing tone destroyed her resolve, and she sensed that whatever she said to him at the cemetery would no longer matter. It would no longer be the truth, but would be tainted by her need for his forgiveness, her anxiety to resolve between them what perhaps could not be resolved.

Nevertheless, she went ahead with her plan. Early that afternoon she picked up Jack and drove toward the cemetery.

They were distant with one another and sat in the car like strangers going to an unwanted but unavoidable destination. When Jack suspected what that destination was, he turned and gave her a knowing look. He'd seen her trick and would not be emotionally duped by what she, too, had begun to think of as a cheap, sentimental subterfuge.

She would have changed her mind and turned around, but they had reached the cemetery gates. She turned in and drove along the long, circular, bumpy dirt road toward the back, past the children's section where Debbie was buried, and up the other side where Sam was buried. She parked the car and walked ahead of Jack toward her grandfather's plot.

It was crowded here and treeless. There was little extra space between the plots, and Sunny walked carefully, her eyes on the tombstones that she passed. Most of the writing was in Hebrew, some of the stones having lines and lines of it, a history of that person's life: daughter or son of so-and-so, born in such-and-such a place, married to so-and-so, parent of these children, died at this age. Though she could not read Hebrew, the letters were achingly familiar. She walked past all these histories unable to understand, but knowing that the past was there before her if only she could see it. Some of the stones had small, inset oval porcelain photographs showing how that person had appeared in life. But more often than not they were vandalized, used for target practice by local boys with BB guns. Many photographs were cracked and chipped so that only a section of the picture was left, or none at all, and where there had been a perfect porcelain image now remained a scarred surface of white. Atop the tombstones were small pebbles, remembrances from people who had come to visit and to mourn.

Her grandfather's plot was still stoneless and without grass, and the earth had not yet settled. At the top of the mound of soil where the stone would go, there was a row of pebbles. Sunny remembered she'd brought no stone for her grandfather. She had so many at home from the quarry, so many pretty ones Sam might have liked, and she was annoyed at herself for having forgotten the tradition.

Jack stopped beside her. Behind them, beyond the dirt road and the children's section, was a wooded area, the trees tall and still bare of foliage. Before them was the main road. Sunny heard the cars speeding past the cemetery as she looked at the earth.

"I forgot to bring a stone," she said, hoping that he would return to the road and pick a pebble at random so that she could place it, no matter how plain, how gray and sharp-edged, with the other stones of remembrance.

But Jack stook there with his arms folded across his chest, his mouth twisted into a stubborn grimace.

"What the hell did you bring me *here* for?" he muttered.

Her mouth opened, closed. "I. . . I wanted to talk to you."

He gave her a smirk that said, Go ahead, then. Talk.

She imagined offering him a dry smile, to tease him out of his resentment. But this image angered her. Why was *she* the one who had to put forth all the effort? Who the hell did he think he was? She felt the anger rising in her. She didn't want to let it out but could not stop it, and she blurted, "You're nothing but a goddamned ungrateful bastard, you know that?"

At this, he looked almost pleased. "Is that what you wanted to say to me?"

"No. It wasn't. There were a lot of things I wanted to say to you, Jack, but all of a sudden it's clear to me I'd be wasting my breath. You wouldn't hear me. Your mind is all made up. You know what you *want* to know, and you don't want to hear anything else. So why should I waste my breath? Hey, fighting with you, and fighting with you *here*, is the last thing I want to do. But you put me in that position."

"No! *You* put *yourself* in that position. *You* called *me*, remember?

You drove *me* here. It was *you*."

She shook her head, feeling hopeless. It was no use. Too many years had passed. He'd had too long to entrench himself in bitterness. Nothing she could say would change a thing, and she'd been a fool to even try.

In spite of all these rational decisions, she held out a hand to him that was half gesturing and half reaching. "Jack, I love you. You're my brother." He made a grimace of disbelief, and she said more firmly, "You're my *brother* and I *love* you."

Something crossed his face that she didn't understand. It was almost as if her love made her vulnerable, as if he would use it to hurt her. "Jack, I was six years old when you were born. Do you understand that? Six years old! I didn't know what was going on!"

"But you found out soon enough, didn't you? Didn't you?"

"I don't know. I honestly don't know. But the point is that it wasn't my decision. I was just. . ."

"You were just following orders?"

The comment made her angry, and she gave him a dirty look. "I was going to say, 'I was just a child.' But like I said, why waste my breath? You're determined not to understand."

"Why don't *you* try to understand? How do you think *I* feel? All those years I thought we were friends, all those years I thought I could *trust* you, and you turned out to be a goddamned liar, just like everybody else."

"Jack. . ."

"All those years," he repeated, his eyes filling with tears. He gazed at the mound of earth. "All those years when I wondered about her, all the times we used to talk. The times at the *quarry*. . . ." He glared at her, and in his eyes she saw that here, then, was the symbol of his anger. They'd been closest at the quarry, sitting on that flat sandy rock, gazing off at the stark beauty, opening up their hearts to one another. Even there, she had lied.

The tears spilled over, and he wiped them away, almost as if he were angry at the tears themselves. "All those times we used to sit on that rock and talk. Why didn't you *tell* me? Why didn't you just say, 'Jack, it's not that she doesn't love you. She's not here with you because she's dead.'"

His lips quivered, and Sunny reached out to him, but he slapped her hand away. "No!" he said, and looked at her with eyes so filled with hate that it startled her.

"I hate you," he said, the words deliberate.

But they sounded strangely childish. "Jack, you don't hate me."

"I *do*. And if you want to know how much, ask your girlfriend."

She gave him a grim look. "Leave her out of it. She has nothing to do with this. My relationship with her is a separate matter. I'm talking about you and me. And as far as you and me are concerned, we're family. No matter what you feel now, I'm still your family. And that'll never change."

"No." He shook his head. "No. You're wrong all the way around. And I'm telling you that I don't want any *part* of this family. As far as *I'm* concerned, you can all drop dead!"

But his very choice of words had undermined his statement, and he knew it. She saw the flicker of memory in his eyes. *Drop dead.* It was what Sam had said to Rose in moments of exasperation. Punctuating a string of Yiddish curses, he would shout, "Drop dead!" When she and Jack overheard from another room, they'd wondered, couldn't you say *drop dead* in Yiddish? Why had he spoken those two words in English?

"Jack. . ." she said, and reached out to him once more.

But he backed away. His glance darted to the iron gates, to the road and escape. Holding out his hand to ward off any touch, he headed toward the exit. As he did, he stepped right in the middle of the mound of earth under which Sam was buried.

The footstep seemed planted in the center of her chest, and her mouth dropped open in protest. But she couldn't say a word. Her insides felt shriveled, and she stood as though frozen, watching him as he walked across the rows of graves to the road. She stood there, her eyes on the tall iron gates where she had last seen Jack's image. Then she turned and headed back toward the car.

She took a slow, winding path. Her thoughts were still on Jack, and she hardly saw the stones or the names engraved upon them. Midway to the dirt road, she stopped and looked around. Beyond the road she saw the woods, the trees tall and close together. There was a sweet smell of spring in the air.

As she was about to go on, she happened to glance at the gravestone near where she stood. Seeing the name, she gave a sharp intake of breath, for she hadn't known exactly where she was until this moment.

This stone was different from all the rest. Without Hebrew, without history, without pebbles of remembrance, it was bare except for the name—Eva Rosenthal—and the date. The name stood out boldly; but the gravestone, small and all alone, felt to her like an outcast among the rest.

The name was like a small defiant statement: I am here, even in death.

But if someone never came here, to the past, if they never happened to come to this exact spot, they wouldn't know she'd ever lived. And she *had* lived.

In a moment Sunny remembered the gray-shingled house, the back bedroom where Sam slept, his big old bureau with the mirror attached. She remembered sitting on the bureau with her back to the mirror, turning around to peek at herself every so often because Auntie E was cutting her bangs.

She'd turn back and squint her eyes closed, and feel the cold of the kitchen shears Eva was placing carefully against her forehead.

"You're gonna be gorgeous, kid! After old Auntie E gets finished, you're gonna be a living doll. A real knockout. You're gonna have 'it.' You know what *it* is? Well. . . I'll tell you when you get older."

Sunny's eyes filled with tears, for with the memory came the realization that she'd forgotten. Or more to the point, been made to forget.

Crying and wiping the tears from her face as they fell, she walked toward the car.

"And how much do you love me?" Evie would ask, and Sunny, or Sonia (for she was still Sonia then), would giggle and answer, "A bushel and a peck."

"And?" she'd demand.

"And a hug around the neck."

"And?"

"And. . . a barrel and a heap."

At a look from Evie, she'd finish, "And a talkin' in my sleep."

"About youuu," they'd sing in off-key unison, "about youuu. . . ."

There was a look in Evie's eyes that made you want to wake up from the sleepwalking that was your daily fare and meet her energy spark for spark. She was always *doing* something—yelling or laughing or crying. More than anyone Sunny had ever known, Evie was full of life. It was unfair that someone so full of life should be forgotten in death. She seemed a woman without history, existing only as a name on a stone.

At the car, Sunny looked back to where she'd stood. She bent and found a pebble, returned and placed it quickly, almost defiantly, on Eva's stone. Then she returned to the car and to the city.

On Monday, when Grace was out of the office, Sunny phoned her mother. After they'd chatted awhile, she said, "Listen, Ma, I want to ask you a question. Why didn't anybody tell Jack the truth?"

There was a pause. "That's a long story," Sylvia said. "Ask your father."

"But I'm asking you."

"Your father has a better memory."

"I know my father has a better memory. I'm asking *your* memory."

"I don't really remember. It was your father's decision."

"Mom!"

"What?" she said in all innocence. "Why are you asking?"

"I want to know."

"Where did you go with Jack?"

"To the cemetery. To visit Grandpa."

There was another pause. "Listen," Sylvia said, "I just thought of something. Don't ask your father."

"Don't ask my father?"

"No. Don't ask him about Jack."

"Why?"
"Because."
"Why?!"
"Because!"
"Well I would just like to know why, that's all."
"Because your father and Jack have not been getting along lately, and he's very touchy about the subject."
"Oh God..."
"Don't say *Oh God* like that! I *live* here with the *two* of them. You don't. You don't know what it's like. And you don't know what it was like *then*, either, so don't go condemning what people did because you don't know what *you* would have done if you'd been in the same situation. It wasn't so easy, believe me."
"You're right. I'm sorry. I apologize. But I still want to know."
"Well, you'll have to ask another time. And I'd prefer it if you ask your father. But not now."
Sunny sighed. "Okay, I gotta go. Danvers is giving me the evil eye."
They said good-bye, and she hung up the phone. Imperial Dynamics employees were not supposed to make personal telephone calls, but it was one of those rules that no one followed and no one enforced. Or rather, it was selectively enforced. If an employee was liked and accepted, the supervisor looked the other way or offered a scolding smile. If an employee was not liked, it was one of a whole range of minor offenses that were grounds for reprimand. Sometimes reprimands for minor offenses added up and became grounds for dismissal.

Sunny was liked and accepted so she used the phone at will, without bothering to check who saw. But the person who was liked and accepted, she often thought, was not herself. If she ever became herself, she wondered—and wondered more and more as time went by—what then? If she said to Danvers, for example, "You and your promotion are giving me a royal pain in the ass. And by the way, you look like a goddamned rabbit. I wish you'd get those glasses fixed so you don't have to keep wrinkling your nose just to get them to stay in place. And your stupid jokes aren't funny, either." What then? Would she be so universally (or rather so Imperially) liked?

Sunny. Sunny and her sunny smile. Yuch, she thought, it's enough to make a person want to puke.

One day a week or so after she took Jack to the cemetery, Sunny and her sunny smile disappeared from Imperial Dynamics forever.

Sunny wondered later, Was it that Louise had caught her on a bad day? Or had she been unconsciously flirting with the idea of coming out?

Coming out. As... as whatever she was. As herself. Was it perhaps that after thirty years of living her life as other people expected— or appearing to live her life in such a way as to make other people comfortable—that she just plain wanted to be herself? She wanted to be herself everywhere, always. She yearned for that: to carry around her self like an inner peace, always to be relied upon, secure in the knowledge that no matter what happened, she knew who she was.

She'd been thinking about buying a new car, and she happened to see a sign on the bulletin board that Louise was selling her car. Sunny had doubts about doing business with Louise, but thought that it wouldn't hurt to ask. One afternoon when Louise was coming back from lunch and the upstairs offices were empty, Sunny, who was standing by the window, called her in and asked her about the car.

Louise began speaking. In the midst of a thought she said, "Actually I want eleven hundred, but I figured if I asked twelve, it would give me a hundred leeway in case people tried to Jew me down."

As Louise had neared the phrase, Sunny had expected it with a sixth sense. By the time she heard it, she had several different reactions ready and waiting to spring into her thoughts simultaneously. First of all, she thought, You stupid *goy*, if that's what you're going to do, then what are you *telling* me for? At the same time, she felt exhausted and angry. But she asked herself coldly, What did you expect?

She took a breath. "You know, Louise, I really resent you saying that. I'm a Jew, and I think it's a nasty thing to say."

Louise looked at her with wide eyes and open mouth. "What's a nasty thing to say?"

"Jew me down. I think it's a nasty remark."

"I don't know what you mean."

Sunny sighed. "It implies that Jews are sneaky cheats, and I'm *not* a sneaky cheat."

Louise's head continued to proclaim her innocence, and now she said, "But you're wrong."

"Louise, don't tell me I'm wrong. I know what the phrase means. I've certainly heard it enough."

"No. I didn't *say* that!"

"What?"

"I didn't say *Jew* you down. I said. . . I said *chew* you down."

This was not at all what Sunny had expected, and for a moment she stood there, her own mouth slightly open. She let out an astonished blurt of laughter. Then she said, "Louise, don't hand me that shit. We both know what you said. There's no such phrase as *chew you down*. I mean, gimme a break. I'm not an idiot, you know."

"No, honest! I did! I *did*. I said, 'chew you down!' "

Sunny waved her hand in dismissal. "Louise, I don't even want to talk about it if you're gonna lie. *I* think what you oughtta do is say, 'Sunny, I'm sorry I offended you,' and that would be that. I'd accept your apology, and that would be the end of it. But if you're gonna *lie* about it, I for one do not want to continue this conversation."

127

"I'm *not* lying."

Sunny pointed a finger into her face. "You're a goddamned liar, and I don't want to talk about it anymore, so please get outta my office. *Right now.*"

"But I didn't *say* it!"

Sunny's face was cold and angry. "Fuck you, Louise. Just fuck you."

Louise's lips quivered, and her face began to cry. *Louise* did not cry, or else, Sunny thought, her tear ducts were clogged or broken, for no tears emerged. Sunny looked around to see if anyone was observing and heard Louise wail, "You said 'fuck you!' You said 'fuck you,' and I *like* you!"

Sunny slapped her open palm to her forehead. "*Oy vey*," she murmured, for again this was not at all what she had expected—Louise being the victim and herself the villain. She was thinking, How can she *like* me when *I* think she's just a *jerk*? What was worse was that Louise had brought a hand up to her lips. Catching sight of those raw gnawed-down fingertips, Sunny was filled with a compassion she did not want to feel.

She sighed, and in a gentler tone said, "Look, Louise. Let's forget about it, all right? You go your way and I'll go mine and that'll be that. Okay? I know *Jew me down* is an expression a lot of people use. I don't think you made it up. I'm not blaming you. We're both adults. Let's forget about it. There's no need for the entire universe to know that you said 'Jew me down' and I said 'fuck you.' "

"But I said 'chew me down!' "

"Oh!" Sunny's hand came up once again, this time over her closed eyes. She knew that Louise wanted her to say, 'All right, all right, you said chew me down.' And she almost said it, just to get rid of her. But at the last moment she imagined the look on Louise's face—a sly and smug victory that she'd fooled Sunny or badgered her into accepting the lie. The Lie. The lie that anti-Semitism was a Jewish paranoia. But I *won't* accept it, she thought. I don't care if I lose my goddamned job over it. I'm not going to pretend she said 'chew me down'! There's no such phrase! Is there? she wondered.

"I *like* you," Louise was saying, "and you said 'fuck you!' "

Opening her eyes, Sunny spied a letter opener lying on the desk. She wanted to laugh and say, with dry humor, "Louise, do me a favor and vacate my office before I take that letter opener and stab you in your goddamned rotten heart." But she didn't say it, not wanting to risk a wail that all of Imperial Dynamics would hear: "You said you were going to take that letter opener and stab me in my goddamned rotten heart!"

She saw that they were at an impasse. Whatever she said would be repeated at a wail, and she didn't trust herself not to say something in the heat of anger that would sound very different when held up to inspection by the head of personnel. The whole thing was absurd. "Louise," she said, "this is for you." She stuck her middle finger in the air. "And just to show you I'm not prejudiced, here it is in Italian." She gave a hefty slap to the bicep of her upraised arm. "As a matter of fact, Louise, I even know it in Yiddish," she said, sticking her thumb between her first two fingers. "Now I'm going to the Ladies Room," she concluded, "and I'd appreciate it if you were out of my office by the time I return." And with that, she left.

When she got home that night, she told Kay she'd decided to get the car fixed. Kay agreed that it was probably a good idea. Sunny nodded. "Listen," she said, "I have a totally moronic question to ask you, but did you ever hear the phrase *chew me down*?"

Kay looked at her.

"You heard me. Chew me down. As in ..." and she made little bites in the air.

Kay shook her head slowly. "Are you sure you're not thinking of chew me *out*?"

"No."

"There's chew me *out*... and there's blow me down. Didn't Popeye say that? Blow me down, ye hardies. Or somebody. Captain Hook? Captain Queeg? Captain Bligh?"

Sunny smiled.

"What happened?" Kay asked, and Sunny told her. When she finished, she mused, "Maybe Louise was right. Maybe there *is* a phrase to *chew someone down*. You know? Maybe it means that if they tell you a price that's too high, you start chewing on their toes and by the time you get to their ankles, they're a foot shorter and ready to lower the price."

Kay was smiling. "Sounds highly unlikely to me."

Sunny shrugged.

There was no question about it. She had "won" the argument with Louise. But what did that mean? It had felt good to express her anger. But as the days passed, she began to wonder, What about Louise? Had she learned anything? She thought, She learned not to say "Jew me down" to a Jew. And if she *did* think the phrase was *chew me down*, I'm sure she thinks *I'm* some kind of *maniac*.

She felt frustrated. She wanted Louise to feel what *she* felt. She wanted Louise to understand.

When Kay asked her about the latest development in the situation, she jokingly played The Victor, narrating how Louise avoided her. But inside, she felt frustrated. She wanted to do something but didn't know what.

She knew that same kind of thing would come up again. Perhaps not with Louise, but certainly with someone else. She saw herself reacting to Louise, perhaps even as Louise saw her: cool, haughty, ironic, disdainful. It wasn't what she felt at all.

A few days after Sunny's run-in with Louise, Kay got a letter of acceptance from Columbia.

At first she was delighted. She would be a Columbia Law School student, a successful practicing attorney. She took great pleasure in imagining Jack as a gas station attendant, greasy and cold, or standing on aching legs in an unemployment line. It made her feel less vulnerable. She would think of all this as a childhood affair that was part of her past. Part of *their* past. At Columbia, Jack wouldn't matter at all.

But when she told Sunny about the letter of acceptance and saw Sunny's face, she realized that Sunny had not magically changed her mind about where she would live. She repeated what she'd said before. She would not move to New York. She would not leave Buffalo.

They talked for a long time.

Finally Sunny said, "Look, I know it's going to be a hard decision for you, but I can't leave Buffalo. Not now. I'd feel like. . . like I was leaving everything behind. Maybe I'll be able to do that some day. I don't know. But not now. I can't. I just can't."

Kay didn't know what to do.

She hadn't realized how much she'd actually counted on Sunny agreeing to move to New York City until Sunny refused to do just that. Now she was in a dilemma. If she went to Columbia she must leave Sunny. But if she began school at Buffalo and then Sunny discovered what had happened and left her, it would have been a mistake to stay. If Sunny was going to leave her, *she* might as well leave Buffalo and go to New York! But if she had her choice, she would rather stay here. With Sunny.

What should I do? she kept thinking. What should I do?

Sunny would not go to New York. Jack would not disappear. Though Kay knew from the way Sunny acted that Jack had said nothing definite in the cemetery, she also knew that there was always the next time.

Sunny phoned Jack and left a message, but he didn't return her call. To Kay, she called him "The Sniper."

"That's his style, you know? He comes out with these zingers when you're least expecting it, and then he disappears." Saying this, she frowned and turned away, for it wasn't what was on her mind at all. It wasn't honest. She kept picturing Jack and herself on that flat sandy rock. She kept hearing Jack say, "I wonder what my mother was like. Do you think," and he'd pause and look at her. Even now she could see his eyes. "Do you think she gave me up because she didn't want me?"

She remembered how she'd shrug and glance away. "I don't know," she'd lie. "Sometimes things are more complicated than that." He'd always accepted this answer from her, though he didn't quite understand it. He trusted her to tell the truth.

She remembered her father, his finger threatening at her eye, his voice a command of authority: "Don't you *dare* tell him. It's not your *place* to tell him. You stay out of it. It has nothing to do with you."

She'd accepted it then, but now she wondered. If it wasn't *her* place, then whose place was it?

Outside, it was beautiful, and she resented having to miss spring because of work. What made it worse was that it rained that weekend, causing Sunny to look up at the apartment ceiling and say, "Hey, come on now. What is this? You have something against wage earners?"

She wanted badly to go to the quarry. She even suggested to Kay that they don the matching vinyl parkas they'd bought one weekend last summer when they'd gone camping and go to the quarry in the rain. "Come on, it'll be fun," Sunny promised. But Kay replied, "It won't be fun. It'll be wet."

On the beautiful spring days, the work days, Sunny would stand at the window looking out over the parking lot and dream of the courtyard behind her.

The four wings of the office building were shaped in a square. In the center was a courtyard, the Executive Courtyard, accessible only through the executive offices on the other side of the hall. The courtyard was graced with climbing ivy and white birch, and in the middle of a grassy space, crisply trimmed ground cover spelled out the words *Imperial Dynamics* to the sky. The Executive Courtyard was off-limits to all but the executives and, of course, the gardener. Sunny wondered if her ambitions at Imperial Dynamics had less to do with money and power and more to do with the calm green courtyard view from across the hall.

Perhaps, she mused, she unconsciously thought of it as a synthesis of the world of the quarry and the world of Imperial Dynamics. But it was an impossible synthesis. Impossible, she realized, because the two worlds were mutually exclusive.

Imperial Dynamics was a place where life was narrowly defined, as though through tunnel vision, focusing on the one goal of profit and excluding consideration, awareness, and concern for all else. In the quarry, everything was integrated; each facet, each bit of life moving independently, yet part of the web of the whole. Here, everything was separate, yet focused on one goal. She didn't quite comprehend it all, or comprehend how and why it had gotten that way. Yet she knew that her instincts were right. At the quarry, she was important. She *felt* important. She belonged, as everything else belonged. Here, she was nothing. Devalued, disrespected, used. When her usefulness was at an end, she would be discarded.

Her ambitions, however, would probably stay just that at Imperial

Dynamics. She was sure ("I can feel it in my bones," she muttered to Kay) that Louise would find a way to use what had happened, use it to her own advantage.

She hoped, of course, that whatever happened between them would stay between them. But she found out soon enough that this was not the case.

It was a week or so after the incident itself, and she and LaSan were in the foyer of the Ladies Room, standing in front of the mirror.

LaSan had been back at work for over a month, looking much better than before she'd gone on sick leave. Grace had told Sunny that LaSan was being treated by a combination of diet and medication, and that if she were careful, she would not need surgery. Sunny hadn't talked directly to LaSan about her health as yet.

She was planning on doing just that when the door from the hallway swung open, and Louise breezed through. Or she *began* to breeze through until she caught sight of Sunny and LaSan. She looked from one to the other. Though the two of them hadn't spoken a word, the sight of them standing side by side must have given her the impression that they were standing side by side united against her, because she shot them a resentful glance and pushed open the door to the toilet/washroom.

Sunny and LaSan's eyes met in the mirror, and they smiled. But they didn't speak until Louise swung back through the foyer and pushed open the door to the hall.

The door closed behind Louise, and Sunny shook her head. She put away her comb. "How've you been feeling?" she asked.

LaSan had removed her glasses and was peering in at the small compact mirror at her eye make-up. "I went to the doctor last week," she said. "He told me I was under too much emotional stress." She glanced into the wall mirror at Sunny's reflection, and her mouth twisted into a slight grimace that commented silently on the doctor's diagnosis.

"Well, you could always blow up Imperial Dynamics," Sunny suggested. "It might help. Who knows?"

"*I* wish they'd just decide about this damned promotion. I was talking to Danvers, and I *asked* him," she said, careful of her pronunciation. "But you know Danvers. . ."

"Yeah. He looks at you with that *rabbit* face. I mean who would've ever thought a bunny rabbit could be so *ugly*?"

LaSan smiled.

"You know," Sunny went on, "to tell you the truth," she said, "I wouldn't mind if *I* got the promotion, and I wouldn't even mind if *you* got the promotion, but if *Louise* gets the promotion. . ." she shuddered.

"Well, that's what's gonna happen." LaSan snapped her compact shut, replaced her glasses, and looked in the mirror again. "I gotta go on a damned diet."

"They couldn't possibly give it to her."

LaSan gazed at her.

Sunny sighed and leaned against the wall. The outer door opened and one of the typists walked in. She'd lost her purse, she said, and couldn't find it anywhere. She went into the inner room, and Sunny said, "Well, I guess I gotta get back to work." But she didn't leave. The typist came out, told them that if they saw her purse. . . . They nodded, and she left.

LaSan lit a cigarette.

Sunny folded her arms across her chest and stared at LaSan, her expression serious. "Well, there's only one thing to be done. We've gotta get rid of Louise."

LaSan met her gaze and said, her face and tone just as serious, "I heard you already tried that."

Sunny's mouth fell open. LaSan smiled.

"What did you hear?"

"Oh, not much. I heard her tell that little girl from the Computer Room. . ."

"Donna what's-her-name?"

"Yeah, that's her. I heard Louise tell her that nobody around here really knew you, you had a dark side."

"A *dark* side?"

"That's what she said." LaSan glanced at herself in the mirror and muttered, "Bitch oughtta see *my* dark side."

Sunny, who had just closed her astonished mouth, gave a short laugh, like a snort. "What else did she say?"

"That you made her cry."

"Crocodile tears, that's all they were. Not *even* crocodile tears. Well, that's it. There's no question in my mind. We gotta get rid of her. I'll put arsenic on her goddamned fingernails, *that's* what I'll do," she muttered. LaSan, who'd been inhaling on the cigarette, laughed, coughing slightly, as she shook her head. She stubbed out her cigarette, and Sunny held out her hands as if to say, "What else can I do?"

That night after work she said, "Now why does that Louise have to be such a *shmuck*? LaSan's not going around saying," (and she whined), "Sunny's plotting to dab Louise's fingernails with arsenic." She was glad to say this because the person she said it to was Grace.

She had decided to take Kay's advice. There was no sense in letting things go on as they were. That night at quitting time Grace had complained, "Oh I'm so *tired*. I can't believe I have to go home and cook dinner."

"What're you having?"

"My favorite—cream of leftovers."

Sunny smiled, and on an impulse said, "Hey Grace, how'd you like to go out for a drink?"

Grace looked at her. "Sure. Sounds like a winner to me. Lemme call The Husband." She went to the phone, and Sunny heard her say,

"Listen sweetie, you know Sunny, the girl I work with? Well, she asked me to go out for a drink, and I was wondering if you'd mind." These were the words she used. Her tone, however, implied something serious—a problem that Sunny had, perhaps; a problem only Grace could solve. When she got off the phone and saw that Sunny had been listening, she shrugged. "He's more likely not to hassle me if I give him some drama. If he thinks I'm just going out to have fun, he'll give me a hard time. Men are so dumb," she added, and laughed.

Once they'd gotten to the bar, a small neighborhood place not far from the factory, and were seated at a table with their drinks, Sunny remarked casually that she and her friend Kay had gone to her parents' house for Passover.

Grace nodded and sipped her drink. "Did you have a good time?"

"Yes, it was very nice. Have you ever been to a *Seder*?"

"A what?"

"A *Seder*. It's the ceremony when we celebrate Passover. You've heard of Passover?"

"Sure, it's the Jewish Easter."

Sunny looked at her. This remark was a bit too complex for an opening move, and she'd decided to ignore it when she realized that Grace was showing no surprise at the turn of conversation. "Grace," she asked, "did you know I was Jewish?"

"Sure. I knew."

"How long have you known."

"I don't know. A long time."

"But how did you know?"

Grace put down her beer. "Oh! What do you think I am, an idiot? I just *knew*. I had the feeling you were when I met you. But since you didn't talk about it, I figured, you know, maybe you didn't want anybody to know."

Sunny blushed. "But. . . why didn't you ever *say* anything?"

"Why should I *say* anything? And what the hell should I *say*? Uh, the Cleveland order is on the desk, and by the way, Sunny, I know you're a Jew?"

Sunny nodded thoughtfully. Grace had bought the first round of drinks, and she now went up to the bar for the second. It was Happy Hour: drinks half price, free popcorn and pretzels. She brought back a bowl of pretzels to the table. They sipped their drinks and munched on pretzels. Sunny said, "Well listen, Grace, if you knew I was Jewish, why did you use that obnoxious phrase?"

"What obnoxious phrase?"

"Jew me down."

Grace looked at her. "I don't think it's obnoxious. I think it's a compliment."

Sunny looked at her, "A compliment?"

The two women sat at the same bar, at the same table, munching pretzels from the same bowl, but they seemed to be in different worlds. "Tell me why it's a compliment," Sunny said.

"Because Jews are smart. They're good business people. They know how to get the price they want."

Sunny saw that Grace was quite sincere.

"I admire Jewish people," she went on. "They have a lot of class. They're very intelligent. They must be. They've worked themselves up from nothing to be so rich."

Sunny's head dropped as though she'd been knocked out. Grace gave a short laugh. "What's the matter?" she asked, but Sunny sighed and shook her head, not knowing how to explain.

They sipped and munched awhile longer. Sunny said, "Did you hear about my run-in with Louise?"

"Not from Louise. But LaSan mentioned something about it."

"What did she say?"

"Just that she overheard Louise saying something about you to what's-her-name from Computers. But Louise won't talk to me. She thinks I'm going to give her *malocchio*. Did you know LaSan had a run-in with her once?"

"No, I didn't."

"It was before you started." Grace reached for a pretzel. "I don't remember the specifics, but they had an argument about something, and LaSan called her evil."

"Oh, no!" Sunny laughed, knowing how Louise would take it. "Well, she *is* evil, in a pathetic kind of way. I mean, I don't think she's so much evil herself as she is stupid enough to be *used* by somebody evil."

Grace shrugged. "Anyhow, Louise freaked out. I guess she thought LaSan was going to put some kind of voodoo curse on her." She smiled. "LaSan said she wished she *knew* a voodoo curse; she'd put it on her in a minute." She got up. "Think I'm going to put something on the juke box. Maybe if this place has some music, we can get in the mood and pick up some guys." She winked suggestively, and Sunny laughed.

That weekend it rained again, a heavy spring rain that soaked the earth and ran off the city street toward the sewers. The sewer in front of the Dew Drop Inn was clogged, and the water made a pond through which cars drove, splashing, and in which children played.

Sunny looked at Kay but did not comment.

In the evening they sat on the porch, holding hands, and looked out at the rain. "It's like an observation deck," Kay remarked about the many-windowed porch, and Sunny nodded.

The rain fell in the night, dripping off the new baby leaves of the two maple trees. It fell past the neon light of the Dew Drop Inn at one end of the block, and past the lighted window of the grocery store at the other. Beyond the trees, the Armory wall seemed dark and impenetrable.

That night, Sunny had a nightmare. It was about a river, a dark river of death, and it was called Raven's Brook. She woke with the words on her lips, murmuring them, picturing the dark rushing water. She would have forgotten the water and the words, assuming they meant nothing. But what happened the following Saturday made her remember.

On Saturday she went to the library. She had been doing quite a bit of reading lately, mostly mysteries into which she could escape. They soothed her because of their implicit definition of the world as an ultimately secure and ordered place whose problems were solved, questions answered, and injustices rectified, all by the last page. When she got to the library, however, she didn't go into the room where the mysteries were kept. She was looking, she realized, for something else.

The wide hallway led first to the Children's Room, and outside that room she paused for a moment, thinking it had something to do with Debbie.

She had brought Debbie here as often as she could. Debbie loved the library, loved the funny vertical venetian blinds, loved being left alone in the Children's Room. *Curious George* was her favorite book, and her favorite color was the yellow of the Man in the Yellow Hat. Her favorite part was when George wore the man's hat. Sunny looked in at all the books and all the children.

Then she continued on her way, walking to the card catalogue in the main foyer. She looked up *Jews*. Flipping through the various subdivisions, it was history that caught her eye. She walked to the stacks.

Her eyes scanned titles on spines, rows of books. Her eyes swept across shelves as she walked between two large metal cases. Just as she was about to turn from one side to the other and come back the other way, a title caught her eye. *Ravensbruch*.

The title shocked her. "Raven's Brook," she murmured, and took the book down from the shelf. It was a book about a women's concentration camp called Ravensbruch.

She checked the book out of the library and took it home. She put it on the shelf in between *Bury My Heart at Wounded Knee* and *The Fate of the Earth*, books she'd bought but never read, sensing perhaps that reading them would confirm all her worst fears and make her even more despairing than she was now.

She looked at the books, at their titles, and then she went into the living room.

Kay was on the couch, staring at the television. She'd been withdrawn and anxious since Sunny made it clear that her decision not to leave Buffalo was definite. Sunny feared that it would make them grow apart. She pointed out the beautiful day they could see through the porch windows and suggested that on Sunday they go to the quarry.

Sunday was a warm glorious day, a perfect day in early June, a perfect day to go to the quarry.

Kay hardly noticed. She busied herself with details: making chicken salad sandwiches, rinsing out the thermos, folding the blanket, looking at the dashboard of the car.

When they were almost at the quarry, Sunny said, "You know, I want to talk to you about something. Remember when I went to the cemetery with Jack and I came back in such a bad mood?"

"Yes, and you said that you didn't want to talk about it because it didn't concern me."

"Right. Except I think it does concern you in a roundabout way." She was silent for a while. "Do you remember way back when we had that conversation about family secrets, and I said that it was difficult for me because since we couldn't get married or have any kind of commitment, it was hard for me to know when you stopped being. . . just a lover and became. . . something more serious."

Kay tried to laugh. "Are you asking me to marry you?"

"Not exactly. I'm just saying that I don't know if you've wondered why Jack hasn't been around lately."

Kay opened her mouth, but no words emerged.

"You know, I always thought I was so honest with Jack. I always thought we were so close. But in a way, all that time I was lying to him."

"About what?" Kay asked carefully.

"About. . . well. . . I'm not sure if it's my place to tell you. He's the one who should tell you."

"Why should *he* tell me anything?"

"I don't know. For awhile it seemed like you two were going to be friends. But I think that his being angry at me got in the way. What's the matter?"

"I. . ."

"Don't you feel good? We're almost there. Hey, you look a little green around the gills, kid. Are you all right?"

Kay didn't speak. Soon Sunny pulled over to the side of the road, to the spot where she always parked.

"Come on," she said. "Get some of that fresh air into your lungs and you'll feel like a new woman. Come on."

She got out of the car. Kay lagged behind, watching Sunny walk toward the pathway.

At the pathway, Sunny's pace quickened. She anticipated that just over the ridge, the narrow path through the tangle of growth would turn sharply, and she would behold that vista, starkly beautiful. The Quarry.

In another moment, she was there, stepping onto the flat sandy rock. She wanted to laugh out loud. Why was it she kept forgetting—

the sky, the sand, the water, all the life that lived in these places, independent yet in unison. Why was it she kept forgetting? she demanded of herself. She answered her own question. Because her life was structured to make her forget, forget what was important, what was essential. She heard Kay call her name. Turning, Sunny saw her standing in the middle of the path. "What is it?"

Kay opened her mouth and closed it. As she raised her hand to her lips, Sunny saw that she was shaking.

"Sunny, there's something I have to tell you. Something I should have told you a long time ago." Kay's lips quivered, and she covered her eyes with her hand. She stood still for a moment, riveted, and riveting Sunny's attention. When she took her hand away, her eyes were wet with tears. "Sunny, I have to tell you. It's about me and Jack. I have to tell you. . . about me and Jack."

But Sunny knew. Suddenly, finally, she knew.

Chapter 8

Blood

From the quarry to the city there was no sound but the car's engine and Kay's quiet weeping. Sunny was driving. Her body was driving. Her thoughts and emotions were absent. She had been at the quarry; she was heading toward home; she was not here, now.

As they drove through the city's outskirts, Kay wiped her eyes, blew her nose, and ran her fingers through her hair, giving Sunny occasional surreptitious glances. But Sunny wouldn't look at her. And just as Kay opened her mouth to speak, Sunny reached out and switched on the radio.

When she parked the car in front of the house, she turned to Kay and said, "Get out."

"Sunny. . ." Kay whispered, and the tears spilled out of her eyes.

Seeing this, Sunny gave an abrupt laugh and said, "Yup. You really pulled it off. You really did. You had yourself quite a time. Put quite a little notch in the old Rosenthal family tree."

Kay shook her head as though to say, I didn't mean it, and this seemed to enrage Sunny. "Didn't you!?" she shouted.

Kay jumped, startled, and began to cry in earnest.

"Shut up, will you please? I don't want the whole neighborhood to see you crying. Just go upstairs. But first I want to know one thing. Are you in love with him?"

"No!"

"You're not in love with him?"

"No." She wiped her eyes with the back of her hand. "Of *course* not! I'm in love with *you*."

Sunny gave her a bitter look, and Kay lowered her eyes, ashamed.

"Is he in love with you?"

"I doubt it."

She shook her head. "Then I don't understand. I could understand if you were in love. Those things happen. But if you weren't in love," she glanced at Kay, "then all *you* did was *fuck*." She'd meant the word to be cruel, and her eyes said exactly that. She faced the windshield once more. "What I don't understand is how you could have done that to me."

"It had nothing to do with you."

"It had *everything* to do with me!" Sunny snapped. Kay, knowing that somehow she was right, looked away.

Sunny didn't speak for a moment. When she did, her voice was strangely quiet. "Go on," she said. "Get out."

"Aren't you coming?" Kay asked, but Sunny looked away as though she hadn't heard. Kay opened the door and getting out, saw the blanket and thermos on the back seat. "Do you want me to take the things in?" she asked, sounding almost grateful to be able to speak of the simple things they shared.

Sunny gave her a glance that said they shared nothing.

Kay closed the door, and Sunny drove off. Watching her go, Kay was reminded of other times she'd watched her go, and she knew she was going to cry. She walked up the steps to the front door, walked up the steps to the second floor landing, unlocked and opened the door, and saw Whiskers sitting on a patch of sun on the living room floor.

He'd been sleeping and had woken at the sound of someone coming. He'd stood up, stretched and yawned, and was gazing through sleepy eyes at the doorway when the door opened.

"Whiskers," Kay whispered.

He meowed in response. She walked to the couch, sat down, and burst into tears. Whiskers sat there for a moment, walked to the couch, jumped up, and sniffed tentatively at the air around her face. This show of sympathy, or interest, made her cry all the more.

It was early in the evening when Sunny got home. By that time, Kay was sitting at the kitchen table sipping a cup of tea.

Sunny put the blanket on top of the now-cold space heater and walked into the kitchen to the sink, where she opened the thermos, tipped it and began pouring out the water.

"Sunny. Look. . . we have to talk."

Sunny didn't answer. She only held the thermos at more of an angle, as though she were glad to get rid of the contents and wanted to do it as quickly as possible.

"Sunny. Please. We have to talk."

Sunny finished with the water and turned to Kay, her face emotionless. "What's the rush?" she asked, and when Kay didn't answer, she turned away, her attitude contemptuous. Whiskers had walked into the kitchen and seeing him, her face brightened. "Whiskers!" she cried. She bent down to pick him up, nuzzling her face against his neck.

But he wasn't in the mood. He suffered her attentions a moment, then wriggled to get free.

"Whiskers! You're such a worm!" Sunny scolded, and put him down. He flicked his tail and walked away. Sunny walked away too, leaving Kay alone in the kitchen.

As Kay watched, Sunny began carrying things out to the porch: sheets, a blanket, her pillow, her alarm clock. She took the floor lamp from the living room. She got into her pajamas and robe, made a sandwich, poured a glass of milk, and went out to the porch with the Sunday papers. Sunny put the things down and called Whiskers. When he came, she closed the door firmly behind them.

Kay sat there, stunned. She stared at the closed door. After awhile, she took a bath and went to bed.

The next day when Kay got home from work, she went into the living room and opened the door to the porch.

It looked quite cheery out there. The old army cot was made up into a neat bed. On the nearby plastic table Sunny was using as a nightstand, Kay saw the *chai*.

When Sunny got home from work, Kay was taking a casserole of macaroni and cheese out of the oven. But Sunny was carrying a cardboard pizza box, and Kay knew she'd stopped at the Italian restaurant and gotten her favorite: eggplant parmigiana with ziti, fresh Italian bread, and pats of real butter.

Sunny put the cardboard box on the counter, went into the bedroom to change into jeans and a flannel shirt. Back in the kitchen, she made herself up a plate of food.

"I made macaroni and cheese," Kay said.

"So *eat* it."

Kay's lips quivered, and she began to cry.

Sunny looked at her in disgust. "Look, don't cry. Or if you do, go in the bedroom. This is the kitchen. I don't want you crying in the kitchen because I don't want to see it. You're the one who created this situation. *You* hurt *me*. And if you think I'm going to feel sorry for you, you'd better think again."

"*Me*! What about *him*? He had some part in it too, you know." Now her face was sullen, and she stood in an almost aggressive pose, her fists clenched at her sides.

Sunny nodded. "I know he did. I know what he did, and I know why he did it. Which is more than *you* know, isn't it? And that really pisses me off, because if you had any brains, you might have seen that something was going on. You might have had the sense to ask about it instead of just jumping in and. . . and not giving a shit about the consequences." She waved her hand in a gesture of carelessness. She stared at Kay. "Sure, I know what he did. I know exactly what he did. He got back at me for something you know nothing about. But what I want to know is, why did you do it? Why did *you*? With my *brother*?"

"He's not. . ."

"Don't you tell me what he is. You don't know what he is to me. You don't know anything about it. But that didn't stop you." Her face was full of contempt. "You know, I do have one question. I know why *he* hates me, but what I want to know is, what's *your* problem?"

Kay didn't answer, and Sunny shook her head. "I could have expected something like that from him—he's so full of hate and resentment. But *you*. You. . . you're a *woman*." She shook her head. "But I guess you're not the woman I thought you were."

Kay's face was sullen. "Well, maybe you're not the woman I thought *you* were either."

"Then why didn't you simply come and tell me? Why did you have to go and do this?"

Kay was silent. She lowered her gaze. "I don't know," she said. "I don't know."

"Well, maybe you'd better think about it."

Kay nodded. "Can I stay here?"

"Very frankly, I don't give a shit *what* you do. You know? Like the man said, 'Very frankly, my dear, I don't give a damn.' "

Kay smiled, hoping Sunny would smile too. But Sunny went on. "If you want to stay here, fine, I'm not going to throw you out because I know you have nowhere else to go. But I want you to stay out of my way. You live here and I live here, but that's as far as it goes. Just stay out of my way." She picked up her plate, silverware, and napkin, got a can of beer from the refrigerator, and headed toward the porch.

"Sunny," Kay began, but didn't go on because Sunny stopped suddenly and turned.

Her eyes sent out warnings. "Look, *you*. You're not worth getting an ulcer over. And I don't want to say anything I'll be sorry for later. So leave me alone. And I don't want to have to tell you again." She glared at Kay to make sure she'd gotten the message, then turned and walked to the porch.

When she was gone, Kay set herself a place at the table, dished out some macaroni and cheese, sat down and tried to eat.

When Sunny left Kay on Sunday, she drove across the bridge to Canada. She parked the car at the old spot, the spot where she and Debbie had so many times waited for Frank, and she sat in the car and cried. She cried until she did not feel like crying anymore, and when she knew she was finished and felt secure that she would not cry in front of Kay, she went home.

On Monday morning, she was anxious that she would not be able to keep up a front at work. On the contrary, being at work was a relief. Rather than being broken-hearted and weepy-eyed as she'd feared, she felt angry in a kind of cynical, I don't care, fuck you way. Her anger was haughty: she could feel that cool look in her eyes that almost seemed arrogant, as though she cared too little about anything to let it hurt her.

On the way to work, she'd bought a pack of cigarettes. She hadn't smoked in years, but now she felt the urge to smoke and stopped at one of those chain stores that had begun to wipe out the Mom-and-Pop corner stores once so prevalent in her neighborhood. She felt angry and reckless.

Hey—smoking wasn't good for her health? So who *gives* a shit? What with nuclear proliferation, acid rain, the greenhouse effect and toxic wastes, she was supposed to care about her health? Hah! That was her attitude. And the cigarettes helped. Somehow they helped release her anger. Or perhaps merely expressed it. It did not feel like her anger could ever be released.

So my girlfriend fucked my brother? Hey—that's the breaks. She lit each of her cigarettes with an angry gesture and shook out the matches the same way. She dragged deeply, blew out the smoke rapidly, and as she stubbed out the butts, there was a hard look on her face.

Grace said after awhile, "Jesus, I better not make any nasty cracks about Jews today. The way you look now, you're liable to nail *me* to the cross."

Sunny looked at her.

Grace held up her hands in surrender. "I was only kidding. Uh oh. . . help. Louise! Save me! You're my friend. I always *liked* you. You were *right* about her!"

Sunny laughed. "Grace, you're a fuckin' moron. You really are."

Grace held up her thumbs in self-congratulations. "What can I say? I'm wonderful. You've heard of Amazing Grace, right? Who do you think they *wrote* that about?"

"God, I can't wait 'til you go on vacation."

"You'll miss me. You will."

"Listen. I'm through with missing people. They're not worth it."

A look of taking note appeared in Grace's eyes. She nodded slowly. "I'm not going to ask what happened, but if you want to talk about it. . ."

"Thanks, Grace. I appreciate it."

At lunchtime, she went down to the employees' cafeteria in the basement. It was not much more than some tables and chairs and a row of machines against the wall: cold drinks, hot drinks, packaged food, and a small microwave oven. As a rule, she spent her lunchtime alone, telling herself she preferred the solitude. But on a whim she went down, and at a corner table found Grace and LaSan.

"Well, well, well," Grace said.

"Here's the girl with the dark side," LaSan murmured, and unwrapped her sandwich. "We're gonna have to start calling her Stormy," she said to Grace, who frowned as if considering the name.

Sunny had by then pulled out a chair and sat down. "Actually, I *was* thinking of changing my name. To Sonia. It's my real name anyway, so it wouldn't be a change. But I was thinking of dropping Sunny. It's kind of childish. You know?"

"Where'd you get Sunny from?" LaSan asked.

"It's from my brother," she said, and when she said the word *brother*, her tone did not change. "He couldn't say Sonia when he was a kid. He used to say what sounded like Sunny. And everybody picked up on it."

"I like Sonia better," Grace said.

"No." LaSan shook her head as though the matter were settled. "People should make up their own names if they want."

"Well then why didn't *you*?" Grace challenged.

"I did."

"What is it?"

"LaSan."

Grace laughed in disbelief and said, her attitude being that she would go along with the joke, "Okay, then, what's your real name?"

"Margaret."

"Margaret?"

"Margaret."

"LaSan, get the hell out of here," Grace said.

LaSan shrugged as if she didn't care whether or not Grace believed her and bit into her sandwich.

That night after work, Sunny ate dinner on the porch, puttered around the apartment a bit, and returned to the porch at dusk. She'd thought she would sit propped up on the army cot and read, but instead she sat on a wooden chair and looked out onto the street.

And so began a new pattern to her life. During the day she went to work. At night she sat on the porch. It felt like where she should be. It was a separate space, outside of the apartment, a space where she could put Kay and all that had happened behind her.

Yet in truth she could put nothing behind her. Every evening she sat on the porch thinking, and every evening she felt her anger slipping away. Not her real anger, but the careless, spiteful anger that she wore during the day. It slipped away and left her aching and exposed.

She thought of Jack—the things he'd said, the way he'd acted. She remembered the day of Sam's funeral. She remembered Jack's sneering attitude when she'd reminded him of the quarry. She remembered what he'd said the last time she'd seen him: "If you want to know how much I hate you, ask your girlfriend." And she'd never pursued any of it.

She remembered all the things in between. She'd let them pass her by, knowing and not knowing that something was terribly wrong. She let it all go by when what she should have done was put up her hand and say, "Stop right there. Hold it just a minute, and let's see what the problem is." But she hadn't done it.

She thought of Kay. But it was too painful. She'd always heard the word *heartache* and it seemed like just a word. But it was more than that: it was a real physical pain, a round, hard lump like a rock that pressed against her chest day and night so that no matter what she did, she felt it. On the porch, when she thought of Kay, she could no longer ignore it. She felt a hollow ache for the well-being that had deserted her. Sunny's trust for Kay had built something inside her, and now that it was in ruins, she felt shaken and alone.

Sometimes late at night, she'd lie on the army cot, curled around Whiskers, and cry. He would glance around and sniff at her face to see what all the fuss was. She'd laugh, still crying, and hug him, whispering his name through her tears.

As the nights passed, she thought, too, of herself, of the times she could have told Kay the truth and didn't. She didn't tell her even when she *knew*, when she *felt* that something was wrong—that he was dangerous. But still, she wondered, how could Kay have been so *stupid*? Is she *stupid*? she wondered. But she knew, too, how charming Jack could be. This led her full circle back to Jack and his anger. And the fact that he had blamed her.

Toward the end of the week she began to feel a new kind of anger. It was not the self-righteous anger that had slipped away, nor was it her anger against Jack, an anger so profound that it felt as though he were dead. This was the anger of a woman caught in a lie not of her making.

When this thought struck her, she looked at the clock, stood up and opened the door, walked into the kitchen, and phoned Rose.

The door to the back bedroom was open. She saw the lighted room at the end of the hallway as she walked around the kitchen. She spoke loudly, and not only for the benefit of Rose who had trouble hearing over the phone. "I'll come over after work tomorrow and take you to supper! All right, Grandma? We'll go to MacDonald's," she added, because that was Rose's current favorite.

"Nuh! I can' go."

"Why not?"

"I gotta go to visit my frien'."

"Mrs. Sadetsky?"

To this, her grandmother let out a stream of angry Yiddish. When she was done, Sunny asked, "What'd you have, a fight with Mrs. Sadetsky?"

"Do you know vhat she *done?*" Rose replied self-righteously, ready to commence an English narration of the story.

"You'll tell me when I see you, Grandma. Right now, I'm trying to figure out when I can see you. I'm free every night. It's *you* we gotta work around, kid."

"Kid," Rose laughed.

"How 'bout Thursday?"

"Nuh. I got. . ."

"Okay, then *when?*"

"Sunday."

"Okay. Sunday."

On Saturday she went to visit Rose. Their plans to get together had to be changed because on Sunday there was going to be a special program at the Jewish Center for Senior Citizens, and Rose didn't want to miss it. Nevertheless, she had forgotten about her granddaughter's visit. As Sunny pulled up in front of the house, she saw Rose walking down the street.

"Grandma, you knucklehead," she muttered to herself. Opening the car door, she called out, "Grandma, wait!"

Rose turned around, squinted, saw her granddaughter, and said, "Uh. I gotta valk!"

"Okay, okay, you'll walk!" she called, and caught up with Rose.

Rose walked every day. Sometimes she had a specific destination, and sometimes the destination was the walk itself. She thought walking was the greatest invention since water—a miracle cure-all, a life-giver, a fountain of youth, a general solution to all problems. Besides, what were legs for if not to use them? She walked with a kind of dogged determination. Accompanying her, Sunny remembered that this was how Debbie had sometime walked: her gait and face set in resolution, her body leaning forward in anticipation. When Debbie was still a toddler, Sunny had taken to calling her the Sergeant. "Hey Sarge," she'd call, "come on, it's time for lunch."

Rose walked briskly, and Sunny remarked, "Hey, Grandma, give me a break, will ya? I'm not as young as I used to be."

Rose shrugged. It was meant to be a shrug of modesty, but the look in her eyes gave it away, and for a half block or so she quickened her pace even more. She wore her pink jogging suit and white oxfords that looked like nurse's shoes.

Sunny had heard some time ago about the famous pink jogging suit and was curious to hear Rose's version of how the suit had come into her possession. "Nice outfit," she remarked as they walked along. "Where'd you get it?"

"Vell," Rose began, "I'm gonna tell you. A voman at deh Center give it to me. She gained alotteh veight, and deh suit didn't fit, so she said to me, 'Please, Meeses Rosent'al, take deh suit. You such a luffly voman, I vant you should have dot suit.'" She glanced at her granddaughter as if to say, How do you like that? "'A luffly voman,' she called me, 'a luffly voman.'"

"Well, if you ask me, you look mighty spiffy."

"*Vuss* is *duss*, spiffy?"

"It means. . . a sharp dresser."

Rose nodded, agreeing with this evaluation. "Dot's me."

When they reached Prospect Park, Rose's destination today, she insisted they sit on the park's outskirts so that she could watch the street. After they sat, she proceeded to talk about the changing neighborhood and the passersby. If she knew them, she acquainted Sunny with intimate details of their lives and their family troubles; for if she knew them she had asked, and most likely, disarmed by her frankness, they had answered. If she didn't know them, she conjectured.

Finally, when Rose paused in her catalogue of the neighborhood, Sunny said, "Grandma, tell me about Eva."

"*Ay-yi!*" Rose exclaimed, meaning that it wasn't such a simple thing to tell. "It vas a long time ago."

Sunny waited, knowing the exclamation served as a preface. But Rose did not go on. She seemed to have forgotten the request and was gazing across the street at a bakery.

"Grandma?"

Her gaze still on the bakery, Rose began to speak, and her words, her tone, her gestures, were leisurely and deliberate, not to be hurried along by anyone else's whim. She enjoyed talking and loved having an audience, and she would take her time whether Sunny liked it or not. As she spoke, she gestured liberally—her hands, her head, her shoulders—all of it emphasizing her meaning.

"My muddaih. . . she vas a sick voman," she began, and counted the illnesses on her fingers. "She vas di-betic, she had kidney trouble, she vas es-metic. It used to be music here," she explained, pointing to her windpipe, looking to see if Sunny understood.

"Mmm, music," she murmured impatiently, wanting Rose to get to the point.

"My muddaih. . . she vent t'rew an awful lot vit' us."

"With her children."

Rose nodded and held up her hand, frowning. "*Sha*. My muddaih— vasn't much money—and she used to manage fah deh liddle money to buy flour to bake bread. Ah! Now I can taste de bread, vhat a delicious bread dot vas! Dot's vhy ve so strong," she explained. "It vas *real black corn*. It vasn't any yeast. She used to make *big* vuns, like *dot*," she said, encircling her arms wide, and Sunny smiled, for her grandmother, like the exaggerating fisherman, was indicating a pumpernickel that would have had to weigh twenty-five pounds. "And leave it stay," she continued, "in a *big pot*, 'bout ten pounds flour, to sour." She paused in the recipe to explain, "Deh bread vas sour."

"Mm-hmm," Sunny nodded in encouragement, for her grandmother was answering a question she hadn't been asked.

"It vas *delicious*," she murmured nostalgically, falling once more into the reverie of the bread. "Ah. *Geshmack*! I can't fuhget deh taste. . . ." And she shook her head at what was lost forever.

Then, apparently feeling that she had made *this* point sufficiently, she switched abruptly to another track. "Yankel had alotteh bodies to him, and. . ." She frowned, searching for the proper words in a language that after over sixty years still felt foreign. "I t'ink he vas fifteen."

"Wait a minute. I don't understand."

"Ve didn't have nutting to eat," Rose explained.

"But who was Yankel?"

"Yankel?" Rose said, annoyed to have been interrupted in her narrative, and looking at Sunny as though she were little more than an idiot. "He vas my bruddaih. And Yankel," she continued, "used to take deh bread and leave us viddout *bread*. And give it to his bodies."

"His what?"

"His *bodies*, dey lived in deh same place. Deh same. . . deh same *place*. It vas a place. *Shtetl*, ve called it."

"Oh, you mean his *buddies*."

"Yah. His bodies. And my muddaih, she said to me. . . *Sha!* She said," and here Rose, with a warning finger wagging into Sunny's face, spoke in Yiddish, her voice deliberate and full of expression. It sounded something like, "vatch'en em vil ditz nemetz da *broit*," and Sunny, half understanding, asked, "But what. . ."

"Because da rest of us, ve vuddent have nutting to eat."

"The rest of the family."

Rose nodded once, emphatically.

"So your mother told you to watch Yankel."

Again that emphatic nod. "So I vatched him. And I told my muddaih," here Rose frowned and shook her head, "dot he is deh von vhat steals deh bread. And he vanna *kill* me. So he took a stick and he pot me on deh head. And he took a pail, a *big* vun, and he t'row it on me. But he didn't kill me."

"He didn't kill you."

"Nuh! Didn't kill me."

"Good," Sunny said dryly. "But I don't understand. What does this have to do with. . . does this have anything to do with Eva?"

"Vay. ." Rose held up her hand cautioning patience. "So any-vay," she went on, warming up once more to her story, "I'll tell you about Yankel. Vell," she began, and frowned, looking for the thread to her story. Finding it, she nodded, satisfied, and continued. "My faddeh, he vas a religious man. *Religious*!"

"Zadie with the Cane?"

"Yah. He vas a *chazzen* in deh *shul*, he done dot voik. He made money fum dot in deh Oldt Country. But vhen he comes to dis country, he don' voik because he is oldt, and he lives *mit* me an' Pa."

"So. Vun day. . . ve get a letteh." She held out her hands, indicating that it had come out of the blue. "Fum Yankel." She threw up her hands and dropped them. "An' he says he can't find voik, he's got nuttink to eat, an' ve gotteh send him money to come oveh."

"Where was he, the Old Country?"

Rose nodded.

"Was he married?"

"His vife died."

"Did he have any children?"

"Nuh. So lissen. So my faddeh sends deh money so Yankel should come." She looked at her granddaughter to see if she was following, then said, "You know dot *Rosh Hashonah* is a very religious holiday. And my faddeh vas religious. So *Rosh Hashonah* is coming, and he sends a telegram, he says dot deh money didn't come, he didn't get deh money."

"Yankel?"

"Yankel!" she said in emphatic annoyance, for about whom else were they talking? "And deh ship is going off. . . and it's gonna be alotteh trouble. He should send him more. But he had deh money."

"Yankel *had* the money? He had it all along?"

"So he had deh money! But he vahn *more* fum him."

"From Zadie?"

Rose nodded. "So. . . *Rosh Hashonah*, I made my faddeh to go and sign in deh bank and take ahlt deh money because deh ship is gonna leave. And my faddeh vas raisin' hell. He vas hollin' and hollin' and screamin', '*Rosh Hashonah*, God'll punish me!' and he said—he *loved* me, my Faddeh. I vas like a *son* to him, I was *smott*. But he vas hollin' at me—he says, 'You preganan' now, God vill punish you too. Because you deh von vhat made me to take it ahlt.'"

"The money."

"Yah."

"From the bank."

"Yah."

"On *Rosh Hashonah*."

"Yah."

"Who were you pregnant with?"

"Eh?"

"Who were you pregnant with?"

"I vas preganan' vit' Eva."

"With Eva. . ."

"Yah. Dot's a long time ago. Let me see, it vas. . ."

"So tell me what Zadie said, he said you were going to be punished because you made him go to the bank on *Rosh Hashonah?*"

"He said, 'I'll be punished and you'll be punished. You might gonna have a dead child, furn vhat you done.' I vas preganan'!"

Sunny nodded. "And then Aunt Evie was born?"

Rose nodded.

"Did he like her?"

"He loved her. But he find it ahlt dat it vas *all a lie.*"

"He found out about Yankel? How did he find out about Yankel?"

"All a lie, he find it ahlt."

"But how? How did he find out?"

"Deh man in Can-e-deh, he sent him a letteh, and he told him evvyt'ing, vhat a *gonif* he is."

"Yankel."

Rose looked at her, exasperated. "Let's go. Come on," she said, stood up, and began walking in a brisk stride toward home.

Sunny caught up with her, asking, "Where is he now? Is he still alive?"

"He's a *gonif*, dot's vhat he is." She wagged her finger at Sunny, warning her to steer clear of him. "He's very crooked."

"Is he still alive?"

"A *gonif!*"

"But is he still alive?"

"*Vuss?*"

"Is he *still alive?*"

Rose gave her a look that said not as far as *she* was concerned, he wasn't. "He's a *gonif.* He came oveh to Can-e-deh, and he voiked in a bakerie. He saved a little bit money, and he bought clothes, and he used to *sell* 'em to deh French people on *payment.* A *gonif!*"

"Uh-huh."

"He has alotteh money, Yankel. But he vuddent give you a penny. Dot bestid. . ."

"Is he still alive?"

She shrugged. "He must be 'bout eighty years old, I believe."

"Where does he live?"

"He lives in Montreal. He's a *gonif.* He's very crooked."

"What does he call himself?"

"Eh?"

"What does he call himself?"

"He calls himself Jacques, dot's vhat he calls himself. Dot's a French name. But he vas Yankel. Deh *mean* vun."

"Oh," Sunny said, remembering the way the family referred to Rose's brothers. There was the artist who'd lived in New York City, and the one who'd gone to Argentina. There was the socialist who'd moved from Russia to Canada to Israel, and the teacher who'd come to Buffalo and worked as a janitor in City Hall. There was the blind one, a musician, who'd been killed by Hitler. And there was Yankel, the mean one. And of the sisters. . .

She tried to think, but Rose interrupted her thoughts with, "Dot bestid, dah *hell* vid him."

"Wait a minute, Grandma. Isn't Yankel the one who sent me the blender when I married Frank?"

Rose gave her a look which meant she should not be so easily fooled. "Hmph!" she grunted sarcastically, indicating that any gift Yankel gave would have attached to it an ulterior motive. "Dah *hell* vid' him. My faddeh had to coise me fuh dat, he coised me tehr'ble. Ah!" she said, shaking her head.

They had reached the house and Rose asked, "You vanna sit on deh stoop?"

"Sure, let's sit on the stoop. But I want you to tell me about when Evie went away, why Zadie made her go."

Rose sat, and Sunny sat beside her.

"Jewish people," Rose began, "believe dot in deh time of *Pesach*, you should open up deh house fuh deh people vit' no place to go."

Sunny nodded. Yes. She knew what was coming.

"So vun time, Zadie, he vent to deh *shul*, and he meets a man. . ."

"You mean the *shnorrer* from Chicago?"

Rose shrugged. Whether he was a *shnorrer* from Chicago or a courageous man who'd lost his job with Cook County because of McCarthy was not for her to judge. "So he stayt, and he stayt, and Zadie diden vann t'row him ahlt, because vhen he comes, it vas *Pesach*. And Evie spends time vit' him, and time. . . I said to Zadie," and she began to speak in Yiddish, her eyes beseeching, her hands making the impassioned but hopeless gestures of one who knows she will not be heard. Then she shrugged. "But he vudden listen. An' he taught dot vhat she done, it vas a *shanda*. An' he vas hollin' and hollin', an' she said she's gonna leave, and he says, 'Go!' " She paused here and held her hands out as though it were the end of her story. "So. . . she goes."

"Didn't you try to find her?"

"She vas my *child*," Rose answered. "But. . . ve couldn't find her. Pa vent in Chicagie and looked and looked. Two veeks he looked. And den his boss he says if Pa don't come back, he's gonna get rid fum him. So he comes back."

Rose was looking across the street, and for the first time in her narration, she seemed tired and unwilling to go on.

"And then?" Sunny prompted her gently. "What happened then?"

"Ve get a phone call. Fum deh 'ospital in Chicagie. Deh people say she is dead, and ve should come. So Pa goes, and he comes back, and he has Evaleh. . . and deh baby."

"And my mother and father took him?"

She nodded.

"Because we were living out of town?"

151

She nodded again.

"And nobody said anything?"

She shook her head.

"Because of Zadie?"

She nodded and said, "Because he said it vas a *shanda* dot people should know. You know vhat is a *shanda*?"

"A shame," Sunny murmured, "a shame." She sighed deeply. "But Grandma, why didn't you just go against Zadie? She was your daughter. Why did you let her go?"

But as she said the words, she knew it was not that simple. There were currents of chance as well as water. Sometimes you could suffer all your life for letting go, but your suffering didn't change what had happened.

The sun was low in the sky, and the street was suffused with a pale light. "It's time to go in soon," Rose said.

Sunny nodded. She shifted her weight, leaning toward her grandmother so their shoulders touched, and the two women sat in silence as the sky darkened into night.

The next day, Sunny went to work. Though Monday was uneventful, by Tuesday there were rumors. There was something in the air.

At lunch Grace relayed the information that that morning, Betty, Mr. Danvers' secretary, had told her that on Friday, Louise had gone into Danvers' office and stayed "quite some time." Grace paused and looked at Sunny and LaSan meaningfully. "And I'm sure," she went on, "that Louise and ol' Roger didn't have a mad passionate affair on his desk."

Sunny gave a glum sigh. "Danvers' office is on the fourth floor, right?" She was referring to the rumors floating around the fourth floor (where Louise had several cronies in Accounting) that Sunny was Dangerous and had a Violent Temper that could flare up for No Reason At All.

LaSan twisted her mouth to the side in a grimace of distaste and indicated by her glance that Grace and Sunny should look across the room to where Louise sat huddled with Tina, laughing.

Tina's purse had been found last week at the back of the supply cabinet minus money, credit cards, and identification. In the Ladies Room, Sunny had overheard Louise being horrified to Tina. A theft? At Imperial Dynamics? How horrifying! Sunny had found Louise's horror amusing since the entire foundation of Imperial Dynamics was theft: of raw materials, time, labor, and anything else that could be stolen.

But now, glancing over at Louise whispering toward Tina's ear, she was not so amused.

Later that day, passing Louise in the hall, she felt distinctly uneasy.

When Louise and Sunny first passed in the hall after their "chew me down" conversation, they'd ignored one another. The second time, Sunny glanced at her briefly; the third time, longer. But Louise wouldn't meet her eyes, wouldn't (it seemed to Sunny) acknowledge her existence.

It had gotten to the point where, when they passed in the empty hall, Sunny wanted to go up to Louise and say, "*Look* at me, goddamnit. I'm *here*. I'm alive!" She imagined herself stopping Louise in the hall, her hand on Louise's arm, her eyes insistent. The image was familiar—a woman in the hall, her hand gentle, her eyes insistent—but she couldn't quite place it.

When Louise passed her in the hall this afternoon, however, she looked up to meet Sunny's eyes. Sunny was prepared to give her a simple hello, a no-grudges-held-let's-start-from-scratch hello. But Louise's eyes and her smug smile said, You wait. Just you wait.

It made Sunny feel defeated. Not because of the likelihood that Louise would get the promotion, but because of the implications of that promotion. If Louise were promoted, they would no longer be equal. Louise would have more power. Any attempt by Sunny to approach her would be seen in terms of that power.

Rumors or not, however, interpersonal relations or not, the work of Imperial Dynamics had to be done if Sunny wanted to get a weekly paycheck. By day she did that work.

By night she sat on the porch and looked out at the stage that she saw from her own private balcony. It was June, and her vision of the Armory was obscured by the lush growth on the two maple trees in front of her house.

The Armory still dominated her vision. But the neighborhood was changing and changing fast. The Dew Drop Inn, once a neighborhood bar, was now a hang-out for men who had a self-conscious air of violence about them. They drove loud, roaring motorcycles, and wore leather and chains; and their women had an attitude of bravado and carelessness.

The corner store had closed down. The storefront had become a video games parlor, a place frequented by adolescents, mostly boys and a few tough-looking girls. Sometimes at night, Sunny heard the roar of motorcycles, sometimes, young voices full of rage. She and Mrs. Mancuso complained to each other about the changing neighborhood. Mrs. Mancuso would say, "I remember when there was all families here. We all knew each other. *These* people, *they* don't care about their children." By *they*, Mrs. Mancuso meant different things at different times. Talking to Sunny, now, she meant people who weren't ethnic, people who weren't respectable, since she considered Sunny a respectable girl who came from respectable people.

As the week passed, Sunny started feeling better. She hardly saw Kay, for they tried not to be in the house at the same time; or if they were, not in the same room.

She felt better at work. She'd begun to joke around with Grace and LaSan, and Grace said that she was glad to see Sunny back to her old self.

On Thursday after work, she went to the bank to cash her check.

It was crowded, and she had to wait in a long line that snaked back and forth and ended at the door. As she stood there, she got into a conversation with the woman behind her. Sunny was a friendly person. She enjoyed making contact with strangers through small talk. She could sense that the woman was lonely.

The woman seemed to be in her early sixties. Almost at once she mentioned her mother, who had died recently after a long illness.

At first they'd begun talking quite logically about being in lines. They'd been chatting about this for a few minutes when the woman leaned forward and with a confidential air said, "Well, once *I* was in line at the big bank downtown, and it was crowded just like this, and all of a sudden this little old lady *pushed her way* to the front of the line."

In an instant, Sunny knew what was coming. It was something in the air. She could sense it, could *feel* it, and she felt exposed. Like a target. A well-established, convenient target.

And the woman said, "Just pushed her way! She went up to the teller and she said. . . ." And the woman hunched her shoulders and clasped her hands together like a 'little old lady' and spoke in a mincing voice, a parody of a Yiddish accent that invited contempt, as though the accent itself were contemptuous as well as the person who used it. " 'Can I hef, can I hef, can I hef my munney? I vant my *munney,*' " she whined. She gave Sunny a look that said, *You* know what I mean.

Oh God, Sunny thought, half in sorrow and half in complaint, What am I going to do? She answered her question with a question, You're looking to *him* for help? Sunny took a breath and asked, "Was she Jewish?"

"*I* think she was."

"Oh. Well, *I'm* Jewish, and. . . *I'm* waiting in line."

"Oh, I didn't mean. . ."

"Maybe it was because she was old and her legs hurt from standing in line or something. You know? I don't think it was necessarily because she was *Jewish* that she was. . ."

"Oh I'm *sorry,* I didn't mean *you.*" And before Sunny could ask who she did mean, the woman said, "My mother had some *very* good friends that were Jewish."

At this, Sunny wanted to laugh. Some of your beloved dead mother's best friends were Jewish, she thought, so you're on safe ground, is that it?

Yes, the woman went on, this one Jewish lady her mother knew (and Sunny thought, Get your story straight, honey, was your mother surrounded by Jewish best friends, or was it one lady she knew casually?), this one Jewish lady had even taught her mother to cook Jewish. She'd taught her to cook, and here she said a word Sunny had never heard.

"What did you call them?" she asked. "Brughels?"

"Oh yes, they're a *very* famous Jewish food. Haven't you ever heard of them?" And there was a look in her eye that said, See? You don't know *everything* about being Jewish. You're not such an expert.

"I don't know. I never heard of them."

"Oh yes, they're *very* famous."

Sunny sighed, looking at the dwindling line of people before them and tried to change the subject, wishing she had worn her *chai*. Then maybe this wouldn't have happened. She was exhausted. But on the way home, she felt better. She thought, At least I said something. At least it was a start.

She thought about the woman in the bank and about the Jewish woman she'd described. She could picture her grandmother doing exactly that kind of thing. Not because it was a bank and she was Jewish, but because she was pushy. She'd been pushy since she was fifteen years old, and she'd pushed her parents into agreeing that she go to America all by herself when only one brother was settled there, in Buffalo, New York, thousands and thousands of miles away.

She could picture Rose pushing her way to the head of some line, and she wondered if in fact it *was* Rose that the woman had described. Rose *was* desperate about money. She'd been hungry in the Old Country and couldn't forget it. She'd gotten out because of money, because her parents had scrimped and saved for the fare, and she couldn't forget it. She was alive because of money. Others, who could not get out, had died. And she couldn't forget it.

Sunny thought, I wish I could have told that woman in the bank about Rosie. Maybe then she'd understand.

Kay was waiting when Sunny got home. She was sitting in the living room, watching TV. Though her eyes didn't move away from the screen when the door opened, it was clear that her attention was focused on Sunny and that she was waiting.

"Hello," Sunny said, without emotion.

"Hello," Kay answered, friendly but keeping her distance as she'd been asked.

Sunny put her pocketbook on the easy chair, greeted Whiskers, and went in to take a bath. She came out in an old yellow cotton smock she wore in warm weather. It was sleeveless and had big pockets, or "pockies," as Debbie first called them. She made something quick for supper and ate it hungrily out of the pot as she boiled water for tea. "Do you want a cup of tea?" she called in to Kay.

"Yes. Thank you," Kay said, and waited.

She'd hoped Sunny would bring in the tea, or at the very least call in that it was ready. She was disappointed to see Sunny head out to the porch, saying, "It's in the kitchen." In the kitchen, Kay sipped the tea, her face thoughtful. When she was done, she rinsed out her cup, set it upside-down on the drain, and walked to the edge of the living room. The first thing she saw was that the *chai* was gone, and she brightened. "I see you're wearing your *chai*," she began, but stopped abruptly. For it wasn't true. She hadn't seen Sunny wearing it. For all she knew Sunny could have thrown it down the sink.

Sunny looked up from the newspaper. "It has nothing to do with you," she said.

Kay saw the *chai* around her neck. "You know," she said, "it's been almost two weeks. I think we should talk." But Sunny's cold distant expression did not change, and Kay blurted, "Without you looking at me like that!"

"Like what?" Sunny asked, and her eyes were cool and mocking.

"Like *that*!" Kay said, angry. "So. . . so *cold*."

"Oh. You don't want me to be cold? What do you want me to do, open up my heart to you? To be. . . *vulnerable*?" She pronounced the word distinctly, reminding Kay of their private joke about that word and the fact that it was no longer a joke they shared.

Kay shook her head, sighing, and turned away. But Sunny stood up, lit a cigarette, and followed her into the living room. "You know," she said, and Kay, who'd reached the kitchen doorway, turned around.

Sunny sat in the easy chair, her spine curled, her legs crossed, ankle over knee. Her arms were folded across her chest, and her gaze was unfocused on the middle of the room. "I've been doing a lot of thinking," she began, "and it's not only that I'm hurt over what you did. It's the reasons why you did it. That's what I don't understand."

Kay opened her mouth to speak, but Sunny cut her off with, "I don't want to hear any explanations. I don't want you to *explain* to me." She looked at Kay. "I want *you* to understand. Because there's a lot of things *I* don't understand." Her gaze returned once more to the middle of the room. "And the thing I don't understand the most is. . . whatever our problems, whatever was wrong, we should have worked it out between us, and you involved somebody else."

She stopped. "I know I have my faults," she said. "I know I'm not perfect. I know I'm not the most wonderful person in the world to live with. But didn't you understand that I was. . . in *trouble*?" She sighed, letting her arms fall from their tight hold. She glanced at Kay. "Didn't you see that I *needed* you, that I needed *someone*?"

"Then why didn't you *tell* me?"

"I did. I just didn't tell you in words." She was silent a moment. Sunny sat up straight. Her teeth were clenched. She took a deep breath and let it out through her nose. She said, "That's the *other* thing. I mean, what are you—stupid? Did you need it spelled out for you?" She stood up, angry. "And that's *another* thing," she began and walked to the porch. But midway there she stopped and turned suddenly.

Kay saw that Sunny was shaking, and she thought, She didn't want to go out to the porch. She wanted to distance herself so I wouldn't see her lose control.

Sunny clenched her fists. "That's another thing," she said, her voice cold. "I *disrespect* you. Do you understand me? I've lost *respect* for you. Are you *stupid* to have fallen for his shit? I know that ungrateful bastard is charming, but you must've been stupid to. . . ." She could not find the right word, and she shook her head, her eyes telling Kay that she would keep silent, but they both knew what she had done.

She rubbed her eyes and sat on the arm of the couch. "I mean, this year. . . this year," she said, pressing her open palm to her chest, "I wouldn't wish on my worst enemy. And you," she made a shrugging gesture with her hand, and let it drop, "you hurt me. You kicked me in the gut while I was down. And that's not right. That's not fair. And *most* of all. . . I'm disappointed in you. Because I thought you were a fair person and you're not."

She looked at Kay and stood up, started to turn toward the porch, and stopped. "You know, people make mistakes. If you had come to me and said, 'I made a mistake,' it wouldn't have been pleasant, but I'd like to think that somehow we could've worked it out. But you lied to me. All that time that I was trusting you, and loving you, you were off somewhere else, watching. *Knowing*. And lying."

She paused, shaking her head, still bewildered. She looked at Kay one final time. "And so I don't trust you," she said, and walked out onto the porch.

Kay stood there, her lips quivering. She turned and walked into the back bedroom, lay down on the bed, and burst into tears.

In the living room, Whiskers was sitting on the floor. He yawned, stretched, and ambled out onto the porch, rubbing against Sunny. But she ignored him, and he walked away, going back through the living room and the kitchen, down the hall to the back bedroom, where he jumped up on the bed and sat down a foot or so from Kay's face and watched her cry.

"Whiskers. . ." she whispered, and gave a sob. "I'm sorry, Whiskers. I'm sorry. I'm sorry, I'm sorry, I'm sorry." Crying, she reached out for him. But he moved away from her embrace. He was offering comfort at this point, not trust, and he walked to the foot of the bed, around to the back of her legs, where he lay down and made himself comfortable.

After awhile Kay stopped crying and lay there quietly, looking at the wall and thinking.

Her thoughts kept drifting back over the past year. She thought of times Sunny had needed her and how she had responded. She remembered how she'd offered support, but only superficially; how she'd offered her arms, but not her heart. She remembered all the times when she was off in a mental corner judging Sunny's moods and trying to protect herself. She saw that she had not entered the relationship with the same intentions as Sunny but had never been open about that fact. She hadn't intended it to be so serious. When that happened, she'd turned her back and pretended she was committed, all the while harboring secret feelings. It was difficult to put the pieces together, but as she did, she didn't like the picture she saw of herself.

She saw a new picture of Sunny, too. She'd once seen a gallant Amazon doing battle with the world, and when that image had crumbled, she'd been disappointed and angry. Later she'd seen a weeping wretch who clung to her in desperation. But Sunny wasn't that, either, and Kay knew it.

Sunny was neither Amazon nor wretch. She was a woman—imperfect, but determined to be strong.

Kay understood that she was beginning to respect Sunny. Realizing this, she knew she was falling in love. It was ironic, and she would have liked to share that irony with her best friend. But her best friend didn't trust her.

She felt a sorrow in her chest, like a terrible heaviness she could not escape because it was inside her.

She looked at the clock. It was after ten, and the sky outside the windows was dark. She got undressed and got back into bed. Whiskers had by this time left, presumably to rejoin Sunny. Kay lay there a long time, alone, then fell asleep.

In the middle of the night, she woke. Her brain was spinning with thoughts, and though she couldn't sort it out at first, she knew that she was angry. After awhile, the thoughts fell into place.

If there had been a situation between Sunny and Jack, why hadn't Sunny told her? Why hadn't she warned her? Why did I have to see something was wrong? she asked herself. Why didn't she just tell me?

She felt self-righteous, as though she'd finally hit upon the chink in Sunny's logic, finally found the way to justify herself and her actions. She imagined waiting for Sunny when she got home from work the next night, pointing an accusing finger at her and saying, Wait a minute, Sunny. You had a part in this too!

But no, she told herself. No. Take it slow. See what happens. Don't accuse her. She didn't accuse you.

Sunny disrespected her because she'd been stupid. If she wanted Sunny to respect her, she had to be smart, to act carefully, to think. Take it easy, she told herself. Don't go jumping in. See what happens. Try to be friends first, and *then* you can sort it all out.

At lunch on Friday, Grace approached the corner table of the employees' basement cafeteria and stood there with a knowing look on her face.

Sunny had been sitting with her spine at a slant to the plastic chair, and she was gazing up at the ground level window, through which she could see an evergreen and some tulips in bloom. One seat away, LaSan was eating a mixture of carrots and cottage cheese out of a plastic container. There was a look on her face of distasteful forbearance.

When Grace approached the table, the two of them looked at her, looked at each other, looked back at her, and waited for her to speak—which she did as soon as she'd wrung the maximum amount of drama out of the situation.

"Louise told Tina," she said, sitting down and leaning toward them, "that she knew a clerk at a record store, and he said he thought he remembered Tina's credit card. And he said that a *black* man used it."

LaSan's mouth stopped chewing. Then it started chewing very quickly, while Sunny, whose mouth had fallen open, watched her. LaSan swallowed. "*What?*"

Grace nodded. "Yup."

"And Tina believed her?" Sunny asked.

Grace shrugged. "I always said Tina was a balloonhead."

LaSan shook her head, her lips tight, her eyes angry. "Was he supposed to be a friend of *mine?*"

"I don't know," Grace said, "but Louise told Tina she couldn't understand how her credit card got into the hands of some East Side junkie."

"What!" LaSan blurted, for she knew what Louise meant by "East Side."

"Wait a minute," Sunny said, "do you mean to tell me that Louise told Tina she *happened* to know this clerk, and he said he *happened* to remember some black guy coming in and using a credit card saying Tina?"

Grace shrugged, smiling, and LaSan shook her head and sighed.

"Well what *I* want to know is," Sunny went on, "where *is* this place? I wanna shop there. Hey, I'll go in and say I'm Willie Nelson, and I want some free samples. Listen, if I get the same clerk, I'll have it made."

LaSan was angry. "Shit," she said. "When I use *my* credit card. . ." she complained, or started to. The complaint ended with a shake of her head. She glanced down at her food, then closed the container and put it away. "I gotta go," she said. "I can't get upset about this." She lit a cigarette, stood up, and headed toward the stairwell.

Grace glanced over her shoulder at LaSan. "Maybe I shouldn't've told her like that. *I* thought it was funny. She got so upset."

"Maybe you would've too, if you were black."

"Yeah, but she's gotta watch her ulcers."

Sunny shook her head. "That bitch Louise. . . ." She looked at Grace. "When did she tell Tina this? Was it before she talked to Danvers?"

"I don't know."

"I'll bet she did. And what kills me is she's got it both ways. She's saying, Don't give the promotion to a nigger who can't be trusted, and she's staying lily-white while she says it. You know? With that goddamned prissy friendly helpful face of hers. She's a goddamned trouble-maker. She's a *snake*! I wouldn't even *insult* snakes by calling her a snake. I would like to find out if she told Danvers any of this shit. Shit about *me*, too," she said, thumping her forefinger to her chest. "You know? And I want to see just who gets this goddamned promotion! That's what I want to see."

"Pretty high talk for a woman without a union," Grace murmured, and Sunny said, "Shit."

"Friday," Grace sighed. Shaking her head and reaching into her pocketbook, she pulled out a sandwich wrapped in wrinkled tin foil. "Friday, Friday, Friday." She opened the tin foil. "Thank God it's Friday. What? Did he give me peanut butter and jelly again? I keep telling him: Tommy likes peanut butter and jelly. I hate peanut butter and jelly."

On the way home from work that night, Sunny drove to a large supermarket that had a small kosher section, and she bought some *Shabbes* candles. At home, she looked through cardboard boxes in the spare room until she found the brass candlesticks that were a gift from her mother's sister. They were unappealingly new looking and always would be, treated as they were with non-tarnish coating. But they looked like they could be used for *shabbes,* and that had been, she suspected, her aunt's intent in giving them.

She couldn't remember the prayer exactly, and she didn't know if the Hebrew she said was the Hebrew she was supposed to say. But she didn't think it mattered. It gave her comfort to light the candles, to press her fingertips lightly against her closed eyes as she had seen her mother's mother do, rocking back and forth in her own consoling darkness.

That night she sat on the porch again. She sat there a long time. Once, she touched the *chai* that lay against her throat and remembered Kay's words, "I hope it reminds you of our life together." Now the words had a different, bitter meaning.

She went to bed but couldn't sleep. Between the Video Palace and the Dew Drop Inn, there was little peace on a warm spring night. She tossed and turned, plumped her pillow, annoying Whiskers who kept looking up, sleepy-eyed, and giving petulant meows. "I'm *sorry*, Whiskers," she said, "but *we share* this bed, you know? I mean I'm not comfortable! You're a cat and maybe it's easier for you to get comfortable. I'm a human being, and I have a lot on my mind."

He blinked at her, disinterested in her explanation, yawned, and closed his eyes, trying to recapture his mood of comfort. But Sunny wouldn't lie still, and finally he jumped off the bed, stretched, and walked through the open door into the living room, not looking back when Sunny called, "Whiskers! Goddamned cat has to have everything his own way," she complained to herself, and sighing, closed her eyes once more.

Finally, Sunny fell asleep. It was a fitful sleep, however, and several times she woke from dreams of a violent city to hear the sounds of angry voices and machines. After awhile, she fell into a heavy sleep. She slept for some time, and was suddenly wakened by someone screaming.

Her first thought as she sat upright was that it was Kay, but she realized it was coming from outside. She went to the window and looked toward the Dew Drop Inn.

Outside the bar, in the street, a tall, burly man was swinging a bat over his head, and as she looked, he brought it down with a sickening sound on the head of a man who had fallen to his knees. By the glow of the street light, she saw blood splatter onto the street, and the man screamed again. A car drove by, swerving to avoid them.

"Oh my God. . ." she whispered, pressing her hands to the window. Without knowing she would do it, she cried, "Stop!" and banged her fists against the glass. "Stop! Stop! Oh God, please stop!"

She stood there, her fists clenched against the glass. It was silent, and becoming self-conscious, she looked at the houses on either side to see if anyone had seen this frantic woman banging on the glass as though it were a cage, and she were raging for her freedom.

Then she thought, if they'd seen her panic, they surely would have seen the reason.

Someone must have called the police, for she heard a siren. The burly man heard it too: he tossed the bat under a car and ran.

A squad car pulled up. She saw police officers talking to bar patrons, but no one, apparently, knew anything. The victim was taken away in an ambulance, and the officers, shrugging, got back into the squad car and drove away.

The night was quiet once more. Sunny went back to bed. She lay there a long time, looking through the windows, past the leaves, to the Armory. She heard a night bird cawing as it swooped down to the Armory roof. Back and forth it went. It seemed, as she listened, that there were two birds. She imagined they had a nest and were catching mice or other food and bringing it back to feed their hungry, clamouring children.

Toward dawn, she had a dream.

She dreamed it was morning, and she was standing on the steps of the downstairs porch. It was a lovely day, the air sweet and uplifting. As she stood there, she happened to glance at the luxuriously spreading bush beside the steps. Its leaves were brilliantly green and vibrant with life. On one of the leaves she saw a bug. It was clearly a bug, yet clearly more. It had a round red and black bug's body like a lady bug, but was more spotted. Its face was a bug face, but its eyes, she saw as it woke and looked at her, seemed almost human. Human? Perhaps not human, but sympathetic, warm, compassionate.

It yawned and stretched like a cat would, or a dog, front legs reaching forward, back end up in the air. It made her laugh. The animal blinked at her lazily, smiling, and made itself comfortable again, placing its sleepy head on a front foreleg. Watching, she understood with a burst of love that there was nothing more glorious in the world than to lie on a leaf on a summer day.

The bug blinked again and gazed sleepy-eyed across the street to the base of the Armory. She followed its gaze and saw some children playing. She and the bug looked at each other and smiled indulgently, the way people sometimes do when they say, "Children. . . ."

But time was passing. The earth was turning, and the shadow of the Armory was lengthening slowly but surely toward the children. Her heart began to pound with fear. She wanted to cry, "Look!" But she sensed that the children were too busy playing to hear, and that the bug could not comprehend what the Armory's shadow meant.

She woke with her heart pounding.

She lay there awhile, then got up to start her day.

She had planned to go visit Meryl that afternoon. In the morning, she baked a batch of oatmeal cookies with chocolate chips because Meryl liked them that way. When the cookies were cool, she lined a shoebox with clean newspaper, piled in the cookies carefully, and closed and taped the box.

By the time she left the house, it was early afternoon. She stood on the porch steps a few moments, looking down at the bush and up the street toward the Dew Drop Inn.

She went to her car and put the cookies inside, closed the door, walked up the block toward the bar. At the curb, she stopped and looked into the street. The blood was still there. Faded already. Even as she watched, a car drove over the spot. She saw the tires circle the spot and watched them spin as the car drove up the street. She wondered, Were there now molecules of blood on the tires? Where would the car go?

She glanced up and down the street. It was a regular day, a Saturday in June. People were going places, doing things. She realized as she looked around that she was standing in the wrong place. Something was wrong. She couldn't see what she wanted to see. Then she knew: she couldn't see herself.

Sunny crossed the street to the other curb. Standing in front of the Dew Drop Inn, she looked down at the blood again and up at the house in mid-block, the windowed porch where she had pounded her fists. As she stood there, a van went by. She barely saw it, but she knew that she'd seen it before and realized what it was.

On the entire side of a new van was painted a pornographic rendition of a torture chamber. Against a gray stone wall, a big-bosomed woman was hanging by her wrists, her long blonde hair obscuring her face. Another big-bosomed woman lay on a wooden plank, bound and screaming. There were iron torture devices hanging on a far wall. And to complete the picture were two pale gnome-like men wearing hooded cassocks. They had pointed ears, long crooked noses and long fingers, and they reached toward the women, leering and drooling.

This picture was on a van that drove through the streets of the city. She had seen it once in a supermarket parking lot. She'd stood there alone, her arms full of groceries, and for a moment she'd thought she'd gone mad. But it was real, and she was enraged. She'd imagined herself heaving a bucket of red paint on the picture and running. Later, she'd remembered how clean the van was, how well-kept, how shiny. She'd thought, He probably thinks it's a work of art. He's probably very proud. Maybe he even painted it himself.

Now, she watched it disappear down the street and with it the blood of a man who'd been beaten.

Her gaze fell to the street. She had an urge to get down on her hands and knees and sniff at the spot, like an animal. It struck her as ironic that on this very corner blood could be splattered, and torture flaunted as art, but if a woman knelt to smell the pain of another animal, she might be carted away and locked up.

As she stood there, an old stray dog came out of an alley, its haunches and ribs pathetically outlined. Overhead, birds flew; and in the tree across the street, a squirrel sat watching. This, too, had once been the quarry in a sense, and now the only animals that lived here were those that could survive alongside Man.

She walked to the car. As she did, she touched the *chai* at her throat. She thought of Kay and was reminded of their life together.

She spent a nice afternoon with Meryl. Meryl was full of news about the Depot and the Encampment, the military budget, and the possibility that Joe might get laid off from his job. Rachel was three months old and beginning to smile.

She stayed for supper. Before she left, Meryl gave her a jar of fresh carrot juice and instructions to bring it to Rose before she went home. "Now don't forget!" Meryl called out the door as Sunny got into her car.

"You're such a *nag*," Sunny muttered. "I won't forget!" But she did, and instead of going to Rose's, she went home.

The apartment was empty. On the kitchen table was a note. It read, "Sunny, I've gone to the park, Kay." She picked up the note and stared at it. When she opened the cabinet under the sink, she saw other notes, crumpled and thrown away. She picked up one, and another. Holding the note Kay had left, she sat at the kitchen table and put down the juice.

The *juice,* she remembered, and sighed. You, she thought to herself, are a knucklehead.

There was a pencil on the table. She turned over Kay's note and wrote, "Kay, I've gont to Rosie's and will be back later, Sunny."

She found Rose sitting on the stoop, enjoying the warm spring air. "*Oy! Geshmack!*" Rose said when she saw her granddaughter.

"Here," Sunny said, sitting down beside her. "I got some stuff for you."

"Vhat's dot?"

"This is bread I made, and this. . ."

"Is dot vhite?" she asked skeptically.

"No, it's not white. It's whole wheat. God forbid I should give you white bread. I only brought you half a loaf 'cause I didn't know if you'd finish it, but if you finish it, let me know and next time I'll bring you more."

"Vhat's dot?"

"That's carrot juice from Meryl."

"Did she peel it?"

"No, Grandma, she didn't peel it. Jesus Christ, you'd think we're trying to poison you. Here, drink it. It'll put hair on your chest," she said, and smiled, remembering that it was what Evie used to say about eating onions.

Rose nodded. "I gotta drink it now, so deh vitamins, dey should still be good. Dot Vitamin C, it goes avay qvick, like dot," she said, rapping her fist into the air since she could not snap her fingers any more because of her arthritis. She unscrewed the cover and drank. "*Oy, geshmack!* It's so sveet!"

"Yeah. She added an apple so it'd be sweet."

Rose stopped drinking. "Did she peel it?"

"No, she *didn't* peel it. It's all in there: peels, pits, core. She probably threw in a few leaves, just to make you happy."

"Leaves?"

"Just drink it, Grandma."

"You vant some?"

"Yeah, I'll drink. . . . *Oy, geshmack!*" she cried, and Rose laughed.

She handed the juice back to Rose and gazed across the street. From the clothesline beyond the vacant lot hung several large sheets. It would be dusk soon, and Sunny wondered if the woman would lean out her window and pull in the line before night. If not, the sheets would be damp with dew the next morning and would have to dry in the sun again. She imagined the wonderful smell, imagined the woman pressing her face into fresh sheets as she took them off the line.

Rose was handing her the juice. She drank and said, "Grandma. . . did anything happen out in the yard that day, the day Grandpa died?"

Rose gave a shake of her head, not back and forth, but side to side. "Ah!" she said, commenting on all the troubles she'd seen.

"Did anything happen with. . . Jack?"

Rose sighed. "Jack came to get deh money vhat ve been savin'."

"The money you put away every week for us?"

"I diden vanna give it but Pa says, 'Give it, it's his money.' " She shrugged to indicate that though she knew she'd been right, she'd had to give in to the forces that opposed her. "I said to Pa dot he is just like Eva—he spends alotteh money, don't know how to save it."

"Did you say it in English?"

"In English?" She thought. "Nuh! In Yiddish, I say it."

"Did Jack understand?"

Rose looked at her, and it was clear from her expression that this was the question she had wanted to avoid, and now that it was here. . . ."I t'ink he undehstand."

"So what happened?"

"Vell. . . I go off into deh house, and I see Pa is talkin' to Jack. Outta deh vindeh, I see it. Pa is talkin' an' talkin', and Jack, he goes like dis," she said and shook off an imaginary hand from her arm, "and he points at Pa like dis, and he yells somet'ing."

"Did you hear it?"

"Nuh! Diden hear not'ing. And den. . . Jack, he goes ahlt, and I'm sitting in deh kitchen, and a banging comes on deh door, and somevun comes and says to you muddaih, 'Messes Rosent'al, come qvick, you faddeh is fallen down.' " She looked at Sunny with a kind of shrug to show that her story was at an end. "An ve go see. . . an' Pa is lyin' on deh grass."

They sat in silence for some time. When the sun set, there was a chill to the air. "You vanna sveateh?" Rose asked. Sunny shook her head. "You *got* a sveateh?"

"I got one at home. Listen Grandma, I have to ask you a question. How come Aunt Evie was living at home when she was almost thirty? How come she wasn't married?"

"Uh!" Rose said, as if Sunny had hit upon a source of exasperation. "She diden vahn no husband."

"She didn't want to get married?"

Rose shook her head. "Nuh! Diden vahn."

"So why didn't she leave home? You know, just go out and get her own place."

Rose shook her head again. "Ve diden do dot."

"You didn't. . . you mean an unmarried girl couldn't live on her own?"

"It vas a *shanda*."

Sunny looked at her. "Who said?"

165

"Eh?"
"Who *said* it was a *shanda?*"
"Pa."
"Grandpa?"
"No. *My* faddeh."

Sunny nodded. "You know, Grandma, I think it was a big mistake not to tell Jack from the beginning. He always used to wonder about his mother. He always used to ask *me*."

"Yah. It vas a big mistake. A *big* vun."

Sunny shivered. Rose slapped her hands down in decision and stood up, announcing that it was time to go in. As Sunny climbed the stairs, something struck her. When she and Rose were settled in the living room, and Rose had turned on the television for her granddaughter and her granddaughter had turned it off, she asked, "Grandma, why did Aunt Evie name him Jack?"

"Eh?"

"Why did she name him Jack? I mean, isn't it true that according to Jewish Law, you can't name a baby after somebody living? She must've known about your brother Yankel."

"Yankel, dot bestid."

"Isn't that the same name? Isn't Yankel the Yiddish for Yacov? Isn't that Jacob?"

Rose gave her a look, as though about to impart a great piece of information. "Vell, I'm gonna tell you. I t'ink she done it *auf tse luchas*. She vas dot vay sometime."

"What does that mean?"

"It means. . . it means. . . it means *auf tse luchas*."

"Thanks, Grandma. You're a big help."

"He is like dot too."

"Who?"

"Jack."

She smiled, not understanding, and yawned. She took off her shoes and lay down on the couch. A glass fruit bowl was directly in the line of her vision, and she gazed at it sleepily. It did not contain fruit as it was meant to, but was a catchall for thread and thimbles, old photographs, safety pins, and old letters.

She remembered Kay's notes, all thrown away. They'd begun and ended with different words and different phrasing, but they'd all said the same thing between the lines: I love you. Please forgive me.

She blinked sleepily, and when her eyes opened, she found herself looking at an old photograph. It was the women of the family.

That was how they took pictures: the women gathering for one portrait, taken by Mo; the men gathering for the one Sylvia took. In this one, Sunny, still Sonia, was a toddler, held in her mother's arms. Perhaps Mo had tried to get her to smile, for she was laughing and turning away from the camera shyly.

Sylvia was managing a tired smile. Norma stood posing at her side, trying to look grown up. Next to Sylvia was Rose, grinning, as she always did when posing for posterity. Her arm was around the back of her daughter, Eva, her hand on Eva's neck.

But Eva, dressed in a cardigan sweater with a scarf tied jauntily at the neck, was turned away, looking at the camera resentfully. She did not want to be there. It was obvious from her pose and from her eyes.

The picture shocked Sunny. She had seen it before, but she'd never really *seen* it. She'd idolized Eva. When she was a child, she'd always wanted to be a secretary, just like Auntie E. She thought of Jack as Eva's son and suddenly felt tired. "Grandma, I think I'm going to take a little nap, okay?"

"Of course, my dahling child. *Gay shlofen, meine kinder.* You body needs alotteh sleep. You need sleep!" she said, leaning forward so Sunny could get the message. Sunny gave a tired little giggle but was too tired to ask, Grandma, how can I sleep with you yelling at me like that? She closed her eyes and was asleep.

The next thing she knew she was being shaken, and a voice was calling, "Sonia! Vake up! It's by you 'ouse!"

"What? What? *What's* buying my house?" She sat up, rubbing her eyes. The sky outside was dark, but the sky on the television screen was full of flames. "It's dot place!" Rose was saying. "By you 'ouse!" It was the Armory.

"Oh my god. Kay!" She jumped up and grabbed her keys, heading out the door. "I gotta go, Grandma. Call my mother and tell her I'm okay!" she called over her shoulder, for she was already running down the stairs.

Half way home she saw the flames. Please, God, she prayed, let her be all right. And Whiskers, too. Please.

She parked the car a block away and ran toward the crowds that stood behind the police barricades. Looking up past the thick jets of shooting water, she saw the Armory towers illuminated by fire. Smoke rolled overhead, and burning embers fell from the sky.

Fire engines and police cars were everywhere, and snaking hoses criss-crossed the street. The firemen worked intently, trying to do their jobs in spite of the crowd. But it was the crowd that drew Sunny's attention: she was looking for Kay.

She made her way through the tangle of people, their faces illuminated by firelight. She saw that their reactions depended on the proximity of their homes to the fire. The people who lived across the street from the main part of the fire, those whose homes were in immediate danger, were tense with fear. Yet there were couples holding hands, strolling around, eating potato chips as though they were watching an entertainment. The Armory Fire in Living Color.

She saw Mrs. Mancuso, who was weeping silently, her hands shaking as she lifted a handkerchief to her eyes. Her husband had his hand around her shoulder. He was trying to comfort her awkwardly while his attention was fixed on the other hand, which held a cigarette. As he brought the smoked-down cigarette to his lips for one last long delicious drag, his wife snapped, "Can't you stop *smoking*? Isn't there *enough* smoke around here?" Seeing Sunny, she blurted, "Cancer sticks! He has to have his cancer sticks!" and went on weeping.

Mr. Mancuso gave an almost imperceptible shrug that meant his wife was upset, and Sunny shouldn't pay any attention to her. She nodded to him and said to his wife, "Is the house all right, Mrs. Mancuso? Have you seen my friend?"

Mrs. Mancuso nodded yes for the house and no for the friend.

"Were you here when it happened?"

"No, we just got back," her husband said.

"Thank *God* the worst of it is on the other side. Thank God," Mrs. Mancuso murmured.

Sunny patted her arm and moved off to find Kay. She asked several people, "Was anybody hurt? Are there any injured?" but no one seemed to know. There were rumors of ammunition stored in the Armory, rumors of napalm.

Turning toward the fire again, she looked up at the Armory roof in violent flames and remembered the night birds. If their nest was there as she'd imagined, what had happened to the babies? Looking up through the smoke, she wondered if somewhere in the sky, the night birds were swooping down in large widening circles, one and then the other, cawing out in fear for their children. She felt tears come suddenly to her eyes. As they did, she felt a hand on her shoulder. Hardly breathing, she turned and saw Kay, her face tense with anxiety.

"Sunny," Kay whispered hoarsely. She looked like she was about to cry. She'd taken her hand away, but now she reached out hesitantly and asked in a voice that sounded strangely polite, "Are you all right?"

Sunny nodded, and they were in each other's arms.

"Sunny," Kay kept saying. "Sunny. . . Sunny," and Sunny knew what she meant. She nodded and began to cry herself while there in the crowd they clung in an embrace—like mother and child, like sisters. Like friends. Like lovers. Like women.

Chapter 9

The Quarry III

The Armory fire was front-page news and normally would have been a focal point for gossip in the Buffalo offices of Imperial Dynamics. Probably among many people unaffected by the decision about the promotion, it was. "Wasn't that something about the fire?" someone would ask, and information would be traded, much of it to do with one's proximity to the event or experience with similar events. "My brother-in-law lives over near Niagara Street, and *he* said. . . ." Or, "Well *I* was in a fire, and let me tell you. . . ."

But at the corner table of the basement cafeteria, the mood was glum. That morning, the decision about the promotion had been announced: Louise Deckert was being promoted. The promotion would take effect on Monday, July 6th, several weeks hence. In addition, the Big Boss from General Office ("Good old B.O.," Grace muttered) had decreed that the Buffalo office should undergo reorganization. One element of this reorganization, they'd already learned, was that Grace was being transferred to the Mail Room. At this point they knew nothing else, but Sunny had the feeling that somehow Louise would be put in a position of power in relation to her.

She had the feeling because of something she'd seen in Louise's eyes when they'd passed in the hall that morning: a smug warning and a confirmation of victory.

Sunny had narrated her hallway experience with Louise, and

169

LaSan had nodded. She said that she'd heard that Louise was going to be made Supervisor of five women, including Sunny, LaSan, and Tina.

"*Tina!*" Sunny groaned. "Oh God, I can see it all now."

Across the table, Grace was sitting resting on her elbows, her hands covering her face. She was shaking her head. "Oh God, I don't know what I'm going to *do*," she complained. She was talking not about any of the organizational changes at Imperial Dynamics, but about her daughter, who had dyed her hair purple. "Oh Dear Lord. It wouldn't be so bad if there was somebody *else* in the family with purple hair. I could just say, you know, she takes after Aunt *Josie* or somebody."

"Grace," LaSan said, "Why don't you shut up about your damned daughter. She probably looks better like that." And with this she lifted her spoon to her mouth, giving a look of annoyed distaste at the diet cottage cheese.

When they were almost done eating, Louise approached the table looking cheery and enthusiastic. "Girls! Isn't it *wonderful?!*" she cooed, and gave Sunny and LaSan a look fraught with so much meaning that they exchanged a glance.

LaSan pushed her chair back, gathering her things. She stood up, looked Louise in the eye, and said, "I got *business* to take care of."

She'd said it so disdainfully that Louise flushed and stood frozen as LaSan, looking languid and bored, nodded good-bye to Sunny and Grace and headed toward the stairwell.

Louise said something and looked away. Sunny didn't know what she said. She was staring at Louise's fingernails. One of the cuticles was ripped and blood-stained. Sunny watched Louise walk away, her back stiff and self-conscious as she sat down across from Tina and began to talk.

Grace had been watching LaSan as she disappeared around the landing. Now she turned to Sunny, shaking her head and grinning. "Woman makes a great exit, doesn't she? You wouldn't know she's only going up there to wash her Tupperware."

"Why *does* she leave early every day?"

"She goes to call her mother."

"Oh."

"You oughtta ask her to tell you about her mother some day. Her mother's a riot. Ida. . ." she murmured, and then sighed, for her thoughts were already returning to the problem at hand. "What am I gonna do? The husband is gonna *shit* a *brick*. He is. I know he is. He's gonna just shit a brick."

"Why, it's not your fault."

"Yes, it is. *I* was the one who told Connie I thought punk was cute. Oh God," she looked up at the ceiling. "Lord, I know I've used your name in vain, and you really hate it when people do that and then come begging favors, and I don't want you to think I've undergone instant repentance just because I happen to have a little bit of trouble, but if you change Connie's hair back to brown by three-thirty, I *swear* I'll make a novena. I'll receive Communion every Sunday at six o'clock Mass." She paused a moment, and pointing her finger as a reminder said, "But it's gotta be by three-thirty when The Husband gets home."

"You know," Sunny said. "I think we should get Louise a promotion present. A set of phony fingernails. Really. Because every time I get to working up a good hate for her, I always happen to glance down and see those goddamned gnawed-down fingernails. You know?"

All afternoon Grace groaned about her daughter and her husband, crooning out every so often, "When the deeeep purple hmmm. . . la-la-laa-la-la-la-la. . . ." At quitting time, she shook Sunny's hand in a solemn farewell and said, "You're not gonna have Grace Catalano to kick around anymore."

"Tell me all about it tomorrow, dear."

Grace sighed, and headed toward the door. At the door she stopped and turned. "I heard you had some excitement last night."

Sunny looked at her askance, her smile ever-so-slightly suggestive. "You mean you *heard* about that?"

Grace laughed. "Aha, now I *will* be here on Tuesday," she promised, and headed down the hall.

Sunny covered her typewriter and the terminal, got her pocketbook, turned off the light, and left.

When she got home and opened the door, she found Kay at the kitchen sink, rinsing spinach for a salad.

Sunny hesitated, shy about their reawakened intimacy, not quite sure what to say or how Kay would respond. One look at Kay's face, however, told her that Kay was feeling the same thing.

"Hello," Kay said, and Sunny smiled.

In spite of what Sunny hoped for, however, it was not that simple. She knew that a real and lasting intimacy was based upon the truth.

Mid-way through supper, Sunny fell strangely silent. And after they finished eating, when Kay pushed back her chair, Sunny put out her hand and said, "Wait. I want to tell you about Jack."

At first, Kay had not believed Sunny.

Then, she was angry at the way Sunny had told her.

Next, she was angry that Sunny had not told her to begin with, though she understood by the end of that first long conversation *why* Sunny hadn't told her. But still. . . .

The following weeks were a time of turmoil. Kay's anger peaked and waned. Several times she felt so despairing of their relationship ever working that she wanted to pack her bags and move out. But she did not.

She received a notice of a three thousand dollar assistantship to the

U.B. Law School. She called the school that day, accepted the offer, and sent a letter to Columbia telling them of her decision. At first she was elated about the assistantship and its implications. She and Sunny went out to celebrate. After they returned home, however, Mrs. Rosenthal phoned and invited them to a Fourth of July cookout, and Kay was reminded of all that lay behind them. She felt sure it could never be resolved. When Sunny hung up the phone, they argued.

"Take responsibility!" Kay shouted at one point. "You had a part in this. Okay, I know what I did. I made a dumb, stupid, foolish mistake. But *you* had a part in it, *too*. You lied to me from the very beginning. Maybe you didn't think it would matter, or maybe you didn't know *how* to tell me, or even if you could *trust* me. But nevertheless, you lied."

For Kay, that argument more than any other "cleared the air," as Sunny said. It was a "good" argument, as opposed to the "bad" ones, the ones about what kind of coffee to buy, or whose turn it was to take out the garbage.

They decided to go to the Rosenthals' cookout. Jack would not be there. He was moving in with some friends, and would be painting his room that weekend.

Sunny had been about to add that in the future she did not intend to alienate herself from family functions just because Jack might happen to be present, and she did not want to choose between Kay and family because Kay could not tolerate his presence. She decided, however, to say nothing. The air was clearer, but still tenuous.

Saturday, the Fourth, was a beautiful day, and in the morning the two women stayed in bed being lazy. As they lay there, Sunny on her side facing Kay, and Kay on her back, Whiskers jumped up and walked up the lump of Kay's body from her legs to her chest, where he plopped himself down and blinked at her. "I can't believe that this is the same cat that used to hate me," Kay said, reaching out and ruffling behind his ears. "He would never *look* at me, and now he acts like he *owns* me. He treats my body like his own private island," she said.

Sunny smiled. She was gazing at the bookcase under the window where, on the top shelf, she'd placed *Ravensbruch,* still unread. That week the library had sent her a second overdue notice, and she'd made a sad joke to Kay about the Library Police banging on the door in the middle of the night and taking her away to the sub-basement of the library, below the stacks, where there was a special Library Jail. She told herself that she should either read the book or return it. But she could do neither, even though she knew her behavior was neurotic and unproductive. The problem was that she could neither face that particular horror, nor forget it.

At noon they drove to the little side street off the lower end of

Elmwood Avenue and went upstairs to get Rose. When they pushed open the front door, they heard Rose talking in a loud voice, half in Yiddish and half in English. She was talking on the phone. When she saw Sunny and Kay, she said good-bye and hung up.

She said, "Hello! Hello! You luffly goil!" to Kay. To Sunny, she said, "You muddaih. . ." and shook her head meaningfully.

"My mother *what*?"

Rose held out her hands in a gesture of innocence. "She don' vahn me to be independen'. I'm in-de*penden*'. Dot's me." She nodded emphatically. "In-dependen'."

"Why doesn't she want you to be independent, Grandma?" Sunny asked, with a glance at Kay that said, Listen to this. "What is she doing?"

But to this, Rose gave her granddaughter another meaningful look, as though the information were knowledge she would not share.

Sunny nodded skeptically and murmured to Kay that this needed further investigation.

When they arrived at Mo and Sylvia's, it was obvious from the way the two women acted that they were at loggerheads. Rose flaunted her disdain, making cracks about Sylvia's cooking and housekeeping. To each little zinger, Sylvia would reply, "Ma, I'm not paying any attention to you."

After a number of "not paying any attentions," Rose went into the back yard to visit her dear son who (she lectured in a voice loud enough for those in the kitchen to hear) should never have married such a woman, a woman who did not even know how to cook or keep house.

"My mother-in-law, the *baleboosteh*," Sylvia muttered dryly to Sunny. To Kay, she vowed, "I am going to kill that woman. I am going to kill her. I was going to kill her last week, but Pa yelled down from heaven, 'Please! Keep her a little longer, please!' "

They laughed, then fell silent. "Pa always used to say, 'When I'm gone, you'll see.' He used to clean the house," she explained to Kay. "And guess who took the credit for it? Three guesses," she said to Sunny. "Uh! *Gottenyu*," she sighed, as her mother had sighed before her, and shook her head.

"So what's the story?" Sunny said. "Why won't you let Grandma be independent?"

"Is that what she told you?"

"Of course."

Sylvia shook her head. "Do you know what she's doing? She started a *junk* business."

"What?"

"You heard me. You know I noticed she had all this *stuff*," she said to Kay. "And for everything she's got a story for how she got it. And

173

she *sells* it. Or she trades with the people in the neighborhood for favors."

"Listen, Ma," Meryl said, just having come in from outside, "Grandma has the instincts of a con artist, long suppressed. I mean, think about it: Rosie Rosenthal. Doesn't that *sound* like a con artist? You know, she's raised her children, and done her work, and *I* think she oughtta be allowed to live her own life if she wants."

"Including going around picking garbage?"

"Hey, you'd be surprised what people throw out these days."

Sylvia shook her head. "Do you know what she did? She bought a dish drainer for twenty-five cents and sold it for seventy-five cents. And then she goes and *talks* about it at the Center. It's embarrassing! Does she *need* fifty cents?! I'll *give* her fifty cents."

"Ma," Meryl explained, "she doesn't want you to give her anything. She wants to earn it herself."

Sunny was frowning thoughtfully. Kay said, "Wait a minute. If that's the same dish drainer she got when she was with us at the Flea Market. . ."

"Right," Sunny agreed. "She paid *fifty* cents for it, not twenty-five."

At this Sylvia threw up her hands in exasperation. "She wanted me to think she made an extra quarter," she said, as if this justified her exasperation.

At that moment, they heard Mo bellowing from the back yard, "Where's the goddamned hamburgers?"

"Here." Sylvia opened the refrigerator and held out the platter to Meryl. "And tell your father," she directed, "to either watch his language or lower his voice. No, never mind. I'll tell him. It's time to eat anyway. Do we have everything?"

Later in the day, after the eating and the cleaning up, everyone was relaxing. Sylvia and Kay were in the house, and Mo and his son-in-law were sitting at the long folding table near the back door. Rose and her great-granddaughter Rachel were sleeping on a blanket under the tree. Sunny and Meryl sat in the back yard by the faded mural.

Meryl was embroidering on a large piece of muslin. "By the way," Meryl said, "how's it look over there, at the Armory?"

"Pretty messy."

"Unbelievable," Meryl murmured, and turned the material over to check the tightness of a thread.

Sunny watched her. The embroidery with all the colored threads reminded her of a sweater she had sat and watched someone knit. Who? Her aunt? Her mother's sister? Yes. She'd called it a Fair Isle sweater, and Sunny had watched as her Aunt Dotty knit the strands of so many colored wools into a pattern. It was impossible seeing the finished piece to follow each color individually, the reds and blues and greens. Though the "right" side was pretty, on the inside it looked all a jumble of colored lines. To understand the finished piece, she'd decided, it was necessary to see the separate skeins of wool and the labor that put them together.

"One day to the next," Meryl was saying, "and the Armory's gone."

"Well, not 'gone,'" Sunny said, for the wall facing her house was still standing.

"Wouldn't it be nice if it were that easy? Swords into plowshares. . ." she murmured. "You know, maybe when we wrap the ribbon around the Pentagon, we'll be able to levitate it out into outer space. Of course not that outer space would want it."

"What ribbon?"

"This one," Meryl said, and held up her embroidery.

"What's that?"

"It's going to be the date of Rachel's birthday. See how I'm working it into the design?"

"But what *is* it?"

"It's the Pentagon Ribbon. Women from all over are making things on pieces of muslin to show what we love and what we'll lose if there's a nuclear war. They're going to sew all the pieces together, and in 1985, on the fortieth anniversary of Hiroshima, we're going to wrap it around the Pentagon."

Sunny snorted. "Wrap it around the Pentagon. . ."

"Yup. And the calculation is that from the rate pieces are coming in, we'll have enough to wrap it around twice."

"Twice!? Around the *Pentagon?*"

"Twice. Around the Pentagon. You should make a piece."

Sunny shrugged. "What would I put on it?"

"I don't know. What do you love?"

She looked around and saw the lovely summer day, the growing things, the wildflowers against the fence. . . . "Wildflowers," she said.

"So, put wildflowers on it. You know how to knit, knit a design of wildflowers."

"Fair Isle," Sunny murmured.

"You didn't see my pictures of the Encampment?"

"No."

"They're in my embroidery basket."

Sunny got the photographs and looked through them one by one while Meryl kept up an enthusiastic monologue about the Encampment, the Ribbon, and the August first demonstration. Meryl said that there was going to be a civil disobedience on the first, and she and her friend Francis had been talking about participating along with the other women.

Finally Sunny, who had been listening with increasing skepticism, said, "And are all these wonderful women going to end the threat of nuclear war?" She'd meant the question seriously and was surprised to hear her voice sounding so flippant, as though she were trying to convince herself not to care.

Meryl glanced at her, stuck the needle in the material, and pulled it through the other side. "I *hope* we're going to end it. Because if *we* don't, I don't know who will. And if we don't do it *now*. . . ." She didn't finish the thought. She shook her head and sighed, and made another stitch.

Sunny nodded. "Who's this?"

"That's Francis."

"She's cute. What does she do for a living?"

"She works with mentally retarded adults. She's a nun."

"A nun?"

"Yeah. Whattsamatter, you prejudiced?"

"Who, me?" Sunny asked innocently. When Meryl didn't answer, she said, "I don't know, Meryl. First you go and marry a *taliener,* then it's 'swords into plowshares,' and now, hanging around with nuns. . ."

"Sister Dearest, 'swords into plowshares' is from the *Old* Testament."

"Well. . . whatever."

"Francis is a very committed woman. She's very knowledgeable."

Sunny nodded. "Nice pictures," she said, putting them back into Meryl's embroidery basket.

She continued to watch Meryl embroider the date of Rachel's birthday and to listen as Meryl talked about the Women's Peace Encampment. At one point, Meryl, in talking about how the Encampment was sometimes perceived, said in a joking manner, "Vegetarians, witches, and lesbians! Vegetarians, can you imagine?"

Sunny did not comment. She'd resented the ease with which Meryl had been sprinkling that word into her conversation. It was all very nice to make progress, she thought, but still. . . .

"Is that your new toy?" she inquired dryly.

"What?"

"That word. I mean, you just got it. Don't wear it out."

Meryl blushed. She knew exactly what Sunny meant.

"Go ahead," Sunny said. "Tell me more about the Encampment.

Later, toward dusk, Sunny and Kay and Rose departed. "Goodbye! Good-bye!" Sunny called, "Good ribbons to bad rubbish!" and she kissed them all good-bye. Mo and Sylvia, Joe, Rachel.

"You gonna kiss me good-bye?" Meryl asked.

"Of *course,* my darling knucklehead!" Sunny said, and kissed her sister good-bye.

In the car, Kay commented that she was thirsty. Rose invited her upstairs for a glass of water, listing, all the way to her house, the beverages she had—juice, and milk, and water—and lecturing the two girls on the importance of consuming sufficient liquids.

Rose unlocked the outside door. When they reached the upstairs landing, the phone began to ring, and Sunny went to answer it. "It's Mrs. Sadetsky," she said, holding her hand over the receiver. Rose shook her head. "Nuh! I don' vahn. Not me."

"But what am I supposed to *tell* her?" she asked. Rose said, "I'm *busy.*"

"Okay." She gave the message to Mrs. Sadetsky. When she turned around, she saw Rose and Kay sitting at the kitchen table. Kay was drinking a glass of water, and Rose was holding out a sweater.

It was dark green and looked like it had seen too many washings. There was a small rip in the shoulder seam near the collar.

"Look," she offered. "Bran' new. You vahn it? Deh lady vhat give it to me said she bought it fuh deh son, but it didn't fit. So she give it to me. It's a good sveateh, it's vool," she said, and handed it to Sunny.

Sunny glanced at the label. It read, "F.W. Woolworth, 100% Acrilan."

"Sure, Grandma. Wool. Now tell me about the choice real estate you have for sale in the Florida swamps."

"I vashed it," she said to Sunny, and repeated to Kay, "I vashed it."

"No, Grandma, I'm not interested."

She shrugged, then thought of something else. "Lissen. . . I found deh letteh."

"What letter?"

"De vun Pa lost. You know. . . ." She leaned forward confidentially. "He is askin' me alotteh qvestions."

"Who?"

"Jack. An' I tell him, it vas a *big mistake* not to tell him. A *big* vun," she said as if trying to convince Sunny, who managed a dry smile. "I think you're right, Grandma."

"Shoo, I'm right. I'm smott, I alvays been smott. I can speak six langviges."

"And all of them at once," Sunny murmured to Kay, who had looked uncomfortable since the mention of Jack's name.

"He is askin' me alotteh qvestions. He is askin' me about you."

"About me?"

Rose nodded. "And I tell him, you a luffly goil."

Sunny smiled. "Thank you, Grandma."

"Vhy not? I saved you life," she said.

On the way home, Sunny began to wonder. What letter was Rose talking about? What did it say? And without thinking, she said, "You know, I'm going to have to ask my Grandmother about that letter from Jack."

Kay did not respond. But a few minutes later, she said, "You know you shouldn't have refused that sweater. You hurt your grandmother's feelings."

"*I* hurt her feelings?"

"Yes. You shouldn't be so proud. It wasn't a bad sweater. There was nothing wrong with it. So the shoulder seam was ripped, so what. You could've sewn it. She *said* it was *clean*. You could've worn it around the house."

Sunny shrugged. "Yeah. Maybe you're right."

"And why are you so goddamned condescending? How do you know that your grandmother's fight with her friend isn't as important to her in her own way as your fight is with me?"

"*What* are you *talking* about?"

"The way you say her 'feud' with her friend. It's so *condescending!*"

"Well, look. Maybe you're right, but why are you getting all bent out of shape? What's your problem?"

"*I* don't have a problem!"

They had reached the house. Sunny shut off the engine. "Look. Jack is my. . . my. . . well, what*ever* he is, I can't help loving him at the same time that I hate him. I'm sorry if you get upset when I mention his name. Jack being my family is something you're going to have to accept. It's *one* of the things you should have thought of *before.*"

And with this, she got out of the car and slammed the door. Kay followed her, angry.

But later that evening they sat on the porch, holding hands and talking quietly. Whiskers lay between them, purring, his paws stretching out over the edge of the army cot.

"I know what you mean," Sunny was saying. "The thing is, though, *why* did I withdraw from you? You know? *I* think I withdrew because I felt I needed to *hide* myself from you. And that makes me mad because you knew what I'd been through. And still, you pursued me."

"I didn't *pursue* you!"

"Oh, you know what I mean! I don't mean you pursued me like a Leaping Lesbian, I mean. . . you fell in *love* with me. And what *I* want to know is, What did you fall in love *with*? It must've been just parts of me. Because there were whole parts I felt I had to hide." She paused, frowning. "Maybe I can't put all of that on you because I was prone to hiding anyway. But still. . . ."

Kay nodded, for she'd been thinking of her image of Sunny as Amazon. "I know what you mean. For a long time there were parts of you I didn't want to see. Parts that were. . . weak. . . ."

"But Kay, I have to be strong for that whole world out there. If I can't be weak once in awhile with you, where *can* I? Where can I show those things, who can I go to if not to someone who loves and understands me? Isn't that what our relationship means? I mean. . . isn't that one of the things we're supposed to be for one another? I don't know about you, but that's what I wanted. I wanted us to be *family* to one another. Now if you wanted a casual six-month affair before you left town for law school, then I guess we wanted different things, and we should've been more clear about that from the beginning."

"Wait a minute," Kay said. "Maybe you're right, at least in part. But while you were all involved in your own problems, I was trying to make decisions about law school. And I didn't notice you being any too anxious to help me decide, or to even talk about it. My decision about law school would have determined the possibilities in our relationship. There wouldn't *be* any possibility if I wasn't here."

"But listen, Kay, when you came back home all full of plans about Columbia, I'd just found a lump in my breast. I mean, put it in perspective. You didn't give me any time. I wasn't there for you, so boom! You ran to *him*."

Kay stood up and faced Sunny. "Okay. So I made a mistake. *I made a mistake.* Now are you ever going to be able to *forgive* me for that?"

There was a silence. Sunny sighed and asked, "But how do I know you won't do it again?"

Kay's jaw dropped. "You mean there's another *Jack* lying in wait for me out there?"

Sunny looked at her. In spite of themselves, they both laughed, perhaps more than the comment merited. Kay sat down again. She took Sunny's hand in her own and said, "Look. I can't imagine I'll *ever* do anything like that again—lie to you like that. Betray you. I feel too ashamed. I feel too awful. It's no *fun*," she said with half a smile. "And I know you're angry, and hurt. . . and you have a right to be. But I don't want you to keep beating me with it forever. I want to know if you think you're ever going to be able to forgive me. I'm not asking for a guarantee. I'm just asking. . ." she thought and said the words carefully, ". . . for a realistic appraisal of your feelings."

Sunny nodded. She thought for a moment. "I *want* to forgive you. . . ." There had been a 'but' in her voice, and Kay looked at her. "I want to forgive you," she said, and this time it was only that simple statement.

"All right," Kay said. "That's good enough for me."

They sat there awhile longer. Kay made some warm milk for herself and a cup of tea for Sunny. They drank slowly, petting Whiskers, who was in his glory. They sat and looked at the trees, the street, the Armory wall. Then they went to bed.

The next morning Sunny woke early. Kay was still sleeping.

She ate a leisurely breakfast, cleaned the kitchen, and wrote Kay a note. She went outside, got into her car, and drove to the quarry.

She had been thinking about the quarry since her last painful visit. She had wondered, Was the quarry spoiled forever? Would she ever be able to go there again with that same loving feeling that had once filled her heart?

She parked the car, and walked down the winding pathway, more narrow now because of the lush growth on either side. At the last turn she paused and looked up.

As soon as she did, she knew something was different. She lowered her gaze again, not wanting to see, and continued on her way to the flat sandy rock. Again, she looked up.

The Quarry! It had always announced itself in her heart. But she saw now that the quarry was like an old friend she had never understood. She'd looked for all the good here, for seeing it had made her happy. Now something was different.

She was different. Her eyes were different. It was impossible for her not to see the machines dotting the landscape. Off to the side was a huge construction of stairs and shoots and graters that separated the earth and crushed it, to be sold by the company that owned the quarry. The quarry, she saw, was not an isolated patch of nature, a refuge from the city. It was a part of it all.

She sat down and took off her sandals, and rubbed the soles of her feet back and forth against the gritty surface. Looking out over the landscape, she thought of other times she had come here, and the people she'd come here with.

The breeze was strong. She looked off to the far ridge, and saw the leaves of the quaking aspen flutter. There was a small pond at the base of the hill where she sat. It had been mud last year and now was a pool of water. The water's surface rippled as the wind passed over it. She closed her eyes, feeling the wind on her face.

Yes, she thought, everything was connected, intrinsically bound together. And she, in its midst, had been a fool to think anything but the truth: that she was a part of it and had been so all along.

She sat there for a long time, thinking.

The breeze blew clouds across the sky, and she shivered, rubbing her bare arms. Soon the sky was gray and billowing.

She stood up, looking around one final time, then turned and headed up the path to the car.

When she reached the city, she drove toward the gray-shingled house. She had the feeling that Rose would not be home, but she went anyway. She parked the car and rang the bell. There was no answer. She rang again, waited, and walked around the side, down the narrow alley between the two houses to the back.

The yard was tiny, enclosed by a makeshift fence made of wood scraps and cast-off doors. The ground had been covered long ago, edge to edge, with cement, and whatever grew, grew in the old tins Sam had filled with soil. He grew tomatoes that when still green he pickled in a large barrel in the cellar. The soil he'd so carefully sifted was hardened in the tins, but even now, Sunny could almost taste those sour tomatoes: tangy, effervescent with garlic and dill.

As she climbed the steep wooden steps to the top, she thought about what she would say if Rose asked where she had been. She wondered, Why did they do that? Why had they always hidden the fact of Sunny going to the quarry? "Whatever you do," she remembered her mother saying, "don't tell your *grandmother* you went to the quarry."

But *why?*

At the top of the stairs, she remembered. Years ago, a child had drowned in the quarry, and after that Rose had always become angry and upset when she found out Sunny went there. The family shrugged and sighed at this. Their attitude was, Oh, Ma. . . . Finally, tired of hearing her warnings, they just stopped telling her the truth. It struck her now that Rose had been right to fear. Perhaps she'd seen the wrong time, the wrong place. But she'd seen a child drown.

Sunny leaned forward to peek through the slit of curtain on the window of the back door. She was looking into Sam's room, the back bedroom. Beyond that, the kitchen was empty, and she sensed even before knocking that no one was home. She got the skeleton key from its hiding place and unlocked the door.

Sam's bedroom was now cluttered with Rose's things. On the dresser was an old tube of lipstick that Rose used when she decided to "get spiffy," as she was saying of late. The cover was off, the lipstick was worn down, and there was a toothpick stuck inside so that Rose could get the last bit. Next to this was a strand of plastic pearls, the kind that pop together and apart to form a chain of whatever length the wearer wanted.

"Mmm. . ." Sunny murmured aloud. "Pearls and lipstick. Must have been a special occasion."

The bedclothes were pulled up hastily, and there was an indentation on the pillow. Rose was sleeping here these days.

On the wall above the chair, at eye level, there was a photograph of Sam's family. It was a formal portrait in sepia brown, taken when Sam had gone back to the Old Country in 1928. She looked at the faces.

They were peasants, she could see even from this picture: the men and women in heavy boots, the children in ill-fitting clothes. Sam, a young man, stood at the side, dressed in a suit that looked new and uncomfortable. He was smiling, nervous but proud, the son who'd gone to America and come back wearing a suit.

The woman sitting in the center—that must be Sam's mother, she thought. Her great-grandmother, Chaya Fayga. She wore a kerchief. Jewish women were required to shave their heads when they got married, and after that they wore a *sheitel,* a wig. But she wore a kerchief.

Why did she wear a kerchief? Sunny wondered. She realized there was no one she could ask.

At her knee was a little boy, looking shy and suppressing a giggle. Who was he? Who *were* all these people who had died? They had died, she knew that. Sam had tried to find them after the war, tried and tried again. But from Europe had come only silence.

She'd once seen Sam leaning forward in his easy chair, watching a documentary on the Holocaust. He watched intently, hardly breathing, trying to catch a glimpse among all the Jews in Europe, the faces altered by starvation, disease, and torture, of a face nevertheless somehow familiar. His family. His friends. People from a village that no longer existed. Anyone in all of Poland that he might know. But among all those faces, he never saw one from his life.

She looked at the photograph and tried to associate it with the pictures she'd seen at the library. But between the two images was a void in which her understanding foundered. They were realities that could never meet, yet had met.

The house was empty. She stood for a moment in the kitchen and looked around, feeling how empty it was. Debbie was gone. Sam was gone. Rose would some day be gone. She felt sad and angry. She walked into the living room thinking, Whatever you're looking for, you won't find it here.

But in the living room, when she saw the couch—or rather, when she saw the *shmatte,* an old sheet, that covered the slipcover that covered the couch, a couch whose springs were broken from sitting though whose fabric was like new—when she saw the couch, she smiled.

Unexpectedly, she'd remembered something: Auntie E sitting on that couch with her large purse open in her lap and her hand mirror held up before her face. She was playing for Sonia, looking into her own image adoringly and crooning: "I love you, my sweet em*bray*-sable you. I love you, my ir-re-*play*-sable you. . . . La de da de da de dah de dah! da-da-da-." And she laughed and winked at Sonia as if to say, What a *nut,* to look at herself in the mirror and sing.

Sunny stood there, her fingertips almost touching the easy chair in which Sam had sat. After supper he always fell asleep in this chair, and around ten, Rose would holler at him in Yiddish that he should wake up and go to sleep.

She had been smiling as she looked from the couch to the chair. But she remembered something, a day she had been here with Debbie, and her smile faded.

It was a summer afternoon. She'd been passing through the neighborhood and had stopped in to say hello. Rose had just finished dusting the living room. She was in the kitchen with Sam, cleaning out the refrigerator and arguing. Rose cleaned house like a resentful whirlwind, cursing the dirt as she moved things from one place to another. When she was done, Sam used to joke, it didn't look better, it just looked different.

Sunny had pulled the window shade against the hot afternoon glare and was sitting on the couch changing Debbie's diaper and uttering vague threats: "If you don't stop squirming. . . if you don't learn to *tell* me when you have to go potty. . . I know you can tell me, you're just too lazy. Next time, you *tell* me!"

The bickering in the kitchen had begun to escalate, and though she didn't understand most of the Yiddish words, the meaning was clear. Sam and Rose sometimes sounded like two escaped prisoners joined by leg irons, trying to make the best of a rotten situation and hating every minute of it.

Finally there was a simultaneous burst of angry words from them both, though Rose's was more forceful, continuing the attack as Sam's waned. It ended with Sam quitting the kitchen, saying to himself, "Her father should have slept that night."

He'd spoken the words in Yiddish, but Sunny understood, for it was what he sometimes said at the end of an unwinnable argument with Rose, either muttering to himself as he did now, or flinging the words at her in a parting shot. He wouldn't have said it had he thought Sunny understood, but she'd heard it often enough to ask her mother for a translation. Not wanting to embarrass him by her knowledge, she bent her head to hide her smile, concentrating on Debbie.

Debbie had seen Sam too, and just as Sunny finished with the diaper, she escaped and ran to him.

"Come back here," Sunny had complained, but Debbie shook her head and giggled. Just as she reached Sam, she turned around and looked at her mother, saying gleefully with her eyes that she would *not* come back.

Tears came to Sunny's eyes, and she said, "Dear God, will I ever stop crying about my baby?"

It was a question whose answer she knew. She walked to the door and opened it, and stepping to the landing, closed the door behind her.

The landing was dark, and the wooden bannister, painted with black enamel, was cool, almost slippery beneath her fingertips. Even in the darkness she saw that the landing was crowded with her grandmother's things: a cardboard box, a row of mason jars, an electric broom that undoubtedly needed to be fixed "just a little." A sweater was draped on the curve of the bannister, the dark green sweater she had refused.

She picked it up. It was getting cool outside, and the sweater, though shabby, would keep her warm.

She went home and parked the car under the wall of the Armory. She stood a moment, looking up at the windowed porch. Then she went into the back yard.

Opening the gate, she thought of the quarry and remembered how in the past she'd gone naked there. Too bad I couldn't do it here, she thought, and looked up at the surrounding houses. But a woman naked here would be a woman misunderstood.

She walked to the area that had been Mr. Mancuso's well-tended garden. Now it was a riotous growth of wildflowers and weeds: columbine and spearmint, lady's rocket and dandelions. Some were in their prime, while others had gone to seed, but each grew surely, according to its own internal pattern and its relation to the seasons.

The uncontrolled growth was a source of grief for her landlord. His wife had told Sunny one evening, "Mr. Mancuso can't work on his garden—his back, you know—and it's breaking his heart." She'd spoken with a touch of melodrama, and Sunny had shrugged. But now the abandoned garden seemed like an affirmation of victory, and she felt something akin to delight at witnessing the birth of an energy that, long held back by neatly planted rows, burst forth here from the earth in all its stubborn variation.

In its own small way, it was as beautiful and magnificent as the quarry. The pale gray clouds rolled overhead; the birds chirped in anticipation of the summer rain. Behind her, in the funnel of each web on the evergreens, there was a spider. She wondered if the spiders sensed the coming rain as she did. She heard the rumble of thunder and felt the cool damp wind that prefaced summer showers.

What had she wanted to say to her landlord? She'd wanted to put her hand on his arm, she remembered. She'd wanted to say, "Those are spiders. Don't kill them."

It was so simple. And it was astonishing how prohibited she had felt from saying that to her landlord: Don't kill them. She imagined herself with her hand on his arm, gentle but insistent. It made her think of something, and she frowned, trying to remember. The woman in the hall. Who was the woman in the hall?

And then she knew. It was Meryl. That insistent woman with her hand on your arm—it was Meryl. What had she said? "How do you say to people, 'Wake up and save the Earth.' How do you get them to listen?"

The first drops of rain began to fall. She stretched out her hands and closed her eyes, turning her face to the sky and smiling as the drops fell with a cool shock on her face. She opened her eyes and looked around once more. It was so *beautiful*, she thought almost angrily. So beautiful.

Sunny left the yard, closing the gate behind her, and walked around the house to the front porch.

It was raining steadily, and she sat down on the top step and watched the rain fall. The rain wet the leaves of the two maple trees growing from the patch of earth between sidewalk and street. She looked at their roots.

The roots of one tree were huge and rolling and seemed as though they would raise the universe itself. When they reached the concrete sidewalk, however, though they bulged over a little, they slipped meekly underneath. The roots of the tree looked like any other roots—simple, small, and unpretentious—but they'd lifted the very sidewalk until it had cracked at the seams. Sunny sat looking at the two different trees and at their roots, and as she sat there, it felt as if she were contemplating a life's choice.

She sensed a movement at the corner and, looking up, saw Kay carrying a bag of groceries and hurrying through the rain, laughing.

"Oh!" she complained as she ran up the steps and stood there, wet and dripping, "I wanted it to be a nice day!"

Sunny smiled. "It *is* a nice day."

Kay pointed to the street. "Go out in that rain and tell me how nice it is."

"Why didn't you wait for me to come back?"

"I wanted to surprise you," she said, indicating the groceries.

"What is it?"

"I'm going to make you macaroni and cheese."

Sunny wrinkled her nose in polite distaste, and Kay's mouth fell open. "You don't like my macaroni and cheese anymore?"

"I think I've just about had it with macaroni and cheese."

"Uh-oh. I think we've reached a turning point in our relationship."

"Thank God," Sunny said dryly. Kay, blushing, put down the groceries and gave Sunny a smiling side-glance.

"Why don't we go inside?" Sunny suggested. "You're all wet. I don't want you to catch a cold."

"No, it's not so bad. I want to sit here with you awhile."

"Okay."

"Whew!" Kay sat, and ran her fingers through her hair.

"Here, take my sweater."

Kay agreed, and when she'd put the sweater on, realized what it was. She peered at the sleeve while Sunny watched her, smiling. "Oh *vey*," Kay said, in a terrible Yiddish accent, "who's sweater is *this*?"

"I keep *telling* you, my dear," Sunny said critically, "it's not *oh*. It's *oy*. There's a world of difference between *oh* and *oy*."

Kay looked at her as if to say that there might be a world of difference between the two, but it was a world she was going to try her best to bridge.

Sunny gave her a smile that was skeptical but encouraging and turned to face the rain.

They sat side by side: not so close that anyone would notice, but close enough so that they could feel each other's presence like a warm continuum.

Sunny was thinking of the day she'd watched Debbie at the edge of the quarry pond, slapping her hand in the shallow water and screaming out in joyful exuberance. She'd always wondered what her daughter was saying that day. Now she knew. "I'm here!" she was shouting. "I'm alive!"

She sighed and noticed that Kay was watching her. The two women exchanged a look that was a smile and turned once more to face the rain. The Armory still dominated their vision. But beyond the Armory was the river. Unseen by them, it followed its own inexorable course: flowing on, and on, and on. . . eternal, in eternal change.

Glossary

Auf tse luchas, out of spite.

Baleboosteh, an excellent and praiseworthy homemaker.

Bar mitzvah, the religious ceremony by which a Jewish boy becomes a man. The ceremony for girls is called *bat mitzvah.*

Bissel, a little bit.

Bris, the circumcision of an eight-day-old Jewish boy performed by a *mohel,* an expert in such matters.

Broit, bread.

Bubeleh, a term of endearment; honey; sweetie.

Chai, the eighteenth letter of the Hebrew alphabet. Meaning "life," the *chai* is worn as an expression of Jewish identity.

Chanukah, eight-day holiday, sometimes called Festival of Lights, celebrating the victory of the Maccabees in reclaiming Jerusalem from the Syrians and cleansing the Temple.

Charoses, a mixture of grated apples, chopped nuts, cinnamon, and wine, eaten by Ashkenazi Jews during the Passover *Seder* to symbolize the mortar that the Jews made during their slavery in Egypt.

Chazzen, a Cantor; the singer who leads the congregation in prayer.

Chevra Kaddisha, the Burial Society.

Chometz, something that is not eaten during Passover.

Dayenu, a lively song sung during the Passover *Seder* giving thanks to God for freeing the Jews from bondage in Egypt.

Gay shlofen, meine kinder, go to sleep, my child.

Gefilte fish, ground fish (cod or whitefish) mixed with eggs, matzo meal, and onions, and served cold with horseradish.

Geshmack, delicious.

Gonif, a thief, a crook.

Gottenyu!, Dear God!

Goy, Gentile.

Goyim, Gentile, plural.

Goyish, descriptive characteristic of Gentiles.

Haggadah, the Passover narrative telling the story of the Jewish people's slavery in Egypt and their flight to freedom.

Hak mir nisht kain chainik, don't bother me.

High Holy Days, Rosh Hashonah and Yom Kippur.

Kaddish, mourner's prayer.

Karpas, the greens eaten during the Passover *Seder.*

Kineahora, a phrase that wards off the evil eye.

Kosher, fit to eat according to Jewish dietary laws. In American slang, it means something that's generally okay.

Kvetch, to complain.

Latke, a potato pancake.

Maror, bitter herbs (horseradish) eaten during the Passover *Seder.*

Malocchio, the evil eye (Italian).

Matzo, unleavened bread eaten during Passover.

Menorah, eight-branched candelabra used on Chanukah.

Mit, with.

Nu, So? Well?

Oy, can express a multitude of feelings, from fear to joy to surprise to relief.

Oy a choleria, oh, a plague!

Oy gevalt, an expression of fear or dismay.

Patchie patchie kicheleh,	Clap clap hands,*
Mame khafen schicheleh,	Mama buys shoes,
Tata khafen zecheleh,	Papa buys socks,
A geshundt in deh babeleh's becheleh!	God bless the baby's cheeks!

* This is not a literal translation. *Kicheleh* is a Jewish cookie. But it's a clapping rhyme, so "clap clap hands" is closest to its intent.

Pesach, Passover.

Plotz, to explode; to be aggravated.

Rosh Hashonah, Holy Day that celebrates the New Year.

Seder, the Passover religious service and ritual meal telling the story of the Jew's liberation from slavery in Egypt.

Setz, to sit.

Sha, shush.

Shammes, the ninth candle of the menorah, used to light the others.

Shanda, a shame.

Shayneh maideleh, pretty girl.

Sheitel, the wig traditionally worn by Orthodox Ashkenasic Jewish women after they were married.

Shiksa, Gentile girl.

Shivah, seven days of mourning following a death.

Shlemiel, a jerk, a loser.

Shmaltz, chicken fat. Used also to mean something overly emotional, or overdone.

Shmatte, a rag.

Shmooz, to gab.

Shmuck, a penis; a jerk.

Shnaps, liquor.

Shnorrer, a moocher, a bum.

Shomer, one who prays.

Shtetl, small Jewish communities that flourished in Eastern Europe prior to World War II.

Shul, synagogue.

Taliener, Yiddish word meaning an Italian person.

Traif, food which is unkosher; someone who is unworthy.

Tsatske, a toy, a doodad, a trinket.

Tsoris, troubles, woe, suffering.

Tuchus, buttocks.

Veni ca, come here (Sicilian).

Vey is *meir,* woe is me.

Vuss?, what?

Vuss is *duss?,* what is this?

Zadie, grandfather.

Triangles by Ruth Geller is part of The Crossing Press Feminist Series. Other titles in this Series include:

Abeng, A Novel by Michelle Cliff

Clenched Fists, Burning Crosses, A Novel by Cris South

Folly, A Novel by Maureen Brady

Learning Our Way: Essays in Feminist Education, edited by Charlotte Bunch and Sandra Pollack

Lesbian Images, Literary Commentary by Jane Rule

Mother, Sister, Daughter, Lover, Stories by Jan Clausen

Mother Wit: A Feminist Guide to Psychic Development by Diane Mariechild

Movement, A Novel by Valerie Miner

Movement In Black, Poetry by Pat Parker

Natural Birth, Poetry by Toi Derricotte

Nice Jewish Girls: A Lesbian Anthology, edited by Evelyn Torton Beck

The Notebooks of Leni Clare and Other Short Stories by Sandy Boucher

The Politics of Reality: Essays in Feminist Theory by Marilyn Frye

The Queen of Wands, Poetry by Judy Grahn

Sister Outsider, Essays and Speeches by Audre Lorde

True to Life Adventure Stories, Volumes I and II, edited by Judy Grahn

The Work of a Common Woman, Poetry by Judy Grahn

Zami: A New Spelling of My Name, Biomythography by Audre Lorde